Send My Cold Bones Home

Tristan Hughes was born in Atikokan, Canada, and was brought up around Llangoed, Ynys Môn. He was educated at Ysgol David Hughes, Menai Bridge; the universities of York and Edinburgh, and King's College, Cambridge, where he completed a PhD thesis on Pacific and American Literature. His first book of fiction, *The Tower*, was published to acclaim in 2003. He currently lives in Biwmaris, Ynys Môn.

Send My Cold Bones Home

Tristan Hughes

Parthian
The Old Surgery
Napier Street
Cardigan
SA43 1ED

www.parthianbooks.co.uk

First published in 2006
© Tristan Hughes 2006
All Rights Reserved

ISBN 1-902638-76-X
9 781902 638768

Editor: Gwen Davies

Cover design by Lucy Llewellyn
Inner design by vanwigwam@lloydrobson.com
Printed and bound by Dinefwr Press, Llandybïe, Wales

Written and published with the financial support of
the Welsh Books Council

British Library Cataloguing in Publication Data

A cataloguing record for this book is available from
the British Library

Contents

For my grandmothers: Nain and Grammy

Prologue

1

His final journey may well have been one of his longest; although, of course, I can only speak of the corporeal part of the excursion. It was fifteen miles from his bedroom in Tŷ Carreg to the yard of Eglwys Fach. Fifteen miles, which for Johnny was the whole and true distance home. Not this home, that he was wrenched into, long ago in the last century, by the forceps of one Dr Williams – who, Johnny had once assured me, had left behind as his only legacy the two slight indentations on either side of his forehead – but the immemorial home of the Llanysgerbwd Joneses. Fifteen miles, which was approximately halfway across the island, or, on my map with its scale of 1:10, one-and-a-half inches. Many of us, when the time comes, will have much further to go – perhaps we will not even know where to – but, set within the proportions of Johnny's life, this fifteen miles was a journey without precedent.

Five of us travelled with him that day. A sparse entourage. There were the two brothers, Bob and Bryn, who owned the farm which both Johnny and I lived beside. They were known as Bub and Nut. Bub because he was so heavy-tongued it was how Bob came out of his mouth, and Nut (short for peanut) because he was five feet tall including the heels on his shoes. An odd couple this: the one middle-aged, tall, dark and taciturn; the other no more than twenty, a squat, flamy-haired chatterbox; the two of them opposite and inseparable. Then there was Goronwy, Johnny's ancient contemporary and, as far as I could tell, the only man you could have really called his friend. And then Sioned, the single woman among us, whose connection to Johnny, at that moment, I had little idea of. And finally myself, Jonathon Hall, the sole outsider, who had known him least and maybe best of all.

We drove Johnny down the hill, on the road through Glan-yr-afon. Two black cars together, bumper to bumper, moving slow and stately – a caravan of ebony snails. No one appeared to mind. Other cars, and the occasional tractor, pulled respectfully over onto the roadside when they saw us, their drivers offering a sombre thumb as we passed by. Under the weak rays of an early morning sun, we inched our way to where the road came out beside the straits, where seagulls floated in the air above the water, dipping and rising in arcs so smooth and effortless that they seemed not to be movements at all, only the apparitions of movements. The mountains beyond were as still as tombstones.

Until, in front of us, the walls of the castle appeared. The remains of a mist lingered at their base, while up above, on their tumbling-down turrets, two flags hung limply. We slid past them without looking. Beyond was the town, where already tourists had begun to crowd the high street – octogenarian early-risers, who flanked the pavements and, with the castle already seen and nothing left to look at, stared at us. An old woman in a blue dress took a picture. We carried on along the street, dark reflections against their failing irises, passing through their immobile shadows, until halfway down we turned to the right and headed off beyond their gaze, into the island's interior.

As we crept inland the landscape thinned and emptied. The tall trees that lined the eastern shore dwindled into marooned islands of oak and sycamore. The fields widened into a choppy sea of tiny hills, capped by stunted, wind-bent blackthorn bushes and green spumes of gorse. Outcrops of stone, almost as white as the skybald sheep who stalked through them, jutted through the grass like half-exhumed skeletons. I thought of Johnny's face then, as I had seen it earlier in the weak morning light: the pale, dry skin stretched over intransigent cheekbones; the twin rises of his temples and the little valleys beneath (the remnants of Dr Williams's work); the white and unruly furze of his eyebrows; the thin lips, puckered together in an unfinished expression – of what I could not be sure. An enigmatic face, even then, still half taunting me, half playing with me, half beseeching me; still adjuring me with his small world and the slivers of history that he had sheared from it. I thought of how odd it was that our paths had crossed, and in crossing had led eventually onto this road, at this time, where I now followed him into what he had once called – assuming I would grasp the reference?

knowing I wouldn't? not caring either way? – the barren womb of mother Môn.

And all the while the road itself had been narrowing. In fact, I couldn't tell if this was still the same road at all, or if at some point we had slipped off onto one of the maze-like, capillary lanes that spread everywhere through the island. I had yet, have yet, not been able to comprehend or navigate this intricate web. There is no discernible pattern or order to it. The main roads follow a clear, pragmatic logic, moving as the crow would from the bridge at Menai to the port of Holyhead; or else edging their way, sensibly, from town to town. But beyond this utilitarian grid there unfolds a leafy labyrinth whose principles of organisation – if indeed they have any – quite defeat me; a shadowy network that spiders its way across the land like the mysterious and convoluted swirls on a Celtic cross. I can hardly count the times when, beckoned by these inviting by-ways, I have found myself hopelessly lost, have watched as the tarmac beneath my feet turned into chippings and potholes, until finally I came to a gate guarded by snarling sheepdogs, or an empty field, or the emptier sea.

And then to narrow further, so that the hedgerows crowded in upon us, obscuring the surrounding landscape, funnelling us into a claustrophobic green tunnel. Ferns and brambles began scraping along the sides of the car with a shrill, metallic whoosh; nettle leaves swished by beyond the glass, their soft, stinging down centimetres from my skin. By now I had no idea where we were: I had never been here. I tried to sink back onto the fake leather seat, to resign myself to the twisting, turning progress of the car, but already I could feel the panic rising within me, the fear of lostness, of not knowing. I wanted to ask the others where this was, how far we had come, how far we had to go, but I could see the silent intentness on their faces, their certainty, and couldn't bring myself to betray my confusion, my ignorance. Instead, I bent my body forward – crumpling the black cotton trousers that I had spent so long ironing the previous evening, watching as the sunbeams faded over the sharp creases – and craned my head closer to the window like a travel-sick child, searching anxiously for signposts or landmarks. There were none. There was only the green blur of the hedgerows and, up above, the vacant, cerulean sky.

Then, suddenly, the hedges had parted and the road terminated in a small, stony lot. At first I thought we had reached nowhere, that this was yet another trick these lanes had played on me; but we stayed where we were and after a minute the others climbed out of the cars and so I followed them. The prospect was much the same as those we had passed through earlier – bony hills, wide fields, a meagre skin of windblown trees and gorse – only here you could make out the shapes of houses scattered amidst them. There were not many, a dozen at most, though it was hard to tell exactly. Their flaking, whitewashed walls were deceptively planted in among the creases and folds of the landscape, where they clung to the bottom of the hills like hard, calcified deposits; so that, sometimes, what appeared to be a house would turn out to be merely a heap of stones dappled with pallid lichens. Or perhaps these had been houses once? Certainly, those that remained were such a threadbare collection that it was difficult to imagine people actually living in them; and, in fact, if you looked closer you could make out the unmistakable evidence of desertion: missing roofs, doorless spaces, windows without glass.

I was standing beside Goronwy, who was contemplating the scene with a kind of uneasy resignation, and it was this uneasiness that gave me the confidence to ask:

'Where are we?'

'Llanysgerbwd,' he replied, with a barely concealed note of surprise in his voice. There was no concealing mine.

'This is it,' I said, and then, after a pause, 'but there's nothing here, no one here.'

'There was once,' he said, but he didn't seem inclined towards explanation and so I didn't ask.

Beyond us, about a hundred yards to the left, was a little church.

'Eglwys Fach?' I said.

'Yes,' he said. I turned my eyes down towards the ground, hiding my disappointment among the pebbles below.

It was barely distinguishable from the outcrops of rock that surrounded it. The architecture was rough and stark, giving the impression that it had not been crafted by human hands at all but sculpted by the wind and rain into the fortuitous shape of a building. It was no more than a stone box topped with a triangle of slates. What I had expected I couldn't say, but it had been more than this. I had heard Johnny speak of Eglwys Fach so many times that I suppose an image of it had slipped into my mind: an image of hazy, medieval beauty and modest, miniature splendours; of ivy-cloaked walls and ancient cloisters; the musty memories of Celtic saints and scholars. I had placed it in the centre of a pastoral surround, a rooted, rustic idyll, where grandmothers hurried their grandchildren down the village streets and old farmers, hardy and resilient, met in the lanes and fields, among the shades of their ancestors. I had expected the past, yes, of course I had, Johnny's past – that was why I was here, that was why we were both here – but I had expected the living too. And Johnny himself had said nothing to dispel or diminish this image; on the contrary, I am sure it was he who had encouraged it. Only now, as I stood before the real thing, did it occur to me that, for all his talk, he had never actually set eyes upon the place. Eglwys Fach, Llanysgerbwd, and the land around them, were part of a past that Johnny had no physical memory of. Unlike his father and grandfather, and the long line of Joneses before them, he had neither been born nor lived here – he hadn't even *been* here, until now that is. Instead, he had sat still for eighty years and invested a place fifteen miles from his front door with all the lustre an exile saves for the land he has left or lost or never known, burnishing it until it glinted and dazzled beneath the beams of some mythopoeic sun. Johnny, I realised, had lived on two islands: the one beyond his doorstep and the one beyond his eyelids. And, as I stood in the precincts of the latter, I began to realise that you can never live – maybe nothing can – in someone else's imagination, in someone else's imagined before.

2

The first thing I noticed as we walked into the grounds was the clock. That it had remained in one piece was remarkable. Everything else about Eglwys Fach spoke of long abandonment and disuse: the peeling black paint of the railings, the overgrown yard, the big, cumbersome padlock that had rusted shut on the arched doors. Even the three yew trees that stood sentinel around the site had a look of weariness and desuetude about them, as if they had gradually begun to retire back into the surrounding fields and leave this place to its own slow ruin. There was no sign that anybody had used the church in years (the only proof of any recent human activity was a mound of newly dug earth in the corner of the yard). It looked like the relic of a lost enthusiasm; a child's toy gathering dust in an attic, the photograph of a half-forgotten lover. But the clock, embedded in a small stone rectangle at the front of the building (what passed for its steeple), appeared almost pristine; with a bright white face and two sturdy black hands.

That it still told the correct time was a miracle. At first I hadn't even noticed: struck by the fact of its continued existence it had not occurred to me to note the actual position of its hands. It was only the sudden eruption of a single chime, momentarily interrupting what had become an almost cloying silence, that made me look up again and see that it had just marked the half hour. I checked it against my watch and found it to be unerringly accurate. Where was he? I thought, as I had before that morning. It was quite beyond me how, in the midst of all the surrounding neglect, this clock had persevered; ticking away the seconds as the weeds grew and the stones crumbled, tolling out the empty hours, keeping dead time. But there it was, and I found its presence oddly comforting. After the confusions of the journey it was good to know that it was half past nine here too. None of us had travelled so very far – not yet anyway.

At ten o'clock, precisely, we started to lower him into the ground. There were ten chimes for the tenth hour. On the first stroke we began to ease the coffin downwards, and then, with each plangent repetition, it descended further, until, on the final lingering peal, it silently touched the earth. Dust to dust.

The vibrations of the last chime had only just dispersed, and Goronwy was in the middle of clearing his throat to say a few words, when we heard the first explosion. The sound would have been startling anywhere, but here it resounded like a thunderclap, an apocalyptic echo of the gentle church bells. Goronwy's cough turned into a rasping, spluttering spasm; Bub, who was standing in front of me, choked out a 'bluddyel'; while Nut, whose shock had turned well-nigh instantaneously into a kind of wild glee, proclaimed, 'Well, fokk me!' We others remained as we were, standing politely and quietly around the grave, cloaked in a near impregnable armour of etiquette, as stiff and immobile as the creases on our black clothes.

The second explosion, when it arrived moments later, was almost expected. Nut had already begun eagerly to scan the horizon in the direction of the first one, pushing up onto his tiptoes and craning his neck out of his starched white shirt. His excitement on hearing the second bubbled over into a dash towards the railings of the yard.

'Look,' he called back to us, 'yu can see the smoke an' everything!'

Bub, a look of resignation hanging upon his face, said to himself as much as anyone else, 'Can' evun teke 'im tu a bluddy funerul.'

But by now, as astonishment faded into curiosity, all of our eyes had begun shifting their sombre focus from the glazed mahogany planks below our feet towards Nut's frantic, pointing finger. Even Sioned, who had provided the only tears of the day so far, wiped her cheeks with a handkerchief full of roses and followed the communal gaze. And sure enough, there beyond the railings, behind the swell of the tiny hills, a column of grey smoke was mushrooming its way into the bland blue of the sky. And as we watched its slow progress into the heavens, a second one emerged, just beside it, spiralling up out of the horizon like a grey beanstalk.

We somehow knew the third would be the last. It seemed the right number for sacral emanations, wherever they might originate. As the final reverberations receded we fell back into a confused and embarrassed silence, hiding our eyes from one another in the contemplation of the hole where Johnny lay. Five figures etched in black above the open earth, a dwindling trident of smoke in the sky behind. Nobody wanted the others to know what they were thinking. Goronwy never spoke his few words. Even Nut was quiet. We stood as still as the stones around us.

The chime, when it came – a single one for the half-hour – was like the snap of a hypnotist's fingers. Surprisingly, it was Goronwy who moved first. He bent down slowly, picked up a handful of loose dirt, threw it onto the coffin, and then turned and walked away towards the gates. One by one we followed him, each of us, in turn, casting our fist of dirt down into the grave, where it fell like a dry rain onto the dark wood. Two ravens wheeled above us and the first breeze of the day rippled through the stunted yew leaves. The bottom of the gate scraped against the gravel of the path, once as Goronwy opened it, and then again as Sioned – who was the last to leave – closed it. I took a final look back at Eglwys Fach. It was as though we had never been there. Nobody had spoken.

We were halfway back to the cars when Sioned, in a tone as flat as glass, said, 'It must have been the dynamite.'

3

On the coast, in front of where I still live, for today anyway, there is a stretch of shattered rock called Chwarel Wen. From a distance, or to the uninformed eye, it looks not so very different from the surrounding shoreline: a series of jagged promontories interspersed with stony bays. You might imagine that the same great sweep of time and tide has shaped it all, caressing it into the picturesque rubble that you will buy postcards of when you leave, thinking what a fine and ingenious craftsman nature is. But the rocks of Chwarel Wen have not had so easy a passage into ruin as those around them; nature rarely splits stones as sheer as these. If you were to look closely then you would see the unmistakable signs of men scored on their surfaces; a subtle, by now almost gentle, intaglio, that is quite at odds with the determined violence that imprinted it.

Chwarel Wen was a quarry for a thousand years. I read this in one of those rather worthy tourist guides that tries to slip a little history into its lists of beaches and hotels. A thousand years, it said, in much the same way it pointed out, on the next page, that a night in the Bulkley Arms would cost you £70. It stopped being a quarry sixty years ago. This I was told by Sioned as we all sat in her kitchen after the funeral. Why she had chosen to talk to me about it I wasn't sure. I wanted to ask her how exactly she'd known Johnny but it didn't seem the right time, and besides, she acted like she knew me well enough. The others munched away at the sausage rolls and cakes that were arranged on the table, but Sioned appeared restless and fidgety, unable to properly sit still as though there was always something to be done, and even as she spoke to me she kept a careful eye on their cups, moving quickly every few minutes to refill them. I couldn't really tell how old she was, because although her hair was white and her face lined, there was a twitchy energy in her that made her seem younger. With one flex of her constantly mobile features twenty years would fall suddenly off them. She told me how her father had worked in the quarry, loading slabs of limestone onto the boats that had once docked off its sides. As a little girl she had sat with her mother on the fern-fringed clifftops, watching her father manoeuvre wedges of rock into the dark and distant holds, hauling them up with cranes until they hung in the air, dangling from their chains like giant flies caught in steel spiderwebs. Afterwards, she would ask him where the stones went and he would list the names of places she had never heard of. She repeated them for me – Buenos Aires, Chesapeake, Philadelphia, Valparaiso – and I could tell they were as strange to her now as they had been all those years ago. The rocks of Chwarel Wen had travelled further than she ever had.

Then the quarry had closed, just like that. A thousand years over with and nothing to signify its passing but a huge iron padlock that appeared one day on the gates. Everything else was left as it was. She remembered walking down to the cliffs and seeing the cranes, motionless, holding up emptiness, and the piles of cut stone that would now go nowhere, their jagged edges the only memorial of those others that had gone and lay scattered across the globe, pieces of a jigsaw puzzle that would never be whole again.

They made Johnny the caretaker of the abandoned site. Even back then, apparently, he was deemed well enough qualified in idleness to sit through the afternoons and nights and keep watch over discarded machinery and vacated buildings. It took them years to clear it out. In the meantime, the quarry gathered a reputation as a haunted place. This doesn't surprise me. I have stood myself on the cliffs above it, on many a windy day, watching as the waves beat against its sides, and each time have been struck by a certain other-worldly atmosphere that surrounds it.

Some of this has to do with its prospect. It looks out over a wide, watery horizon, interrupted on one side by a barren headland – and the still more barren island that nestles behind it – while, on the other, a long line of shore slopes far away into the west. In between there is only a distant and uncertain line of sea and sky, out of which, when it is clear, there materialises a series of shadowy, blue-grey hillocks. I have been told, at various times, that these are definitely the Wicklow mountains of Ireland, whilst at others that they are – equally definitely – the Isle of Man. Perhaps as a result of this confusion, I have never been able to see them as resembling anything quite so substantial as actual mountains or islands. Instead, they have taken on, in my mind, a slightly muddled status: not exactly supernatural, but not exactly real either, like those phantom peaks and wandering, blessed isles that drift through the pages of old annals of exploration.

Then there are the tricks of light and atmosphere that play continually above and around it: the constantly shifting clouds, the slanting, startling, sunbeams, the creeping mists and bursts of sea-spray. They are hardly ever still, never the same. Close your eyes for a second, open them, and everything has changed. It is like some conjured, conjurers' realm, as if the whole had once been touched by Merlin's wand and then sent on its protean way. Sometimes I have sat for whole days and studied these transformations, searching out some connective thread, some way of holding it all together, but none has ever shown itself: the airy kaleidoscope has continued its random adjustments – the sun shines, the clouds shudder past, the rain falls, the mists come and go – and there I have remained, confused, surprised, not a wit the wiser. There are moments, particularly in the morning and the evening, when it has made me imagine whole dimensions clashing and churning around me, tumbling through and against each other, until the thought has made me dizzy and I turn to watch as the gulls and cormorants and oystercatchers flicker over the water, like emissaries from another world.

But mostly it is the noise of the sea itself, as it thumps and washes and sluices through the rocks below. It is loud and eerie, a sibilant din, punctuated by the sounds of the water as it pushes through into unseen spaces in the rock and forces out the air within. At low tide I have climbed down the quarry's edge, as far as I can go, and searched out the various cracks and crevices at its base. But they offer no real access to the hidden caves and gaps that must open out behind them. I cannot see what lurks past their pursed and barnacled lips. Pushing my hands through, I have dangled my fingers in the emptinesses beyond; but the contours and extent remain invisible to me – there is only the blind sensation of damp air and briny darkness. The sole intimation of what is there are the sounds themselves: spooky exhalations, strangled siren songs, the spectral breath of stone itself.

However, for those who lived near the quarry back then, and for whom, I suppose, all of this would have been as unaffecting as a pond in the back garden, it was the ghostly detonations that earned the quarry its reputation. They boomed out once or twice a month, Sioned explained, sometimes in the early morning, sometimes as the sun was setting. On windless days they could be heard in the village. They hurried farmers home at night. They quickened schoolchildren's steps. For the fishermen, who caught their echoes out on the water, they were considered bad omens, signs of an empty sea. Working on the premise that a thousand years is far too long for something just to stop, it seemed quite natural, apparently, to suppose that the quarry's spirit – a composite wraith, knitted together out of a millennium's worth of dead and departed quarrymen – had simply carried on its restless ways, breaking up its phantom rocks with its phantom dynamite. And young Johnny, its custodian, began to earn, for the first time, a certain renown for living close to the mysterious edges of things.

All of this was common knowledge to the others at the table. Bub and Nut, whose father must have told them the story enough times to glaze their ears, carried on with their cakes. Goronwy stared at the tablecloth. I was the only one listening.

I could sense Sioned's voice begin to change, to move slowly down towards a whisper. It was as though it were easier if directed at me, but still loud enough for the others to hear; a secret in its delivery but meant to be shared.

'But I saw him,' she said, 'I saw him at it. I was only a girl then, but I played down there, on my own, mind. There were seagulls' eggs on the cliffs and I collected them. And my mother said I was too old for that kind of thing, but I liked finding them and I wasn't scared of ghosts. The first time, I was up there and I saw him walking out over the rocks below, so of course I hid because I didn't want him to know what I was doing, because I didn't want him to think I still liked childish things. I could see he was carrying something, it was only small you know, but I could see it was something. And then when he gets to the water he stops and reaches into his pockets and out come these matches. He's looking around then, sly as a polecat, and me hiding in the bracken, too nervous to breathe hardly, thinking he'll spot me any minute. Only he didn't, did he, because on he goes, lighting up his matches. And then I knew what it was he was carrying – it was a stick of dynamite, wasn't it! I saw the fuse when he lit it, going off like one of them sparkler things the children play with on bonfire night.

'When he threw it into the sea I thought that's that then, it's out now, no harm done. And I was in the middle of thinking what he was up to, playing with the stuff in the first place, and where he'd got his hands on it, so when it goes off, well, it was some kind of shock, I can tell you now. The funny thing was that there was no noise, not to begin with you see: it just went all still, all of a sudden, not normal still but different you know, like the air'd been sucked out of the sky; and then the sea just fell, a big circle of it, dropping down as though there was a plug or something that'd been pulled out beneath. It was then I heard it. Boom. *Arglwydd* it was loud, I can tell you, like a huge drum being banged beside your ear. I almost fainted, right there in the bracken, I almost did. And the water, well up it comes, a great bulge of it, like a massive jellyfish lifting itself out of the sea and then bursting. I could feel drops of it on my face, all the way up there, with my ears ringing and my heart going a hundred miles an hour.

'I thought he was crazy then. Daft, you know. Fooling around with that stuff and everything. Making everyone think the place was spooked and full of bwgans. And people thinking how brave he was, looking after the place, how ghosts didn't scare him, that he might actually be friendly with them. Daft, I thought, but sly as well.

'It was only after a bit that I saw the fish: one or two at first, but then a bunch of them, all over the top of the water, rolling around there as if they'd gone to sleep and floated on up to the surface. Then Johnny reaches inside his jacket, pulls out an old flour sack, and walks down – calm as anything – to the sea's edge, and just sits there, waiting for them to drift towards him so he can grab them and put them in it. And I had to laugh, quietly like, to myself, to think of the whole village with the heebie jeebies on account of Johnny doing a bit of fishing. I really did. But I must have been laughing a little too much, because my feet were shaking, and then I saw that they'd pushed this stone right up to the side of the cliff. I looked at that stone for hours, only it wasn't hours it just felt like them, and however hard I looked it wouldn't come back from the edge – no, it stayed right there on it, see-sawing away, with me trying not to breathe, let alone move, in case that were to push it over good and proper. I remember the gulls drifting past and looking at me, and I'd swear the buggers were laughing then too, only at me this time.

'When it finally did go, my stomach went with it, I can tell you. I watched it falling and I was so nervous I froze, couldn't move an inch, and on it went and I still couldn't move and it seemed to take an age to reach the bottom. But it did. The sound of it hitting the rocks below was like a second explosion, I swear, with all the banging and echoing. He looked up then, of course, and I still couldn't move, just sat there like a bloody statue. When he saw me I didn't know what he'd do, but I imagined the worst, even though looking back now I don't know what that worst could've been. You see mostly I was embarrassed. I thought he'd think I was just a little girl playing some kind of spying game, or hide and seek, or – well you know, that sort of thing. It's hard to explain, isn't it. You see, he was good looking back then – though it's hard to believe it – a very handsome man, and I was young too. For months I'd hoped he'd look at me, but not like this. So I guess that was it: I think that maybe the worst thing he could have done was think of me as a child.

22

'Instead he winked. Just the once, before he turned back to carry on collecting his fish. But it wasn't any innocent wink, oh no, not the kind you give to children; it was one of them winks that you pretend you haven't seen, or understood, but know you've done both. I must have gone red as a cherry, was glad he'd turned away and couldn't see my face, but inside my heart was going a hundred miles an hour again, only in a different way this time. It sounds so stupid now, doesn't it, but after that wink I knew I'd never tell anyone what I'd seen. And I haven't, not until now.'

By now nobody was talking, or eating. I think Goronwy was smiling, or at least the creases on his face were slanted upwards in that shape.

'Yu joking, right,' said Nut, all excited at first, but then, when Sioned's face didn't change, turning ruminative, contemplative almost, as though he were weighing up a loss. 'Me old man spent years putting the frighteners on me about that bloody quarry, didn't he Bub. "Yu shoulda heard 'em," he'd say in this voice, all quiet and deep yeh, like he was doing one of them trailer things for a horror film, "yu shoulda heard 'em, down there in the rocks, lad, going off like cannons, and nobody within a mile of the place." And I halfway bloody believed 'im too, th'mount of times 'e went on about it. I didn't even go there till I wus a teenager, did I Bub. And I was still nervous then, I can tell yu.'

Bub remained inscrutable.

Nut continued to look thoughtful, and then a little despondent and resentful, like a child who's been told there's no such thing.

We sat for a while in silence – not for the first time that day.

'I heard them as well,' Goronwy finally added. 'But what does this have to do with what happened today, Sioned?' he asked.

'They were up in his attic, the three of them. The old bugger wouldn't let me in there you know, after twenty years of cleaning for him; kept the place locked and got in an almighty huff when I asked to go in. But I kept on asking, I did, because the thought of what kind of state it must be in, well, it made my skin crawl. *Esgob*, he was a filthy man, I can tell you, never lifted a finger after himself. If I hadn't been cleaning for him his house wouldn't have been fit for pigs. So the first thing I did when he died was get the keys. I knew where he kept them, in the box with his spare teeth, thinking I wouldn't notice them in there. So when I knew he was dead, well I went straight up there to give it a clean, didn't I. And you should've seen the state of it. Dust everywhere, cobwebs like you've never seen. It was full of cardboard boxes mostly, loads of them, stuffed with pages and pages of paper. I tried reading some of them, but I couldn't understand his writing so I just started wiping the dust off of them, one by one, trying to make the place fit to be in. I must have done about ten before I reached these other type of boxes, wooden ones, and because they were different I opened one and there it was, the dynamite, all mouldy and blotchy and falling apart, but it was still dynamite and it gave me one hell of a fright, it did. I knew better then to touch it because my dad'd told me, when I was a girl, that it was more dangerous when it was wet; unstable you know, only needing a knock to set it off. So I left it where it was and went right back down the stairs and phoned the police.

'When they came they had these men and a van with them, special police they said, that dealt with bombs and stuff. It took them hours to bring the three wooden boxes down – though I suppose they had to check the whole attic for others – and there's me still worried about what a state the place was in. And I asked them what they'd do with the boxes, and one of them said not to worry, they'd take them off a bit, to somewhere safe, and let them off in a controlled way. A controlled explosion, they said, and I told them there was no such thing as controlling an explosion. But they just smiled and said they'd do it away from any houses. And I suppose they must have, too.'

'Now there's timing fer yu,' said Nut.

Bub said nothing. Goronwy continued to stare down at the impeccably ironed tablecloth.

It was the last time Johnny's explosions would haunt them.

Part One

1

But they continue to haunt me.

Sitting here, surrounded by my boxes, looking out of the window at a view that I have come to imagine as familiar and my own, they return. Boom. Boom. Boom. One by one by one. I can still see those three columns rising up into the sky's oblivion, can still hear each separate shock of air. The reverberations seem to echo outwards from an unstill centre, casting a backwards ripple over the past, eddying forwards into the future, agitating the whole until there seems to be no clear before and after, no chain of events, but only the explosions themselves. Maybe Sioned was right, maybe you can't control them.

Tomorrow I will leave everything else behind: this cottage, this view, this island, these people, all of it. Tomorrow this will all pass away and become no more than the memory of a few fields, a sweep of sea, a stretch of crumbled coast, a set of outlandish consonants crammed and impacted on signposts. No more than this. I am something of an expert at leaving. I travel light. A man of the world, a man of worlds. Skipping over the straits I will look back once, maybe twice, and see the flat land beyond the mouth of the Menai recede and vanish as though it were a mere hallucination on the water, will see the small outcrop of Ynys Seiriol shrink and slip away behind the Orme. This place will become nothing more than part of a future conversation, in a location I am yet unsure of, where I will unfold it to show how much of the world is contained in me, how much I have been augmented and enriched by it. Perhaps for one night it will help me win a lover, though there are many better places I could use for that. North Wales is not the best loosener of skirts, I can assure you. Eventually, time and space and transit will whittle everything away – everything except them. And, if it were left entirely to me, I would leave it at that. Boom. Boom. Boom. Nothing more. But it is not entirely up to me at all. I have obligations now, to Johnny, for what I took from him, for what I accepted from him; which was not much, and only what he asked me to, but was enough – in fact everything.

I wonder if I am still angry with him for this. I was to begin with. Because this is an unexpected encumbrance and I will not be able to move on properly and unimpeded until I have shifted its weight off my shoulders. I'm not used to carrying luggage, especially another man's. So let me slough it off here, once and for all, and slip back into that unadhesive skin that is truly mine, that is my real and only legacy, my remaining birthright. And somewhere in all this there will be her as well. Two hers: one I lost and one I made to fill the absence. In my own special way I am about to betray both of them.

2

'When yu first meet 'im you'll think he's an old bastard,' said Nut.

'Oh, right,' I replied, 'you mean he'll be a bit difficult before I get to know him?'

'Listen mate,' Nut said, 'when yu get to know 'im you'll *know* he's an old bastard!'

We were standing in front of the entrance to Bub and Nut's farm, me beside a rusty gate and Nut beside the huge black wheel of his tractor. It was quite rare to see Nut on the outside of this machine. I had been here for two weeks and Bub and Nut were the only people I had met, yet I'd only seen Nut with his feet on the ground twice. The rest of the time he could be seen bouncing about on the tractor's seat as he careered up and down the narrow lane we shared. Those first few weeks after moving in I had lived in almost perpetual fear of encountering Nut and his tractor, which, at various and unpredictable times, would be armed with huge iron spikes that made it look like some terrifying metallic triceratops. What Nut accomplished on these journeys was a mystery to me then, and remains so. I don't ever recall having seen Bub driving and can only surmise that by some long-established fraternal arrangement, Nut did all the moving and Bub did all the work.

'So why yu wanna see 'im anyway?' Nut asked.

Which was a good question. Looking back I am not too sure if at that moment I could have truly answered it. Even now I am slightly unsure what answer would be adequate, though at this point I am dealing more in explanations and justifications than in answers. So let me say here, once and for all, that I sought him out in good faith. There was curiosity, yes, of course there was, but there was more to it than that. I was searching for something, that I can see now, though what exactly it was remains cloudy and obscure to me, or rather it is something I cannot quite form properly into words or motives. Have you ever had moments, sitting in a pub with friends, or talking to someone on a bus, or lying in bed with someone at night, when relating the story of your life begins to exhaust you; when suddenly the whole process of linking A to B to C in order to present the alphabet of who you are becomes a great and onerous burden? There will be your parents, your constrictive school in Milton Keynes, your class rebellion, your first fumbles in the darkness, your gap-year epiphany on Kilimanjaro, your first true love and the damage they did to you; there will be all this and, perhaps, for different people, and wanting different things, you will juggle the

34

details, place more weight and significance on A than C, pretend you have reached U already, or make J the secret key to it all. Nevertheless, the recitation remains an irksome imperative and, adjust it whichever way you want, you are forced to spin it all out to each new person you meet, again and again, like an ancient mariner: and the albatross is you. Well, if you have had these moments, if you have felt this exigency hanging like a corpse about your neck, then I ask you to imagine living a life made up of only these moments, where each day you woke up nothing, nobody, and were forced endlessly to recount yourself into existence. Because this is what my life has felt like. I have never managed to fall into, or weave, the web that would hold and explain me, that would let me rest. But, irony of ironies, to make you understand this I would have to start all over again.

Because, to explain all this properly, I would have to tell you everything. There would be my dreary childhood, spent hopping from dingy house to dingy house, from city to city, from north to south, for reasons that to begin with were never clear to me. Only later, as I grew older, did I start to comprehend the pattern whereby my father, having built up a new store of debt and dissatisfaction, would simply up sticks and leave, hurtling us (there was only my mother and I) on towards the next destination, all the while accumulating fresh reserves of failure and bitterness in much the same way tourists accumulate mementoes and keepsakes – until each of our new houses was more densely decorated with misery than the last. I remember watching the television with my father as a child and how each time the name of a city we had lived in before came up he would shout out, with an indolent rage, 'shithole', and eventually the shitholes would multiply until the whole evening was full of them, so that even now when I look at a map of England and see the names of the places I once lived in – Birmingham, London, Leeds, Bradford, Salford (the list is long) – they all seem just avatars of one archetypal and absolute Shithole. I would have to tell you all of this, even though now, when I recall my earliest days, the only things I can seem to conjure are an endless succession of vans and unfurnished rooms, of tower blocks and grotty terraces, of first days in new schools and streets with new names that, in my memory, have somehow become one single street, long and wearying, that runs through them all like a thread strung with drab, grey beads.

And there would be more besides. There would be how, afterwards, when I had escaped him, I inherited my father's corrosive momentum; setting off on a drifting course that was no better because it was my own and, in fact, all the time simply made me more like him. How in the spirit, or at least the simulacrum, of rebellion, I made his peregrinations look provincial: moving across continents and hemispheres, gathering stamps on my passport like so many trophies, inwardly sneering down my nose at his petty little life while I cleaned toilets in resorts, slept rough on beaches, searched for pennies on dirty floors; despising him from beneath tropical suns, with callused feet and nits in my matted hair; standing on muddy roadsides with my thumb held out, comparing his cowardly flights with my own bold explorations. There would be the friends I left behind, or never made; the stillborn loves, the dissipated hopes, the perpetual movement and, eventually, the grim, gnawing awareness that movement was the only thing I had to hold on to. And the whole while distilling my father's bitterness – which was all he'd given me – into a hatred not just of him and the myriad shitholes that dotted my past, but the entire world that I dragged my portable self through yet was not a part of, and that, in the recesses of my twisted heart, I envied and yearned after. I would have to tell you all of this, to relate the whole dire and pitiful picaresque. But for now I would only have you believe that, in seeking out Johnny, I was somehow attempting to learn how to stay still, to carve out a space where I could be silently myself; was trying to put in place the first part of a jigsaw puzzle that, once complete, would bind me immovably and forever into a here.

'Because he's one of my neighbours,' I ventured.

'Look mate,' Nut replied, 'he's been one of me neighbours since I was born, but I only go an see 'im when I 'ave to.'

3

As Nut clambered back onto the seat of his tractor and set it spluttering and rumbling back to life, I looked out past the gates of the farmyard and beyond, towards where the fields fell into the sea. My first glimpse of the island had been a misleading one. I'd driven down the road from Chester, watching as the hills to my left multiplied and grew into the edges of mountains and the coast to my right sprouted caravans and concrete, until, eventually, the bulge of the mountains had squeezed away this aluminium littoral and swallowed the road itself. I passed through a series of white-walled tunnels that glowed in an unnatural light; and when I emerged from the last of these the mountains had pulled back, like a man sucking in his belly, and left the road to pass unhindered across a low strip of nearly deserted land. When I looked again to my right everything had changed. Where once

I had seen only caravans, the sea and a barren headland in the distance, there was now an island whose long, even line of shore stretched out towards me and ended with a smaller island, that hung off its edge like a full stop. It lay across a wide strait of water that, with each mile, became narrower and narrower, until I could barely make out where the mainland finished and the island began. But that first look had implanted in my mind an image of remote flatness that for weeks afterwards dominated my idea of the place. Even after I had set foot on it, and walked a few miles across its ground, I could not rid myself of this impression. On these walks I would often glance over at the now somehow faraway mountains and imagine that one of their peaks had once broken away and floated over the sea to here, where it had fallen onto the water and spread out like a vast, deflated balloon. Only recently had this image begun to fade (even at this moment its residue remains), and as I surveyed the drooping fields beyond the gates, following them to where they sheered abruptly into jagged cliffs, I began to refine and readjust it: from where I now stood I pictured the island as more like a slightly convex pancake, that sloped down at its sides, making it seem as though everything was gradually sliding off towards its edges and falling into the sea, like the splintering mouth of a glacial river, or the coast of an ice-cap. And perhaps it was this sense of slow and invisible momentum that brought back to me the memory of another, far different and far distant, shore, and the sad and peculiar beginnings of my journey here.

It had begun with a policeman walking up the sandy drive of a dilapidated shack on the bottom corner of Florida. Inside, nestled on a cot bed, I was waiting for a rainstorm to break. The cockroaches knew it was coming, and had started to scuttle frantically over the worn linoleum floor. I listened to the sound of their tiny steps, anticipating the moment when the thick, heavy drops of rain would arrive to drown them out. Instead they seemed to get louder and louder, filling the quiet vacuum that always came before these rains. And then they had become, unmistakably, the slow and steady tread of human feet. Leaping up to the window I caught sight of him, making his way towards the shack, and instinctively calculated my chances of escape. They were next to none. There was no back entrance and most of the windows were bolted shut. Three months before, I had broken open the front door, but had yet to get around to the windows. He knocked twice, loudly, and I stood absolutely still, thinking that it wouldn't take him long to notice how obviously deserted this place looked. Then he knocked a third time and called out my name. The sound of the syllables shocked me. How did he know it? As far as I could remember I had not used my real name since arriving. This was not out of any conscious subterfuge, but rather the exhaustion I have spoken of; because, tired of explaining myself, I often took the easier option of invention. So how did he know it? In curiosity, as much as fear and resignation, I went to the door to give myself up.

My mother was dead. That was what he had come for: to tell me, to let me know. He was not interested in squatters at all. After a few minutes of explanation, and a sympathetic nod, he walked back down the drive and left me. At some point the rain had arrived, though exactly when, I couldn't be

41

sure of. By the time I'd got back inside, the cockroaches had hidden in the corners.

Finding me had been almost pure chance. For two years I had had no communication with my mother. Neither of us had even known where the other was. And then one day, about two months before, I had been sitting on the crest of a sand dune, watching a kite move through the air above the ocean, when an old hippie approached me. He was selling a variety of clumsily assembled trinkets, rings made out of shells, bracelets beaded with coloured glass – the kind of junk they sell on beaches – and I'd glanced over them with neither the inclination nor the money to buy one, when I came across a piece of polished red stone. It was almost entirely unremarkable, just a lump of shiny rock, with a hole drilled in it and a leather thong threaded through to make it a necklace. I pointed to it and he handed it over. Its effect on me was instant. As soon as I picked it up I started quietly blubbering, blubbering until my face was a wet sheen of tears and snot and my ribs heaved and spasmed beneath the thin cotton of my shirt. The poor man didn't know where to look, and when I tried to pass it back he held up his hand and said if it meant that much to me I could have it, gratis. For the rest of that day I hardly moved, just sat there on the dune-crest, holding the thing, moving it through my fingers. It was like some piece of my past had followed me, had sunk down into time and the Gulf stream only to re-emerge here, washed and smoothed, on this beach.

One of my first memories is of a trip to Blackpool with my parents, when I was six or seven. It must have been a Saturday or Sunday, and I remember the day, to begin with, as a series of frictions and disturbances, domestic tremors. I was upstairs in my room, adjusting a collection of rocks I had started making, forcing them into taxonomies of shape and colour – I didn't know their names or origins – when the sound of my parents' bickering started to creep beneath my door. This was unusual for weekends – although all too common during the week – because normally my father spent these two days drinking with whatever friends or acquaintances he had managed to find or hold onto. Ordinarily, these weekend mornings, as he prepared to leave, were my favourite times of the week. The imminence of departure transformed my father. He became jaunty, excitable, playful, a different being entirely from the morose, blank-eyed man whose presence, from Monday to Friday, disturbed my evenings and roused my mother into truculent fits of nagging. From my bed I'd listen, still half-asleep, to the sprightly pattering of his feet over the kitchen floor, followed by the clattering of pans and the cheery whistle of the kettle. The smell of bubbling bacon fat would drift into my room, warm, smoky, delicious, while I slipped in and out of dreams. I would hear him scampering through the hallway, stopping to kiss my mother, shouting goodbye to me from the front step, and then the door would close and the day would stretch out before me, peaceful and quiet, my own. But something this morning had gone awry. My mother's voice, shrill and importuning, was saying something about our never going anywhere on the weekend as a family, while my father, unexpectedly halted in the midst of the preparations for his departure, slammed down the frying pan. As the turbulence below grew, an empty, nervy feeling settled in my stomach. I heard a plate smashing and my father shouting, 'So fuck it

43

then, we'll fucking go.' My stomach felt so light and empty I was afraid I would fall over. I grabbed a piece of red sandstone and held it tightly in my hands. I thought it might ballast me, I thought together we could survive the earthquake.

That journey, in my memory, shuttles forward like a helter-skeltering nightmare: full of abrupt shifts and turns, rapid transits, deferred arrivals – the sensation of falling, the terrifying immanence of landing. There is me, in the back seat of our old Ford Cortina, clutching my stone, staring down at where the rust has eaten a hole through the floor, watching in dread as the asphalt rushes past, fearing its motion will suck me out of the car and into its kinetic blackness. There is my father at the wheel, his lips pursed shut in anger, his muscles tensed and furious, driving too fast, barely avoiding the other cars on the road. And then my mother, looking silently into the side mirror, her huge, glassy eyes wetting up at the corners; objects that appear closer than they are. Together we hurtle onwards, along with the rest of the holiday traffic, one more family bound together in their little knot of misery, headed for somewhere none of us wants to be.

I remember nothing at all of Blackpool, except my mother buying me a kite, and my father wrenching the rock out of my hands and throwing it into the sea. I had watched it loop through the air before falling into the water. Sandstone to sand.

But a whole ocean had not eroded it. Holding it in my hands I could feel myself returning, and it was her face, magnified, preserved, that I saw most clearly. There she was, her pale features scrunched into a grimace of patience and resignation, her footsteps locked into my father's restless, dissatisfied wake. She would never get away; the journey would never end for her. And it now occurred to me – though perhaps this knowledge had been there all along, only I had kept it hidden beneath the image of him – that I had left her behind; that my escape was also an abandonment.

That night I wrote a letter, filling up pages and pages with an overwrought account of what had pushed me so far from her. I worked on it all through the even hours of equatorial darkness, stopping occasionally to look at the moths that had gathered around the light on the desk. I watched as they threw themselves at the bulb, bouncing off the glass that protected the filaments within, then swirling off to regroup in the shadows. I watched as they became increasingly frantic with each failed effort, twisting and jerking on the smooth, opaque surface, hammering it with their wing-beats until they fell exhausted onto the desk. And each time I returned to my letter the more I could see the resemblance between these doomed, spasmodic efforts and the frenetic, hopeless movements of my pen, beating against an absence that I could never properly fill, or explain, or expiate. Looking down at the scribbles that had multiplied on the pages in front of me I realised that the lines of their crazy flight had become my own.

The next morning I sent it, not knowing if it would even reach her, if she would ever open or read it. On the front of the envelope I scrawled down the last home address I remembered, and then on the back, almost as an afterthought, my own address, which was not really mine at all.

And that was how they found me. It was my mother's solicitor who tracked me down. The letter, apparently, had eventually got to her; forwarded several times until it found its way, first into her new house, and then into her hospital room. There had been no time for a reply. But she'd saved it, and in the last weeks she'd passed it on to the solicitor. Afterwards, it was he who gave the address on the back to the British Embassy, and it was they who'd sent the policeman on his errand up the drive. Of course by then it was too late, much too late. By the time I got back she was gone.

I had always thought my family was the depressing and Spartan epitome of what they call nuclear: a central core with no circumambient constellation of atoms. There had only been the three of us. My mother's parents died when I was relatively young, but even before that I had seen them just the once; a fleeting and awkward visit, marked more by their obvious loathing of my father, and disapproval of my mother, than by any excessive interest in their offspring. Afterwards they were rarely, and then never, spoken of. My father had grown up in an orphanage, a fact with which he was terribly fond of availing me whenever he felt that I was showing signs of not appreciating the good fortune of having parents and a roof over my head. He'd given me more than he'd ever had, and more than nothing was deemed a considerable boon in his estimation. And so I had grown up in the belief that beyond us three there was really very little, that we were more or less a self-created entity, a kind of tawdry phoenix that had sprung out of ashes and flapped off on its own sooty, ragged way. We were not very big on genealogy in my family, and on several occasions, when thoughtfully drunk, my father had intimated to me that the name Hall was something he'd casually borrowed from a boy he'd shared a dorm with, for no other reason than that he was good at football. It was a bittersweet surprise then, when, soon after I'd discovered we'd been reduced to two, I was handed an unexpected legacy.

'Ty Gwynt,' the solicitor had said, staring carefully down at the paper in his hand and pushing the words out of his mouth with a slight look of suspicion. It was almost exactly the same look of suspicion that he'd given me a few minutes earlier, when I'd first walked into his office wearing what by now had become my only outfit: a pair of frayed and sun-bleached jeans and a Hawaiian shirt that had worn into more of a Galapagosian one.

'Yes, Tŷ Gwynt' he'd repeated, more confidently this time, adding, 'it's on Anglesey.' I still had no idea what he was talking about and looked blankly back at him.

'It's on Anglesey,' he repeated, and then, when I gave no response, he continued, 'it's an island, just off the coast of North Wales.'

'So what's Tŷ Gwynt?' I asked.

'The name of the house, I suppose,' he replied.

'What house?'

'Your house, Mr Hall.'

So, I had inherited a house. I had also, apparently, inherited a relative; not a living one, of course, but a relative nonetheless, and who was I to be picky about such things?

He didn't have a name, or at least not a name that the solicitor knew. But he had been my uncle – that much he did know. And, although he was dead and untraceable, and although I had never been given the chance to meet him, I was glad that he had once existed. I was glad to have my family increased by one, even if it only added to those absences which now spread across my life and over into my past.

47

The house had been bought thirty years ago, the year I was born, and put into my mother's name. Why exactly my uncle had done this I don't know, and never will I suppose. And so I guess it had been meant for us, to give us a place to start out in. But why had we never lived in it, and why had I never even heard his name? That for the past thirty years she had never spoken about him was a mystery; that she had owned the house he'd given her without once mentioning it was even more of one.

Or maybe it wasn't so much of a mystery. My mother had always hidden things, only usually these were objects of such seeming inconsequentiality that, were it not for the heightened awareness you have as a child for the small details of the world that surrounds you, I would have never noticed them. I remember a blue hat with a lace veil that she carefully secreted in a box in every one of our many attics; a black, leather-bound bible, with gold lettering on the spine, that would always find its way into the drawer that was never used; a particular china plate, embossed with a picture that I sometimes thought was a dragon, which skulked in the secret recesses of all our kitchens. It never occurred to me back then why she bothered to keep these things hidden, although now I can see that this small, but treasured, hoard was in some way her attempt to protect a part of herself from my father; that this ostensibly random cache was in fact a kind of armour or antidote: a static realm of objects immune to the relentlessly centrifugal world in which they were placed, and the husband who resided over it. What I could have never seen, or guessed, was that this realm had extended beyond mere objects to encompass people and places too. My mother had kept this uncle and Tŷ Gwynt stored away in her mind for thirty years. And now, when it was safe to, when there was nowhere left to hide them, she had given them to me.

She'd also left me a note. All it said was: 'This is for you – a home.'

That evening I travelled from the solicitor's office in London to Liverpool. By the time I arrived it was night. I had desperately wanted there to be a grave, but I should have known there wouldn't be one. A final resting place – it wasn't really my father's style. The only thing I had was the address of the crematorium. It was about five miles from the station and I walked there in the soft, late-summer darkness, down unfamiliar roads that led from the bright centre of the city onto narrow, weakly lit streets; streets that forked and multiplied until suddenly they had become once more one long and endless street, lined with anonymous houses and names I didn't know, leading neither forwards nor backwards but only onward, towards somewhere I would never arrive at, or stay, or leave. Looking up I could see the faded orange glow that filled the sky above me, and beyond it the faintest glimmer of a pristine and unreachable blackness. As I walked I must have fallen into some kind of daze or trance because before I knew it the first grey beams of morning light had crept into the sky and the street had run out of houses; they had turned instead into huge castles of brick and concrete, with slanted roofs of corrugated steel and moats of empty asphalt. The street itself had widened, breaking into a miniature delta of white lines and arrows, sprouting tributaries, eddying around islands of withered, dusty flowers. And it was towards one of these that I now directed my footsteps, knowing I would never find where she'd been burnt and that the dispersal of her ashes would have been my father's final victory. And I made my way into the centre of this pale island and placed the red stone on its dry earth and then took the letter I had written – that the solicitor had returned to me – and laid it on top. I waited then – for how long I don't know, only at some point the street had filled with cars, that circled around me before slipping away – staring down at the swirls of ink on the pages, studying their veering lines, until suddenly they had seemed to suggest a direction, a destination: another island, that I knew nothing of, but where I now knew I would go. As I turned to leave a gust of wind, the first of that day, had picked up the pages and scattered them into the air.

4

And so, with the sound of Nut's tractor fading in my ears, and the view of the fields dawdling their way to the ocean in my eyes, I continued the short walk from my cottage to Johnny's. It was late in the autumn and the leaves had begun to fall from the hedgerows onto the pot-holed, gravel surface of the lane, where they gathered together into yellowy-orange clumps. The sensation of walking through them was odd: on the top they were crisp and brittle, but underneath they had settled into a damp, slimy mulch, so that each footstep, as it descended, passed through a friable, crackling surface before becoming embedded in the sludge beneath. It made the ground seem somehow treacherous, duplicitous, and instinctively my steps became slow and tentative. My attention, in turn, shifted down towards the ground, where I now noticed the uppermost layer of leaves rustling and fluttering, although whatever breeze it was that moved them was too small to feel on my skin. And, as I carried on, the conceit entered my mind that these leaves were not actually animated by the air above at all, but by the slithery world below; that the ground I walked on was porous and unstable, like a thin crust of reeds floating on the surface of a bubbling swamp. This thought must have held me for some minutes, because by the time I looked back up I found that I had arrived at the track that led from the lane to Johnny's house.

I had passed this track already, and on several occasions had been tempted to walk down it. But there was always something vaguely forbidding about it that stopped me, a minatory quality which I didn't know whether to ascribe to the track itself – a steep and uneven descent fringed on each side by high, untrimmed hedges of blackthorn that reached towards each other to form a dark, jagged vault of branches – or simply to the fact that Johnny was at the end of it. I stood for some time at its entrance, peering down into shadows where dead leaves spiralled, and then up at the low, leaden banks of cloud that slouched their way across the sky. A flock of silent starlings whirled above me before breaking apart into swift specks of black. I stood there for minutes, maybe longer, taken suddenly by a feeling of lightness, of uncertainty, a sense that I was not here at all but caught once again in one of the blurry junctures that had made up so much of my previous life. And in the confusion of those minutes I thought I saw the shadows below me thicken into the shape of a person. It was moving, and for a shadow its movements were surprisingly sprightly and energetic, so that before I had a chance to make it out properly it had slipped

52

out of my sight. I blinked. I wasn't supposed to see people here. The one thing I knew about Johnny was that he was a recluse. Or had that been Johnny himself? I think I might have left then had I not slipped on a wet slab of slate and tumbled halfway down the track.

From where I eventually landed I could see the bottom corner of Johnny's house. It was made up of a base of large, thick stones, one placed unevenly upon another, giving it a look of higgledy-piggledy solidity, of hastily assembled permanence, that reminded me of a place called the ugly house – or Tŷ Hyll, I think – that sits on a corner of the A5 road through the mountains, just beyond some twee tourist town. I had visited it once and been taken by its endearing grotesqueness. It was built entirely of random slabs of rock, piled on top of one another to form a startlingly asymmetrical cube; all jutting out edges and hard, craggy ledges, like a house morphed out of a landslide or a shrunken, wizened mountain. Walking around its walls I discovered a small garden at the back, enclosed by a white picket fence, and a narrow path that led out of the garden and up a steep slope through a scattering of oaks and birches. I had followed this path for a couple of hundred yards, until its steepness made my footsteps difficult and my body sweat, and then turned to look below me. From this vantage point I could see the path winding down through the trees and into the garden, right up to a tiny green door that I had not noticed before – possibly because it was obscured by the erratic contours of the wall in which it was set – but which now gave the building a half-beckoning, half-interdictory air that made me feel as though I had stumbled upon some gaunt, inedible version of a fairytale cottage. From here it also

53

became apparent how closely blended this building was with the ground around it, strewn everywhere with glacial leftovers, stones left long ago stranded by the melting ice, so that I had thought, if this house is ugly then so is everything that surrounds it – these mountains, these valleys, these steep fields and forests, all of it.

Before leaving I had read, on a rather half-hearted and worn plaque, the story of how the house came to be built. In times gone by, apparently, there had been a custom whereby the poorest peasants were offered the chance to own patches of the highest, least fertile, land hereabouts. It was decreed that if they could build a house in a single day, from the moment the sun broke over the horizon to when darkness fell, then they would be entitled to a certain portion of land surrounding it. The extent of this portion was decided by the throw of a hammer. If the house had been successfully heaped together – four walls and a smoking chimney was the minimum requirement – then the rather exhausted builder would, the morning after, be allowed to stand on the threshold of his new domicile and hurl the largest of his hammers as far as he could into the distance. From where it landed a circle would be drawn, with the house in the centre, and the land contained within this circle would be his. Taking a final glance at the place, and the woods and fields about it, all I could think of was the grim urgency of that throw, of everything that depended on it; of the sore and aching limbs that propelled it into the air and its hopeful, precarious flight, while all the while these trees and rocks had looked passively and uncaringly on. And I was filled again with a sense of the incongruity of the thing, the injustice, of how what we build in need and desperation, and that which nature leaves by chance, can be judged so differently, so that this house is called ugly and everything around it beautiful.

After I'd lifted myself up off the track the rest of Johnny's cottage became visible. It was a squat, two-storey building that clung like a limpet onto the sloping land. It wasn't ugly at all. On either side of its front there was a small window and momentarily I thought I could hear a voice coming from the one nearest to me – or perhaps voices, I couldn't tell – but before I had time to be sure it was gone and I quickly put it down to the rattling in my head after my fall. There was a door in the centre, or rather a door split in two like you get in stables, and beside this door was an old steel bathtub, placed directly below a piece of broken guttering. As I approached it the top half of the door began to open and a head of white hair appeared, followed by a hand and an arm. It was the hand that took my attention. I couldn't quite make out at first what it was holding, just the colours and the shape: it looked like a gasping mollusc, made of glinting, enamelled yellow and a dull, greyish pink. It was only when the hand began snapping the thing together that I realised it was a set of teeth. I watched as the hand shoved the teeth into the rainwater collected in the bathtub – breaking through a covering of leaves that had gathered on the surface – and began swishing them around. I half expected them to spring suddenly into life and go off chattering into the murky depths of the tub. Instead they re-emerged, dripping and glistening, and were promptly shoved into the mouth of a face that I now looked at for the first time.

I wish I could describe how he looked then, but, in my mind's eye, all I can see is his dead face. It is as if some

55

synaptic alchemy has conspired to leave only a cadaver in my head, has inserted a corpse into my memory in place of what was once living, so that I can remember the words he first said but it is a pair of dead lips that speak them, a pair of dead eyes – rolled-up and white – that look at me.

'Who the hell are you?'

'I'm Jonathon, from the cottage down there', I said, pointing nervously in the direction of my cottage.

'Well why don't you just bugger off back to it then!'

'I just came to say hello,' I said, adding, almost in desperation, 'we're neighbours.'

But by then he'd shut the door.

5

'You'll 'ave tu try harder than that, mate,' said Nut later that day in the village's pub, the Dragon, a look of amused delight crossing his features as he spoke.

Bub, who was sitting beside him across the table, added, 'Aye, he cun be a bluddy awkward bugger wun he wans tu be.'

'Yer round,' said Nut. It always seemed to be mine. Part of my Dragon probation, I had thought at the time. I'm still on it.

It was quite early in the evening and there were only Bub and Nut and me in the front room. In the back I could see a blonde girl setting up equipment, for what I couldn't tell. At the bar the barmaid smiled at me and started pulling the others' pints without me having to say anything.

'An' what about you luv,' she asked. I told her and she smiled again. I was still a novelty here. I quite liked it. It made me feel exotic.

On my way back, holding the pints carefully in my hands, I saw the door open. A tall, slender, old man walked in, looked quickly around, and then crossed over to Bub and Nut's table.

'Get one in for Goronwy, will yu mate', Nut shouted. The barmaid was already pulling it by the time I turned back towards the bar.

Back at the table Nut was gleefully relating my encounter with Johnny to the old man: '...an so 'e tells 'im to fuck off 'e does, like I told 'im he would....' As I put the pints down Bub politely stopped smiling and gestured towards the man.

'Goronwy,' the man said, 'pleased to meet you. Jonathon, isn't it?' We shook hands briefly and he thanked me for the drink. 'So, what's your interest in Johnny then?'

'Well, I suppose it's because we're neighbours now,' I said, knowing that was not really true – or rather, it was half-true, but to tell the whole truth I would have had to tell them everything. And how could they have understood?

As we spoke the pub began to fill. A small, balding man came past and nodded at us. A plump, shortish girl bought a drink and stood with her face turned away from us, staring at the dartboard, saying nothing to anybody. There were two women at the bar and Nut waved towards them; one of them flicked a V at him in return.

Goronwy's voice had only one level. It was as though age had drained out its inflections and left behind this thin, parchmenty kind of intonation, too tired and fragile to either dip, or rise, or veer. To follow it I had to filter out the wayward, see-sawing sounds that had begun to form around it. The jukebox had come to life, lights rising up through its interiors and refracting off iridescent silver disks that clicked and spun like wheels in a clock. A song came on. Folky guitars, and words that were all a babble to me, came wheeling into the air. The name Dic Penderyn was in the chorus, lots of times.

'We were in school together,' Goronwy said, 'the old grammar school in town. He's a clever man, Johnny, very clever, though most of these wouldn't grant it. He was the star in school, not me you know, though I did more with what I had and so got the reputation. He left when he was seventeen, left when everything was at his feet and beckoning: university, degrees, careers, a way out and into the world. Just left, without a word of explanation, without a single reason or excuse. There were lots around here who had him down for being lazy anyway, because he read a lot – everything he could get his hands on – and was a dreamer besides; a haunter of horizons and sunsets, with a mooning look in his eye and a liking for loneliness, both in himself and in the places around him. And his leaving, well, that confirmed it for them. Couldn't even stick with his studies, they thought. But it wasn't that. Johnny may be many things, but lazy isn't one of them. I wish I could tell you what it was, only I don't really know because he's never told me. More than half a century gone and not a word about it. Of course, he spoke a lot less after his mother....'

The disks had slipped into a different tempo, coaxed on by Nut and a fifty pence piece, a thumping, repetitive bass line that seemed to joggle the beer in my stomach and send the bubbles fizzing, elatedly, into my head. I was beginning to feel a bit drunk. Bub had appeared with more drinks and there were other people in the bar now, none of whom I knew. A girl at the table beside us laughed and began to dance with her arms, pumping them back and forth like jackhammers; a tight, red top clung to her breasts and her bare midriff was coiled like a thick snake around the top of her jeans. 'Can't get... can't get you... can't get you out...' cried the jukebox, and all the time Goronwy's voice not altering, not wavering, but hanging like a thin foam above heavy wave-breaks. I could only hear it now through the other voices, other sounds, and struggled to trace and decipher it as though it were the faded base of a palimpsest of noise.

'...who was a mysterious woman herself, and never, I think, thought that she really belonged here. But, because she had been moved once was determined never to be moved again, and wanted the same for Johnny as well. Or that's my take on it. Johnny won't discuss her either: another of his taboo subjects. They talk about him, of course they do. The more a person retreats from the world, the more other people rush to fill the void they leave behind. A vacuum is to be abhorred... it's more than I care to think about... *can't get you out...* liable to be filled with all manner of nonsense. And yet me, who perhaps knows him best of all – if know is a word you can use with Johnny – can sense this emptiness at the heart of him, a missing element, like those in dying stars, that seems to exert a disproportionate gravitational pull on every-thing around and about him, so that even to be in the same room as him makes you feel it... *can't get you....*'

In the wateriness of his eyes I could see the reflected disks rotate, filling his irises until they too seemed to glint and spin and sing. At the end of the bar, two black rectangular boxes had appeared, out of which lights began to dart, flashing red, then green, then white, bouncing off the tobaccoed yellow of the walls.

'Just testing,' shouted the blonde girl to the barmaid, 'checking they look arright.'

'They look luuvly tu me darlin',' Nut called out, cupping his hands beneath his chest.

'Idiut,' said Bub, looking over at him.

'Yer round, mate,' said Nut, looking over at me.

'Best just make mine a whisky, thank-you,' said Goronwy, lifting a brow over his whirling eye.

'I'm just loooking....' cried the jukebox.

It was quite packed around the bar now, and I had to push my way through to it. There were older men in battered plaid jackets, and younger ones in nylon trakkie tops; women with bright, shining hair – the smell of spray stung my nostrils as they passed above it. Some of them glanced at me, without smiling. I didn't feel exotic now. I felt like a stranger. The plump girl stood transfixed before the dartboard, watching the arrows arc towards the battered, perforated felt. The bar was covered with dead pints.

'When's she gonna start?' whined Nut.

'Dunno,' Bub replied.

'I remember talking to him once, not so many years after I'd got back from the war, and I was telling him how I'd met a man from Llanysgerbwd in Rangoon, in a bar with a bamboo roof, and that this man had known his father. I was telling him how strange it had felt, to be there in this bar, looking out through the window at the rutted red clay of the road, at the rickshaws bouncing past, and the company of Gurkhas who were splitting cucumbers with their kukris beneath the tall palms, of how strange it had felt to hear the syllables of his father's name and of Ebenezer Chapel and Eglwys Fach, to hear them there, in the humid air, a thousand miles or more from home. And all the time I was talking his eyes shining, staring, as though by staring he might somehow see what I had seen, heard what I had heard... and then started crying, silently, helplessly, Johnny, who you'd never imagine doing anything without thinking about it, his face a mess of tears... only I couldn't tell then if he was crying for his father, who had died before he ever had a chance to know him, or for something else I didn't know about.... You see there's so much he keeps hidden that, sometimes, I begin to wonder if this front he keeps up isn't like some cheap magician's plastic cup, a thing to hide nothing, to cover whatever it is that isn't there....'

'Not buuying... just loooking...' and then the discs spun into stillness and the singing fell to a whisper before fading away. And for a while we all went quiet, as though the jukebox had spun out our voices too.

'She's getting ready,' said Nut, eventually.

'Ladies and gentlemen,' said the barmaid, 'put your hands together for Rhian, who's come all the way from Holyhead to sing for us tonight.' A thin spattering of applause ran through the room.

The young blonde girl was standing between the black rectangles – their lights flashing red, then green, then white – holding a microphone. From somewhere behind her a speaker began spluttering into life, and then she began to sing. The room filled suddenly with applause, and then with singing.

I watched Goronwy watching her, his face lit up by the alternate colours as though someone were turning a kaleidoscope in front of it. The pale translucency of his ancient skin seemed to let the colours through, making the bones and veins and tendons beneath stand out in polychromatic relief, stretched out like a peacock's tale, with two dark circles for eyes. I couldn't see what they were seeing.

'My, my, my,' she sang, swaying with the lyrics, a hand held up to conduct the chorus. 'My, my, my,' sang the rest of them, in sotted unison. Across from me Nut was lost ecstactically in the noise, shouting out each syllable, and even Bub had let himself go; his voice, momentarily freed, rising up with the rest: 'My, my, MY, Du-li-lu.' And despite myself I could feel the pull of it, could feel my pulse respond to the ascending clamour, my lips tremble on the bright edge of the words, two fluttering moths drawn hopelessly to Tom's hoary, hackneyed flame.

By the time I turned back Goronwy's chair was empty; there were only the coloured beams falling through its slatted back. For a second I thought he had simply dwindled away into the colours, dissolved back into a million smoky photons, become a skeleton of light. And then I could hear him speaking beside me, the tone and volume of his speech not altering, making no adjustment to the surrounding din, saying, 'Tell him you're interested in abroad,' and, as I shifted around, there he was, the black spots of his eyes gleaming down, all wry and cryptic, saying, 'tell him you're interested in travel....' He turned to leave then, and I watched him recede through the crowd about the bar, his gaunt frame flitting between them, every now and again lifting a lank arm in farewell, until finally he had disappeared altogether.

The blonde girl was gathering herself to lead one last crescendo, but when it came I found the pull had gone. Inside

63

I had gone quiet and the noise around me felt a hundred miles away, like the distant rumbling of a faraway sea. Only my loneliness was left with me. I glanced over at the girl by the dartboard; she was staring at the singer now and for the first time I saw her face. Her eyes had such a look of contentment and serenity in them that it almost broke my heart.

6

'It's down 'ere yu say?' the taxi driver had asked me.

'Yes... well, I think it is.' I hadn't actually said anything.

'Yu think it is or yu know it is – yu better decide mate, 'cus I don't wantu be taking me car down this lane for nothing.' From the back seat I could see the folds of his belly sagging down towards the gearstick, vibrating imperceptibly as they were quivered by the idling engine. These were the first words he'd spoken to me. Back at the coach station he hadn't said a thing, just waited for me to haul my boxes towards his car and stammer out the claggy syllables of my new address, which I'd carefully copied out onto a sheet of paper. He'd waited, unimpressed, for me to finish before nodding his head at the door. For the next half an hour we'd sat in silence as, out of the window, I watched a bridge pass beneath us, a castle go by, mountains appear, the sea flickering in and out of view.

'So what's it gonna be?'

'Look, I'm sorry but I'm really not certain. I've never been there.'

'Never been there,' he muttered, 'that's handy innit. So what's the name then?'

'Of the village?' I asked, taking out my sheet of paper and nervously preparing another attempt at pronouncing it.

'No, not the *village* mate, we've just gone through that,' he said, not even trying to hide his exasperation, 'the house.'

'Ty... Gwy...'

'Why don't yu give us a look,' he said, thrusting his hand back over his shoulder. I passed him the paper. 'Ah, right, Tŷ Gwynt. Why didn't yu say? Yer a bit off 'ere then, we've already passed it, like.' He turned around and headed back down the road we'd come along. After about six hundred yards or so he swerved abruptly onto an almost identical lane. As we thudded through the first potholes he slowed to near walking pace and suddenly became quite talkative.

'Yer a bit late, aren't yu?'

'Late for what?' I asked, and for one absurd moment I'd imagined that someone might be waiting for me to arrive. Out of the corner of my eye I couldn't help noticing that the meter hadn't slowed down as much as the car had.

'For a holiday. Yu don't get many coming this late in the year.'

When I told him I wasn't here for a holiday, that I actually owned the place, he glanced at me suspiciously in the mirror and I tried to conceal the frayed edges of my fading shirt.

'I used tu live round 'ere – when I was younger, yeh – an' I don't remember that place being anything but a holiday home. There was only people there in the Summer.'

I told him I'd unexpectedly inherited it.

'Well, yer lucky there then mate,' he said, squinting once more into the mirror. 'It's in good nick an' everything I reckon. An' yu've got most of around 'ere tu yerself. Only a couple of farms round 'ere, an' a weird old fella lives down one a these lanes.' He gestured vaguely with his hand towards what looked like a gap in the hedge. This was the first time I'd heard of Johnny. The car jolted as its wheels sank into another pothole.

'One a them recluse types, yu know. Never leaves 'is house, never goes anywhere. Been holed up 'ere since he was a kid s'what I heard; crazy old bugger they say, mad as a fukking hatter, living in a world of his own. When I lived 'ere there was kids who used to go down an' spy on 'im, just fukking about like, an' they said they saw all sorts'a crazy shit through his window; saw 'im playing with dolls an' stuff, an chanting like a fukking priest or something. Can't imagine it meself yu know, staying in a house yer whole life. No wonder 'e lost it. Still, least he won't be bothering yu, mate.'

By now we'd come to what appeared to be another gap in the hedge and we turned into it, revealing a short, muddy track, leading up to a single storey, whitewashed cottage. Behind it there was a copse of willows, in front, some fields, an island, the sea. The taxi had come to a stop and for a moment the driver and I sat in silence.

''Ere we are then,' he finally said. I didn't say anything. I didn't know where we were. 'I'm not taking yu right up to the door mate. Sorry an' that, but the track'll fuk me car.'

'That's no problem,' I said. 'So this is it then?'

'What?'

'The house.'

''Course it is. Christ mate, don't yu even know what yer own place looks like?'

'I've never seen it before.'

'Well, welcome home then, pal.'

I took my own boxes out of the boot and stood for a bit watching the taxi drive away. When it was gone I turned to look up the track towards the house. So here I am then, I thought. And I'd already forgotten its name.

Inside I began to find relics of the summer visitors the driver had told me about. There were some books on a shelf in the sitting room; in the kitchen there was a set of plastic plates and some cans of beans; in the bedroom I came across a children's bucket and spade, two butterfly nets, a collection of shells. I gathered them all together and put them in a pile on the kitchen table, and then sat looking at them. For a while I couldn't understand what interested me about them. But slowly I began to realise that they filled me with a terrible envy; envy for people I'd never seen, but whom I now pictured as a succession of happy families returning sun-drenched and laughing from long summer days and throwing down their tanned limbs in my house; parents reading their books in my living room, children arranging their beach booty on my floor, while far away I played alone with my stones, hiding in some room that I'd not once risked or bothered to think of as my own. These other lives, so different to my own, seemed to emanate from them, to unpack themselves from out of the objects they'd left behind and congregate about me – each one a rebuke, each a reminder of what should have been. They made me feel like I was the visitor here, the one passing through, not them.

Later that day I took them outside and burned them. I watched with pleasure as they turned to smoke and ash, until all that was left was a heap of charred shells. And I made a promise to myself that this cottage, whatever it was called, would be mine now. That I would live here and make sure that the people who'd owned this stuff could never come back. I would learn to live here. I would learn to be like him. And it was at that moment that I'd begun to think of Johnny, before I even knew his name.

7

The sun and the moon hovered over the continents, the one above the Bering Straits, the other somewhere between Iceland and Norway. Half the world caught in a perpetual day, the other in an endless night. Because only time was moving here. I watched as the minute-hand ascended in the West, jerking its way across the great plains, skipping over the Pacific; while the hour-hand declined – more slowly – into the East, inching through Siberia like an iceberg. It was quarter to two.

I'd been waiting at the table for at least twenty minutes and, apart from the illustrations on the clock face, there was really very little to look at. On the far side of the room stood a tall cabinet full of unused china cups and plates, etched with pictures of what appeared to be dragons – or were they dogs? Behind me was a small fireplace, fronted with a bronze grate, in which a tiny heap of coals glowed faintly, sputtering occasionally into the odd warmthless and miserable flame. Everything in the room smelled of coal smoke. In my memory that whole winter smells of coal smoke; it seems to hang like a shroud over it all, creeping into each crevice and corner of the shortening days. And now, like so much else in this country, my memory is inextricably entwined with the residue of fossil fuels.

'Tea?' he asked, appearing suddenly in the middle of the room although I hadn't noticed him come in; a question rendered entirely rhetorical when he lifted the pot in his hand and began to fill two chipped white mugs with tea. It was not the last of this type of question that I would hear.

'So,' he said, sitting down opposite me, 'Goronwy tells me you're quite the well-travelled man.' When he'd poured my tea I'd noticed two brown liver spots on his fingers, and as he talked to me I found myself unable to stop looking at them. They seemed to hover like fuscous butterflies over the table, making me feel as though he were somehow sensing me out with them, was caressing the air about my skin with blind, invisible antennae.

'Been all over the place, he says. Of course everyone seems to be at it these days. It's easier now, isn't it?'

'I suppose it...'

'Got around himself a bit, did Goronwy, when he was younger you know. Went off with the army – lots from around here did, back then in the war; it was how you got to see the world, either that or work on the boats. With a gun or a cargo, that's how you travelled. Usually both. So what took you away?'

72

Away from what, I wanted to say. Instead I prepared some speech about curiosity, restlessness, that sort of thing, but before I had time to deliver it his hands had floated up in a gesture that appeared to imply that there was no need for me to answer. You don't have to tell me everything, they seemed to say, and I was relieved.

'There was one man,' he said, as if in reply to the answer I hadn't given, the real answer that is, the one I'd never intended to give, 'lived not far from here, in a village down the coast, who woke up one day and decided to move to Mobile, Alabama. Without a hint of warning you know, not the slightest little clue, just wakes up and starts telling everyone he meets that he's off as soon as he can sell his things and get a ticket. And at first they all laughed, swearing they'd never even heard of the place, and if they hadn't, then there was no chance *he* had, seeing he wasn't the most cosmopolitan man in the village, not by a long shot. Might find his way to Chester, they said, but this Mobile place, well he'd be lucky if he found it on a map. But he keeps on telling them and three days later he's getting on a bus to Liverpool, and later a man from the village, who works there on the docks, comes home saying he'd seen him, sure enough, getting on a ship to America. They could hardly believe it. Why would he go, they all asked. He'd had a job, lots of family, even a fiancée. So it must be the fiancée, they decide. *Esgob*, say all the women, isn't that an awful way to weasel your way out of a wedding. *Arglwydd*, say all the men, the lad's got a bit of pluck to him, to go that far to stay single. And for ten years he's gone, vanished, disappeared, until he's no more than a half-remembered story in the village – "the man who went to Mobile" – though of course by then it's been embellished a bit and there's oil in it, an illegitimate child, the suspicion of a murder. Ten years, without so much as a peep or a postcard out of him, nothing. And then one day he shows up. Walks right on into the pub. It takes them a while to recognise him then, not because he looks different but because he looks the same; if he'd come in wearing a stetson, a belt with a big brass buckle and a couple of pistols, a pair of chaps, then it would have been easier; he would, quite obviously, have been "the man who went to Mobile", or "the man who went to Mobile and then came home". But he looks just the same as when he left – a bit older, granted – and so for a few minutes he's only some lad who used to live here. And when they do recognise him everyone's asking about the child and the oil and the murder, telling him about the poor fiancée who cried for a month before marrying someone else and turning into a right old bitch (lucky move there they say), and he just looks confused, then bewildered, then a little disappointed in himself for having to disappoint them. The truth, he says, is that he went away because he didn't know who he was.

'It was one evening, he tells them, when he'd been up a ladder at his nain's house, nailing a slate back onto her roof, and the ladder had slipped and he'd fallen into the garden and clunked his head on a chunk of limestone jutting out of the grass. And he's lying there in the garden, feeling his head, checking for holes in his skull, but there don't seem to be any so he's pretty relieved about it – no damage done – only when he stands up he can't remember why he's there, or even where *there* is. Then this strange old woman comes out of the door offering him panads and brechdans and he begins to get the fear in him and runs off into the street. But it's a street he's never seen before and he doesn't know a single house on it. Strangers walk past waving at him, only he's got it into his dented head that they're pointing at him; that they're singling him out like some circus freak or gypsy, and God knows what they'll do to him. So he runs down the street in a panic, runs until the street has gone and become the sea, not knowing which sea, but all seas are made of water he thinks and this makes him feel a little better. There's a narrow beach beside this sea and he walks along it until he comes to a sign with a picture of an island on it, and an arrow painted in red that points to a corner of it, with the words "you are here" written above it. But of course he doesn't know where *here* is – it's just a preposition to him – all he knows is that he's on some island in some sea. And as he walks further down the beach he comes across a piece of flotsam, a rusty oil barrel, and on its side he can make out some flaking paint that has survived the water long enough to spell out the words Mobile, Alabama. At this point he realises that he's not alone on the beach. In front of him, where the pebbles become mud and sand, two men are picking cockles and one of them has looked up and started waving at him and, even worse, has begun shouting something at him. The panic comes back twofold this time and he sprints towards a thin line of dunes at the edge of the beach, where he nestles down amongst the reeds and grass, waiting for the night to come and hide him. It's like he's fallen waking into a nightmare and when the night does come all it gives him is a few hours of comforting, dreamless blankness. The next day he opens his eyes and nothing has changed: there is the nameless sea, there is the unknown

75

village, there is the unfamiliar sky. But the people are unavoidable now: they're out everywhere, walking dogs, fixing boats, fishing, and eventually they start coming up to him and talking. They speak like they know him – some of them even speak like they like him – but he's sure they're pretending because he's never seen them before. And behind the fakeness of their words he senses an undefinable, yet inescapable, hint of menace, like a bee buzzing beneath the petal of a flower. There's this story that he's heard – though where and when he might have heard it is a mystery – that keeps coming back to him. It's about an Englishman arriving on an island and all the natives welcoming him like a long lost friend; they invite him to feasts and dances, they sit around with him on mats telling stories; a few of them even offer him one of their wives. But in the end, just when he's getting comfortable, they kill him and eat him. Now he's pretty sure that this won't happen, but he can't shake off the feeling of foreboding and this story, he imagines, must be coming back to him for a reason. So he decides to tell everybody he meets, thinking that if they think he's leaving – and quite soon – they'll be secretly better inclined towards him, that he's off to Mobile, Alabama (because he doesn't know the name of anywhere else). And before he has time to blink almost, he is gone.

'For the first few years it isn't so bad. Not having a past doesn't seem to be problem: half the people he meets there are trying to get rid of theirs anyway, and when he does need one it's easy enough to borrow one of their cast-offs, or to make one up from scratch. But at some point he begins to realise there's something missing. It's hard to put his finger on. It's as if everything around him is surrounded by a hollow shell,

76

and however hard he tries to get through it, all he manages to reach is the departed echo of some other, primary thing. It's a terrible feeling he says; sometimes he feels like a ghost haunting the world, sometimes he feels like the world is a ghost haunting him. And one day he's wandering down on the wharves at midday, amid the bustle of loading and unloading, of people and cargoes, when he comes across an ancient looking man who's sitting on a crate looking at it all. "This was all empty once," the old man says to him, "the bay, the sea, Christ! this whole damn country." He doesn't say a word more, but he's said enough because this lad knows now that for him it still is empty, and, what's worse, there's a whole continent full of emptiness inside him too. So for two years more he's lugging around this terra nullis in his belly, and it's heavier than you think, this emptiness, he says, heavy enough to snap a man in half. And it would have snapped him too, he tells them, except that one day he's passing the window of a stationery shop, and in the window there's a rack of cards – birthday cards, get well cards, all kinds of them – and one of them's a valentine. He didn't know why he even looked at it, but he did, and on the cover are the words *Mon Amour*. He only needed to see the word once, he says. He knew what it was then. The next year he spent earning his fare home.'

What was I to make of this? Why was he telling me this story? Was I its subject? Was he? In fact, come to think of it, why had he welcomed me in in the first place? I'd arrived prepared with Goronwy's instructions but had never had a chance to carry them out. He'd just ushered me through the door without a word and sat me down beside the table. He hadn't asked why I'd come. And yet, from the moment I'd

77

stepped into his house, I'd had the feeling that he knew, that he knew better than me. There was something in his voice that reinforced this feeling, a quality of knowingness, a teasing, winking suggestiveness, as though this was a game to be played and played at my expense. I didn't know then that it would always be a little like this.

We sat in silence for a bit, as the minutes whirled about the globe. I looked up to see the hours had reached the Steppes. Behind me the fire had reclined into a bed of faintly glowing coals. It was cold in here I realised, uncomfortably cold. Around the brown spots on his fingers his skin had turned a bluey grey.

'They probably told you about me,' he suddenly said.

Not very much, I was about to say, but he didn't give me the opportunity to reply. For a recluse he was turning out to be almost overbearingly garrulous, 'but I wouldn't pay too much attention to their blabbering. Let them talk. They've got little enough to talk about anyway. I remember it was the same when I was a boy. There was a woman who lived in a cottage by the quarry – of course it's gone now; a pile of rocks, that's all that's left of it – who only went out at night. I could see her come out from where I worked in the quarry, each night as the moon rose. She didn't do anything. She just walked down to the quarry's edge and sat down. Sometimes she cried, or maybe she always cried. I could only see her tears if the moon was bright. That was all she did. But after a few years they had her doing all sorts of things: witchcraft, sex, seances, the usual ones. And most of them knew as well as me that her husband had died five years before, dragged under by the ropes on his lobster pots, right off this very bit of coast.

They knew as well as me that she was only mourning, that she was only doing what a hundred other widows do when they sit beside gravestones. But after a while it wasn't enough for them; they had to make these other things up.'

His fingers had gone still but his body was hunched forward, as though in expectation, as though I would suddenly see the reason he was telling me all this. But whatever it was he was getting at, I wasn't getting it. I was playing my part in the game badly. I didn't know the rules. I didn't know the game. The talk of this woman had only made me think of myself. Because wasn't I in mourning too, in mourning for someone without a grave? And hadn't it brought me here as well? There were so many things I wanted to ask him. How do you learn to live in one place and for that to be enough? How do you learn to be alone, utterly? There were so many things, but I was beginning to sense now that it would always be a matter of his telling, not of my asking.

'I'm glad you've come,' he said. 'When Goronwy told me about you I thought maybe you were just the man I needed to see.'

He looked right at me then, but I couldn't quite read the expression on his face.

Part Two

Part Two

1

In the months that followed, Johnny's front room became more familiar to me than my own. When I think about the winter, I mostly picture it unfolding beyond his windowpane. Or perhaps unfolding is the wrong word. During those months nothing seemed to move, at least not through the glass of his window. Picture it instead as a grey stasis, a damp and ambiguous murk.

Of course outside it got wild enough. I remember the wind arriving sometime in November; a few refreshing gusts at first, waltzing in from the sea and spinning the leaves off their branches. But thereafter it became more brutal and noisily incessant, howling its way over the water, screeching up and over the cliffs, droning through the slates on my roof. And as the wind grew everything else receded. The landscape seemed to contract into an elemental residue, as though whatever was not firmly riveted onto the ground had simply blown away. Huge banks of glowering cloud smothered the horizon. Even the colours of the place ebbed and dwindled, bleached by the tumultuous sheets of briny rain that swept in from the west; while those that remained clung like watercolour wraiths upon the darker imprints of cold, naked rock and wet, bare bark.

I say more familiar than my own because, to tell the truth, I was struggling to fit myself into my cottage. Much of the time I felt like the drafts that blew through it were more at home there than I was. When I was a child, my mother had had a ritual for moving in. It was a simple one really. Because they had been so often used, my mother had named the boxes in which we stored our belongings. They were called after the rooms whose contents filled them: there were the bathroom boxes and the living room boxes, the kitchen boxes and the bedroom boxes and so on. When we'd arrive at a new place my mother would always go in first, with me trailing along behind her, and spend half an hour appraising its deserted interiors. I don't know what calculations and measurements she made during this half hour, but afterwards she'd turn to me and my father, (who always waited about twenty-five minutes before following us in – to delay his disappointment, I suppose) with her dark hair falling over her uneasily resigned and unhappy eyes, and begin pointing to various spots throughout the place, intoning, as she went, the names of the boxes. Later, when my father and I had put each box in its appointed spot, she'd usher us out and unpack them. It was only when she'd finished and we were allowed back in that I'd see how she'd tried, as best as she could, to replicate the exact arrangement of objects we'd had in our last building. There, in a living room a third of the size maybe, and differently shaped perhaps, to the last one, would be my parents' framed wedding photo (taken outside a registry office, with my father already chafing in his suit and looking away) halfway up the right-hand wall as you came in, just where it had been before. There, on the new bathroom door, would be the outdated calendar full of outback jokes that she could never bring herself to throw out. There was all of it, everything we owned, heroically, pitifully, pinned and pushed into place, into an imperfect approximation of before.

My father, for his part, would lose interest in wherever we'd arrived almost immediately. For the second half of the journey there (the first half was usually dedicated to heaping his vitriol on where we'd left) he'd blather incessantly about the new place he'd lined up: 'Jon,' he'd say – always addressing me because he must have thought that because I was a kid I would've forgotten that he'd made this speech countless times before, 'wait'll you see where we're going. It's nothing like that shithole we've been in... no, no worries there. Be glad to get out of that bloody cupboard, won't you, into a proper place. 'Cus let me tell you, from what I've seen....' And on and on, like he was Father Christmas, not realising that I'd stopped believing him well before I'd stopped believing in fat men coming down the chimney. And I'd know that he hadn't seen a grey brick or concrete block of the building we were headed to, because the first signs we were about to leave were usually a letter or an unfamiliar newspaper, a couple of surreptitious phone calls and maybe an argument, but never, not once, an actual journey of reconnaissance. We always set off towards the unknown, the banal and familiar unknown, with him droning on and on and on about somewhere he'd not even seen, his eyes fixed intently on the road ahead, imagining I'd be excited like he was – a man who believed in, who loved, who thrilled to only the places he hadn't yet arrived in.

I thought about my mother's ritual often during those first months. And I tried, sometimes for hours on end, to re-enact it. I'd stand in each room of my house and attempt to envision how I'd arrange and decorate it. But, as the weeks crept on, nothing came to me and my own boxes remained untouched in the corner of the room I slept in. I flitted in and out of spaces that were almost as empty as the landscape outside had become; a winter palace, pared, stripped, vacated, which I rattled through like a wind. And the longer I stayed there the less I seemed able to remember. One morning I woke up and sat for a whole hour on the edge of my bed, paralysed by the view through my window of the weak light emerging on the surface of the sea, my mind numb and blank, my past as adrift from me as this island was from the mainland, not just another country but another planet, another dimension, spinning and spiralling away of its own volition – distant, blurred, invisible.

After a while I found I could no longer even picture my mother properly. Her image had dwindled and faded like the colours outside. And when I tried to bring it back I discovered that, inexplicably, it was somebody else who appeared, staring at me with a look I knew I'd never once seen on my mother's face.

2

When not at Johnny's I was usually with Bub and Nut. Nut, for some reason, had taken me under his young wing. I think at first this was because my outsiderdom placed me automatically below him on the rungs of an unspoken hierarchy based, as far as I could tell, on age, lineage and origin. And though I bettered him in one of these categories – being seven years his senior – my deficiencies in the others ensured I languished well beneath his heels on the ladder. Being naturally exuberant – often to the point of hyperactive over-excitement (all those hours sitting on his tractor seat couldn't have helped) – he often appeared constrained and fidgety around Bub and the others, as though he were being held back on some invisible leash. But when I was around that leash seemed to slacken, giving him ample scope to vent his energies.

He began by introducing me to his interests, which appeared to centre mainly on Formula One racing. My initial glimpse of this took place on my first visit into the Nut and Bub household. It was a wretched day at the beginning of December and I had spotted Bub through my window, flailing a weighty fencing hammer about his head in the teeth of – as I'd realise a few weeks later – a fairly moderate early winter gale. For a few minutes I watched as he teetered and swayed and jerked in the wind, trying to balance and aim the hammer, looking for all the world like a drunken Father Time on a weather vane, brandishing a scythe made of lead. I waited a few minutes more, long enough for him to crush several undeserving cowpats, unsure whether offering my help might not be considered rude or insensitive, before going out to offer it anyway. But Bub seemed quite happy with the offer, and allowed me to spent the next hour or so crouched below him clutching fence posts, watching the uncertain trajectory of the hammer as it descended and thudded onto the wood, inches away from my fingers. Afterwards he stood in the wind, pointing towards his farm, and forced out a few strangled syllables, one of which I made out as 'tea'.

I'd never passed beyond the gates of Bub and Nut's farm before, though I had stood in front of them several times, and when I now entered the yard I was filled with the distinct sensation of being watched. In one obvious respect I actually was being watched. There were two old black-and-white sheep dogs slumped in the corner of the yard who, from the moment I stepped inside, began eyeing me with an indolent suspicion that threatened every moment to burst into a more energetic hostility. These dogs, I'd begun to realise, were almost a generic fixture of the island. If you looked closely you'd find them everywhere, in yards, under hedges, behind gates; I mean, if you really looked, if you kept your eyes wide open when you walked or drove around, then you'd quite likely see a thousand canine eyes staring back at you, wondering what you were doing here and not too sure if they were that happy that you were. And, if you then waited long enough, as likely as not a furtive figure in wellies and oilskins would sidle up along some hedgerow in the distance and cast a similar glance in your direction. These island Cerberuses were nothing if not the animal extensions of their masters. But it was more than these dogs that made me feel like this. Perhaps it was the windows of the farmhouse – a small, single-storey bungalow dashed with grey and white pebbles – and the way the drawn curtains twitched in the draughts that filtered through the glass, making it appear as if the hand of some undiscerned watcher had just that moment let them fall shut. But there was also something less specific that worked on me, something I couldn't quite put my finger on at the time and find hard to describe now. All I can say is that everything in the yard seemed to be concealing something: the rickety sheds with their flapping doors and shuddering, corrugated-iron shutters, the mysterious tangles of metal debris gathered in the corners, the empty barrels, the plastic fertilizer bags that fluttered like ensigns around fence posts and strands of barbed wire – all of them suggested some hidden thing that was not so much beyond my sight as looking at me. With each new gust of wind the whole place appeared to blink.

As Bub ushered me in the door I heard Nut clattering around in the kitchen. He was struggling with a drawer full of

89

cutlery and when we entered the room he met us, holding a big brown jar and a carving knife; there was a slab of white bread in his mouth and a smear of Marmite across his cheek.

'Yu wan' one,' he spluttered, sending a cascade of crumbs towards me.

'I'm fine,' I said. Bub shuffled towards the kettle.

Bub and Nut lived alone together. On that day, you could tell. There was a bachelors' clutter about the place – not so much a mess as an admixture of use and neglect. Parts of the room, like the area around the kettle, were unkempt, while others, like the heavy oak sideboard full of porcelain plates and the walnut chest of drawers, on top of which stood a collection of china cats and dogs, looked utterly untouched, waiting silently and patiently beneath a patina of grey and adhesive dust for the loving cloth that had long ago ceased to caress them. That cloth had belonged to their mother who, several years before, had been moved into the old folks' home in the village. Neither of them really spoke about her, although every Sunday Bub traipsed down there with a bag of fresh potatoes or tomatoes and once, when drunk, Nut had brusquely informed me, 'She's off 'er nut now and runs about in the night in the nod, screaming that 'er cats are dying.' And maybe these ones were. Maybe all the objects we leave behind begin to die without our touch. And what other things in this house I thought, what untrod corners and unworn clothes, what unseen pictures and unheld keepsakes, were wheezing out their final breaths while she shrieked naked and forlorn in the night?

After tea Nut took me to see his room. He seemed to like showing me things. He took a kind of proprietorial pride in the most disparate elements of his surroundings, delighting as much in pointing out to me the drooling, retarded giant who played in the yard of a nearby farm as he did in guiding me round the picturesque nooks and crannies on his own land. To Nut my presence made everything somehow new and interesting, an array of small wonders that I'm sure he half-expected me to bulge my eyes out at in astonishment and admiration. But they only brought home to me once again the sad insight that so much of my life had forced upon me: that whatever new place you go, it's your guide who usually ends up seeing the familiar as a novelty, as somewhere truly different, and it's you who watch as the apparently exotic crumbles before you into an unutterable sameness.

The room was full of racing cars. There were miniature models of them on the bedside table and chest of drawers, posters of them on the wall, pictures of them cut out of newspapers and magazines stacked up on the floor. Nut stood back to give me time and space to digest this revelation.

'This is quite a collection,' I said.

'I got loads of 'em, aye. All sorts! From the sixties an' seventies an' everything.'

'Yes, quite a collection.'

Nut began thrusting various models into my hands, excitedly listing the names of drivers and manufacturers, trilling details of horsepower and engine capacity, top speeds and tractions, while his green eyes began to glaze and shine under his copper fringe. He told me of great races and famous tracks, Imola, Monte Carlo, Monaco, names that I could see for him were not the names of actual places at all, but instead were magical extensions of the cars themselves; a series of petrol-drenched paradises, glistening under the rays of a metallic sun, gleaming beneath the shards of its silver light.

Outside I could hear the wind moaning through the yard and beating its way over the bungalow roof. My thoughts seemed to follow it, blowing along across the rain-soaked fields and leafless hedgerows, whistling around cottage doors and windows, eddying into the maze of roads and lanes. And, for a few moments, I imagined that mysterious tangle of by-ways through Nut's eyes: as a circuit of turns and straights and chicanes, where rattling signs and flapping silage bags looked like chequered flags, where around each corner podiums waited and champagne corks burst; and, for a few moments, there was nothing hidden from me and nothing watching me and nowhere else in the world I wanted to be.

3

Back in Johnny's house another world was being revealed to me, or rather several. Maybe it was all the years spent alone, all the accumulated conversations that he had never had, but there was no silencing him that Winter. Out streamed the words, a steady flow of them that seemed to silence everything else. To tell the truth I still don't know whether he spoke quickly or slowly, only that he spoke without interruption until, abruptly, he'd finish for the day. I think it must have been something Goronwy had said that night, about the emptiness that you sensed in him, but sometimes I felt his voice as disembodied, as words that floated through the air with no corporeal source; as hollow sounds, like echoes returning. Occasionally, when I'd look up from the table, it seemed like the only things in the room were the fluttering brown spots on his hands.

It was during those moments, when Johnny seemed least there, that I began to detect what appeared to be subtle proofs of other presences in his house. They were so slight and apparently inconsequential that for a long time I hardly even registered them. For instance, now and again there'd be a certain scent intermingled with the coal smoke in his room, an unexpected hint of polish or perfume that lingered for a half hour or so before being overwhelmed again by the heavy reek of soot. At other times I was sure I caught the whiff of a freshly baked cake trying to squeeze beneath the door from the kitchen. Twice I discovered strands of hair on the table that weren't Johnny's. One was definitely human, it was long and white; the other one I wasn't too sure about, it was jet-black and unusually coarse and thick, as if it had come from a horse's mane. Among the other mysterious objects I found on Johnny's table were a few desiccated flakes of orange peel, a glass bead, pieces of straw. He always brushed them away before I had time to really notice them, let alone ask about them. But sometimes it wasn't anything so definite as a smell or an object that made me imagine these other presences, sometimes it was only a vague feeling that someone had just left, or something had just been put away. And whatever it was that prompted this feeling, it would eventually be drowned out by the relentless tide of his recitation.

He began with genealogy. I don't remember all the names – though later some were given flesh and bones – only that there were tens and hundreds of them; a great troupe of dancing syllables conjured out of Llanysgerbwd's almost unfeasibly fruitful loins. Then there was biography, the selected lives of those past Joneses who, for Johnny, had taken on a special stature or significance; enough, anyway, for him to single them out from the horde. And lastly there was autobiography: Johnny's life, or at least those strands of it he deemed fit to describe to me.

I don't want by this to suggest a particular sequence to these recollections, that they were unfolded in an orderly fashion or treated as discrete categories, because in Johnny's mind, and on his tongue, they were all spliced together; a composite jumble that defied the unities, that intermingled like the blasted strata of exploded stone.

Nor should I forget the setting. In fact, maybe I should begin with it, as it was the point of origin for all the rest. This is Johnny's Llanysgerbwd.

It was a seaside village out of sight of the sea, he told me. Nestled as it was, amongst the small hills of the island's interior, the water was concealed from its view. But when you live on an island the sea is everywhere, he said, and you don't need to see its water to know it's there. Look up and you can sense it in the sky: in the quality of its light, in the gulls that hover about it, in the smell of it, in the sounds that are hidden in it. He might as well have been born and brought up on a boat, he said, because from the first moments he could remember there was brine in his nostrils and distance in his eyes. Like his father, who was born on a boat: a three-masted barque called the Western Monarch, in the bay of Valparaiso. On the Western Monarch, eight months out of Liverpool with a cargo of coal in its hold and a smaller cargo of cells in his grandmother's belly, which was painfully unfreighted in the captain's cabin and docked in a wooden cradle they had made from boxes on the journey. Valparaiso

Jones they named him. Valparaiso Jones, from Llanysgerbwd by way of the Horn.

There were many like his father in the village he explained, men called Janeiro and Sydney and Philadelphia, sired on the ground and delivered on the sea; men whom you saw only one month in the year – sometimes years – who turned up for a bit with tans and then vanished; a population of absent, remembered men who occasionally left their wives behind to mark their pieces of earthly territory. Because back then there were only really three things you could do on the island, he said, you could farm it, or you could quarry its cliffs, or you could leave it and go to sea. And those who came from Llanysgerbwd did all three. It was these livelihoods that shaped the village, he said, shaped it literally, physically, in a way that oddly inverted what you would expect from those who lived them. It was the sailors who had built their houses in the centre, two-storeyed ones of clean brick for the captains and mates, single, whitewashed squares with one door and one window for the ordinary seamen and fishermen; but all of them clinging together in the middle, each side of the road, while their owners scattered themselves around the globe. Next came the quarrymen, in the second circle, who put together tidy little boxes with stolen stones and filled them with too many children. And then the farmers, whose cottages were spread out in the hollows between the hills, on the very edges of the village, belonging to it only in the way moons belong to planets, strung out along the furthest reaches of its gravity. An ironic patterning, where it was those who never left the village who always lived furthest away from it, and those who were barely there that formed its nucleus.

It stretched along the road for a third of a mile, maybe less, punctuated at one end – the more elevated – by the church, and at the other by Ebenezer Chapel. The former made of river stone that, he said, seemed to have retained the memory of those centuries of water that had smoothed it and on sunny days would flicker like the bottom of a stream; the latter an unfussy grey block capped with austere, Presbyterian slate. The one always looking down the small rise – as though it were its nose – at its parvenu neighbour, squinting its stained-glass eyes and worrying about its near-empty insides. These were the poles of Llanysgerbwd, Johnny told me, its North and South, which on Sundays would divide the village into temporary hemispheres. And around each of them was a graveyard where, once a week, you would see people congregate, standing amongst the graves on which their family names and professions were written – G Jones. Pig Trader 1801–1839, V Jones. Sailor 1881–1906 – clustering about the dead as people seem to do here he said, almost to remind themselves that that they are still here, that they still exist because they have existed before and left behind this reassuring detritus of slate and inscription.

Before long I had heard the names on many of those gravestones, and knew who had lived in almost every house and what they did and who had married their second cousin – a not very bright girl who was useless at sowing and afraid of geese. I knew about the spot above Pritchard's farm where you could see the island's only mountain – which was not a mountain really but the single hill high enough to pass for one – that had been gutted years back for its copper; I knew of the old Penlon estate, gambled away by the son and lived in by his two spinster sisters, who spent their lives painting local flowers and plants and freed their peacocks to roam through the village. Johnny was an encyclopedia of Llanysgerbwd, and no detail of it appeared to have escaped him. And yet there was always something missing when he described the place, something lacking that I could not put my finger on at the time but which left it strangely unreal and unclear to me; a blurred outline that inexplicably reminded me of going to watch *Jaws 3* in the cinema as a child, with a pair of 3-D glasses made of yellow and red plastic that I'd got out of a box of cornflakes, and how Jaws had not looked like a three-dimensional shark at all but like a lump of yellow and red plastic thrashing his way through a yellow and red ocean towards the focus that would ever elude him. The details somehow didn't add up, didn't fit together: although all of them came out of the projector they never seemed to fall together properly into a living image, or even an image of something that might have been alive. After *Jaws* I had cried miserably in disappointment, having been cheated out of what the cornflakes box had promised me – *Jaws*: Just Like in Life – and my mother had tried to comfort me by buying me a magazine with photographs of real sharks in it. But they weren't the same, they weren't what I had imagined those glasses would deliver to me, and I continued to blub ungratefully over the pictures. And my mother had said 'Jonathon,' she always used my full name when she was pissed off with me, 'those are real sharks.' But I remained inconsolable.

I'm not sure if some glimmer of my uncertainty didn't get across to Johnny, because eventually he began to show me photographs as well. He'd vanish suddenly, often in mid-sentence, and leave me with the clock and the warmthless fire and the coal smoke, while he rummaged around in a room upstairs that I never saw. Then he'd reappear and spread these pictures on the table between us, taking up where he'd left off, not pointing at them, not even specifically referring to them, but continuing to talk as though their presence alone provided an unequivocal bulk and substance to his words, a celluloid proof and permanence. And at these times his voice would become subtly more cajoling and insistent, almost incantatory, and his hands would flutter with even greater rapidity than usual, as though he were some wizard trying frantically to conjure a whole village out of an unseen hat.

I can only remember one of these pictures of Llanysgerwd. I don't know why this is. Perhaps it was some lack of attention on my part, the type you always suffer from when looking at other people's photos, photos without you in them or anything that relates to you. Perhaps it was this. But I think there is another reason for my forgetfulness, for the blankness that seems to answer all my efforts at recollection, and that reason is a great deal more difficult to explain. In fact, maybe only that one remaining picture can explain it.

At first glance it wasn't that remarkable, and resembled several others I had seen in cheap brass frames in the tourist shops in town, each portraying some quaint image of the island's antiquity. It was a black-and-white photograph of the village bakery, a plain two-storey building cut in half by a long rectangular sign painted with the name Gwalia Temperance: Bakery & Confectionery. It had two windows. In the first you could see a shelf full of loaves, balanced on top of each other like doughy bricks, and just above them, written on the glass, the words 'Hovis Bread'; while, in the second, 'Cadbury's Chocolate' had been written in a circle around what appeared to be a crest of arms or shield, below which two advertisements were placed, one for Tower Tea, comprised of several oval portraits of absurdly genteel Edwardian ladies sipping from porcelain cups, and the other for Carbosil: 'The New Soda', in which a maid was sitting reading a book in front of a giant clock face (although what this had to do with soda is beyond me). The family who owned the bakery were standing on the pavement. To the right were the father and his son, both dressed in white baker's aprons; the latter with his sleeves rolled up, his hands on his hips and a cap worn jauntily sideways on his head; the former with his hair pulled back beneath a handkerchief of sorts and holding what looked like a paddle. To the left were the women: a wife, her sister and two daughters. They were all wearing long black skirts, that dipped into their waists and then billowed down over their ankles, and white blouses that were tight up to their elbows and puffed out around their shoulders. On the road that passed in front of them, standing just to the left of the women, was a horse-drawn delivery van with its name, Betsy, inscribed on its side. The brother of the baker was holding the reins of the horse in one hand and a whip in the other. A bad exposure had lost everything to either side of the house and family in a haze of white light, and this had spread to some extent across the entire photograph, giving it a slightly unusual paleness, as if it had just rained flour.

But there was nothing obviously special or interesting about it, even though by the time Johnny showed it to me I had already come to know a bit about the people in it and what would happen to them: that the son would die in the trenches at the Somme, aged nineteen (which would date the photo somewhere around 1910, the boy having looked about fifteen in it); that the sister would never marry; that the brother was a drunk and sang Bread of Heaven on the roads at night. No, nothing conspicuous, except when you looked very closely at the faces of the family. When I had, I'd been surprised to find that none of them seemed to be that happy about being photographed. The father's eyes were turned sideways, away into the whiteness at his side, while his son's were directed belligerently and moodily towards the camera. Meanwhile, both the wife and her daughters were staring down at the pavement, with a look that was not – as you might expect – demure, but stern and sad and sullen; a look duplicated to some extent in the brother's face, where it had become pretty much an outright scowl. Nobody in this photo, I began to sense, wanted to be seen or looked at. And the more I did look, the more I got the uneasy feeling that it wasn't just them who didn't want this, but that it was also the photo itself that didn't; that the paleness which had spread across it was not simply the failure of a tardy lens but an attempt to dissolve and conceal itself, to slip away behind the light. And as I held it in my hand I didn't feel like a witness anymore but an intruder, someone who'd blundered in upon a fleeting scene in which they weren't meant to be present.

So perhaps it is some unconscious decorum on my memory's behalf that has deleted those other pictures, has tidied them away into the oblivion they seemed to ask for. I think sometimes we tend to assume that the past is grateful for our attentions, that it lies around craving our gaze and interest, seeking desperately, like an ageing Hollywood starlet, whatever hope of prolongation and preservation we can offer it. But maybe it isn't, not always. Maybe sometimes it just wants to be left alone.

And yet I still wish I could remember them, or that I'd at least been able to keep hold of a handful. Because without them Johnny's Llanysgerbwd is really nowhere – to me anyway. Later I did ask if I could have a few, but Sioned said they weren't there, said that as far as she knew – and she'd never seen them, or even known he'd had them – they'd probably been removed along with the other boxes the explosives men had taken away. So that is that, I suppose. Boom. Boom. Boom. And now they are all just ashes.

4

If Nut hadn't have pointed her out that night maybe nothing would've happened. God knows I wish it hadn't. There are times when I am calm, when I can look askance at the world and all that has happened to me with a certain placidity; an equilibrium that lets me feel that I have reached a kind of Olympian detachment from it all, that I am not still down there on the plains, struggling, explaining, escaping. But I am never allowed to stay there for long. The descent is only ever one treacherous precipice away, one vertiginous plummet. And then the ascent must begin all over again. I met a girl once in Mexico, a long-limbed Californian with perfect white teeth and an over-developed interest in mental pathologies, mostly her own. She told me that this whole up-and-downess, this continuous toing and froing in some people's characters, had a medical name: they called it cyclothymia, a circle of tempers.

I seem to have lived my entire life in that circle, that whirlpool, have spent days and weeks and months and years swirling and bobbing in it. And now, more than ever, I blame him – my father – for this. I blame him for the perpetual odyssey that has become my existence, where the island I got to has turned out to be only a fleeting Ithaca, and where now, in front of me, spreads a dreary, uncertain archipelago.

You see, sometimes when the circle begins to spin I try to reach out for things and people to cling to – to keep me afloat, to get me closer to a shore – and that night, I can now see, she began to become one of them. I would prefer not to tell you this, I would prefer to pass over it and get back to Johnny, but somehow it is part of what I must tell and so I will.

It was about a fortnight after my first visit to Bub and Nut's house. Nut had decided to branch out beyond the Dragon for a night and so we had gone to visit some of the pubs in town. It was a strange town, no more than three miles from the village but altogether different. Bordering the straits, its front was made up of a curving Victorian terrace, painted in various pastel tints, with a half-hearted pier straggling out into the water in the middle. Behind this front was the main street, lined on either side with shops selling tea towels imprinted with red dragons, plastic flags and buckets, prints of Celtic crosses and old women with steepling black hats, as well as several recently opened bistros that used a lot of French on their menus. It was a mixture of cheap tweeness and nouveau tourist riche, and had that forlorn quality that pervades so many British seaside towns, that scent of seaweed and old age and exhaustion. At the end of the street, where it trailed off into long, undulating fields (if you looked closely

104

you could see the miniature flags of a new golf course), stood the crumbling walls of a medieval castle, surrounding a concentric inner bastion of towers. There was something faintly anomalous about the whole place, a vague sense that it was somehow superimposed on a landscape that didn't entirely welcome it. And that night, as we drove in, and I looked across the straits at the bleak shadows of the mountains and above at the shuddering black clouds, there seemed such a glowering hostility in them, such an inimical quality to the twinkling lights of the hillside villages opposite, and the island ones behind, that I half felt like crawling into this castle to hide.

We made our way into the George instead.

At the bar I watched a red dragon flexing beside me on a man's pallid bicep. A shroud of smoke lingered over people's faces, softening their complexions and slowing the already slow drawl of their speech. In one corner a fruit machine twirled cherries and lemons around in the stale light. In the other there was a framed map of the island, with various ships drawn around its shores, entitled 'Famous Ship Wrecks of Anglesey'.

'Mine's a Stella,' said Nut, 'an Bub'll 'ave the same.'

There was a TV to my right above the bar, showing a football game. I watched it for a bit, as I always do, and wondered if the boy who my father said gave me my name ever really made it. I hope he did. But tonight it was the crowd that interested me. Every few minutes the camera would cut from the game and fan out across the ranks of spectators, before zooming in on particular groups, mostly those that included prettyish girls or men with huge, naked, bulging guts, either painted with their team's insignia or else purpling in the cold night air. I was taken by the intensity on their faces, the pinched concern around the edges of their eyes, their pained and eager anticipation. When, eventually, I turned back to the faces in the pub I found them a sorry mirror of these others. On one side of me the man with the dragon on his arm was staring moodily into his pint, as though each of the percolating bubbles that drifted up to the top of his beer and burst were yeasty dreams and hopes. On the other side were a couple of ragged traveller types, a man of about thirty and a girl of about ten years younger. They were both dressed in layers of lustreless black, interspersed here and there with the swirls and smudges of a faded, tie-dye rainbow; a pattern replicated on the girl's face, where a huge bruise spread out across her cheek in livid whorls of black and blue and orange and yellow. For some reason I supposed they must be lovers; there was such a miserable, disappointed togetherness about them. Behind these I saw two old men at a table, their eyes fixed thoughtfully on its coppery coloured top, which was almost the same colour as their ruddy, alcoholic skins. Nothing would happen here, I suddenly thought, and everyone here knew that. Nothing would or could happen. I was standing in a vacuum where expectation did not exist, that was crowded only with lives as squeezed and crumpled as the fag ends in the ashtrays. It was an odd thought, and not an unhappy one to me.

And nothing would have happened either, if Nut, at that moment, hadn't pointed her out:

'Fokk,' he rasped from behind me, 'wus she doing 'ere?'

'Who?' I said, turning around.

'Tammy Retard.'

Who's that?'

''Er!'

I followed his rude finger towards the fruit machine and found her there.

She looked exactly as she had in the Dragon, her eyes transfixed this time on the spinning reels and the flashing, bleeping lights. And it was that look that began to undo me, that serene and contented stare, as though everything she could have possibly wanted was in front of her, was held in the calm, still circles of her eyes.

Up to that point – and well beyond it too, if I am being honest – I didn't really notice the rest of her. It was like her body, her face even, was just the penumbra beyond the edges of those eyes. And there remains a shadowy quality, a blurred indistinctness, about the picture of her left over in my mind. But perhaps this picture is more accurate than I imagine, because everything about her did seem to overflow, to push out against and over whatever tried to bind and bound her. Her clothes were always too small: little tops out of which her breasts and belly bulged; jeans stretched tight across the wide, crescent swellings of her buttocks, and harshly buttoned into the thick, overhanging flesh of her hips; high heels wedged onto her plump, pink feet. Even her bones could not catch hold of her. The delicate lines of her cheeks and jaw were bleared beneath a puffy sheen of skin, while below her knees and elbows had receded into dents and dimples. Sometimes, when I looked at her, it was like I could see some other, half-forgotten person there; another body, another face, submerged.

And, apparently, there once had been.

Bub and Nut told me about it in the pub that night, told me about the day three years before when Tammy had been hurled through a windscreen and come out different on the other side. She was lucky, they said, it was almost miraculous. No one else survived. There had been six of them to start with, crammed full of beer, in a Ford Fiesta, speeding over the bridge towards whatever the mainland promised. Only it hadn't promised the white transit van that was coming the other way. At the very furthest point of the island, where Môn becomes Gwynedd, where it is no longer even a piece of ground but a strip of tarmac suspended over the staits, they hit it. Almost a hundred feet above the water they crumpled into each other, wrapping together like one of the links in the heavy iron chain that held them up. It took three hours for the firemen to pull them apart, Nut said, three hours while this steel knot bled over the road and into the sea. And of all six in the car, and two in the van, it was only Tammy who made it.

Almost miraculous, they said. Hardly a scratch on her. The boy who'd been beside her, her lover, had a battery in his stomach. The girl who was driving, her best friend, was mangled into the dashboard. The rest of them had just dissolved into the wreckage; they'd taken them out piece by piece, digit by digit. Only Tammy had escaped, flung headlong through a shower of shattered glass onto the road. They found her fifteen feet away and couldn't believe at first that she'd actually been in the car.

But the girl who'd been in the car wasn't the one who ended up on the road.

'She wus changed after that,' Nut told me, and I could hear the quiet sympathy in his voice, a voice that was hardly ever quiet. 'A bit odd, like. They never noticed nothin' in the hospital, but something wus bust up 'ere, yeh,' he said, pointing to his head, 'an yu could tell it wus. She hardly says nothin' now, an' she wus chatty as fok before, like. An' she wus thinner too, weren't she Bub?'

Bub nodded, gravely, in witness to this.

'An' she shouldn't be out 'ere,' Nut continued, looking stern and concerned and proprietorial now, 'cus she gets up to all sorts on 'er own, an' if people dunno 'er they'll take advantage.' But neither he nor Bub made a move towards her. It was as though their disapproval was enough to protect her. Or maybe it was they who needed protection: from the idea of her, from the idea that you could be so easily broken and altered, could wake up one day with the taste of asphalt in your mouth and your self lying strewn and shivered all around you.

But I couldn't take my eyes off her. I couldn't see what had been before; all I could see was her stare. And after a while Nut began to notice this, and shook his head slowly from side to side in Bub's direction before turning to me and saying, with a disgusted sneer, 'If yu wan' a go, jus' buy 'er a drink.' And I could feel my shame creeping across my neck and face, rushing up through my capillaries and onto my skin, and I wanted to tell them that it wasn't like that, not at all, that it was something different that I couldn't explain, that I couldn't make them understand. But when we left the pub neither of them spoke to me. They walked in front of me together, cutting me adrift on the lonely pavement behind, between the coloured houses that were now all grey beneath the bitter sky. And as I walked alone I looked across again at

109

the faraway lights and their twinkled admonitions, hearing the sea beating against invisible rocks, and then ahead towards the crumbling walls where I wanted – more than ever at that moment – to hide, feeling like I too was infringing on a hidden world that didn't want me, sensing the ground under the concrete shudder at the touch of my feet. And for the rest of that night I couldn't shake this feeling. In my half-dreams the wind had become Nut's sneering words, while the rain had become that other rain from months before, washing away the very last thing I loved. I tossed and turned to escape them until finally, near dawn, I fell into a dark and silent sleep. But on waking I found that the thought of her comforted me, except that when I put my hands beneath the covers I might have guessed it was more than comfort.

You see, it was only later – maybe only now in fact – that I realised that perhaps they already had understood; that it was me who hadn't.

5

Johnny reached into his pocket and pulled out a human jawbone. After placing it carefully on the table in front of me, he smiled and said, 'I'd like you to meet my father.'

It was, apparently, one of the few things of his father's that Johnny had inherited. There had also, at one time, been two ribs, half a pelvis, and a femur, but they had been commandeered as ballast for his coffin and sunk into the graveyard of Eglwys Fach. Besides, Johnny told me, there had always been rumours that these others were not his at all, but belonged to a Norwegian cabin boy who had had the misfortune, or the luck, to be posthumously adopted into the Jones family.

The jaw itself was not that prepossessing. The teeth had all fallen out, and the bone had turned a dirty, jaundiced yellow. But once upon a time, Johnny said, as he held it affectionately between his fingers, it had been a much-admired jaw, strong and chiselled and sculpted, the stubbly plinth of one of Llanysgerbwd's most handsome faces.

'He was a good-looking man, my father,' Johnny informed me, 'and my taid too, they always said. We were lucky with our genes and came from princes' stock, the remnants of the house of Aberffraw so we were told; though I'd be careful with things like that because round here they all pretend to have royalty in their blood. There are more descendants of princes in north Wales than anywhere else in the world I think, and most of them will let you know it, between mucking out cowsheds or delivering the mail. But, wherever we came from in the beginning, the Llanysgerbwd Joneses were handsome men, and none more so than my father.

'My mother always remembered the first day she really noticed him. She'd been picnicking with some of her friends, on a secluded beach about three miles from the village, when she'd caught sight of a small fishing boat as it rounded the headland and came to anchor in the cove. There were two men in it. As they began to spread out their net, to catch the herrings that were shoaling off the beach, the other girls with her started pointing and giggling, and one of them, Rhiannon Evans, brazenly waved. She couldn't understand at first what all the fuss was about. The only one of the men she could see properly – the other was holding the net in front of his face – was Dai Tŷ Ichel, a fat, clumsy boy who'd thrown an egg at her once when they'd been in school. But when that net was thrown she said, well, what a catch it disclosed, without even touching the water. My father had thick, black hair that, according to her, she could see shining all the way from the

112

beach that day. And then his eyes, which appeared to glint silver against the backdrop of the sky like they were a reflection of the herring's scales that darted below them through the water. After that first glimpse my mother said she couldn't take her eyes off him, that she sat with the others and stared until eventually he looked over at them and smiled. But it wasn't aimed at them all, not even at Rhiannon, whose over-eager hand was still in the air. It was aimed squarely and confidently at her. And then he turned his attention back to the net and left her with the profile that was so perfectly built on this.'

Johnny had passed me the jaw then and let me hold it, as though by having it in my hand I'd be better able to judge its true quality. It was smooth and light and felt so fragile that I'd been afraid if I held it too tightly it might splinter into dust.

'Of course, it wasn't the first time she'd seen him. They were both the same age, more or less, though it had taken my father a bit longer to disembark in the village: fifteen months to be exact, during which time he'd been freighted halfway across the world. No, she'd grown up knowing little Valpo, had shared a schoolroom with him, had run with him through the stubble of the hayfields after harvesting, had played cowboys and indians with him in the gorse thickets that covered the hills. My father was always with the indians, who won a lot more battles on Môn than they ever did across the ocean. But around the age of ten he'd started to disappear. To begin with it was for a month or two, then months, then years, until Valpo Jones became just another part of the childhood she was leaving behind. This disappearance wasn't unusual. Llanysgerbwd had never been big enough for all its sons, and every year a handful of them would vanish. She knew, vaguely, that he'd gone to sea, with his father to start with, and then on his own. There'd even been a letter from him, not sent to her, mind, but to the local newspaper, which every few months published a young seaman's account of his initiation into life before the mast, called "Our Boys at Sea". They were all much of a muchness she said, with lots of stormy crossings and place names she didn't know, and she wouldn't have remembered my father's except that after he died she went to the newspaper office and found it.'

And then Johnny had reached into the same pocket from which he'd taken out the jaw and brought out an equally yellowed wad of paper. Its pages were dotted with brown blotches and the edges were spattered with wax. It took me a while to decipher the writing. It went like this:

Dear Readers

It has been a great privilege for me to be asked by the esteemed editor of our paper to provide you with a letter recounting the events of my most recent voyage at sea. I have therefore undertaken to offer you an unvarnished account of my first circumnavigation of the globe, on board of the *Queen of Cambria* – a three-masted barque of 1000 tons, owned by Llewelyn Williams of Caernarfon and Captained by Thomas Owen of Nefyn.

We set sail from London after much preparation, and three very pleasant days that I spent in the company of one Thomas Edwards, once of Llanysgerbwd but now living on King's Cross Rd, where he is fortunate enough to have taken possession of a respectable tavern, frequented very often by seamen like myself from his own country. He made eager inquiries about many of the villagers, and has asked me to pass on his greetings on my return. Mr Edwards was kind enough to introduce me to a variety of local entertainments, the highlight of which was a rousing evening of hymns held at the London Welsh Society. Mr Edwards proved to have a very fine voice indeed, a fact which I think explains the many friends he has cultivated from within the theatrical profession.

After embarking we suffered several weeks from nasty blows, calms and head winds, during which time I was unexpectedly stricken by a case of *mal de mer* that lasted for two whole days and left me in a most miserable state. Our first mate, a bruising, big fellow from Caernarfon was, I regret to say, entirely unsympathetic to my plight during this period, and on several occasions cruelly accosted me in front of the rest of the crew, asking me what kind of men they bred on the island of Môn, if we were all brought up holding our mothers' hands and spent our time collecting flowers with our sisters, and if I needed a little *sws* from my nain to make me better, and other such things. He is a brute of a man this mate, and the others on the crew have taken to calling him Merv Mountain, partially on account of his size and stature, and partially on account of his rude and overbearing manners. However, I fortunately regained my health and after that Merv spread his cruelty more liberally throughout the crew.

Thirty-one days out we raised the beautiful island of Madeira. It offered a welcome strip of green on the horizon, and from afar I entertained the fancy that it might be my own native island, a thought which soon filled me with a terrible hiraeth and sad memories of all of you at home. I think at this moment our Captain must have caught sight of this in my expression and gained some intuition as to my feelings, because he offered me a kindly nod from the quarter deck and called out that one day in the future we would be looking out like this towards the mouth of the Menai, after which I felt much better. Our Master is an excellent man, both serious and thoughtful, and at all times has evinced a great inclination towards our improvement under his care, even offering us the opportunity of hymns and Bible discussions in his own cabin on Sundays, an opportunity that, I am sorry to relate, not many of us has taken advantage of, despite the promise of sharing one of the many fruit cakes his wife supplied him with for the voyage.

We lay in the port at Funchal for two days, taking on fruit, potatoes and various other fresh provisions. There was a Portuguese chap in our crew – named Manuel but who we all called Man – and he was delighted to be somewhere where he could speak his own language, keeping up a constant and ardent chattering with the men from the port as we loaded the ship. We were allowed one night of leave on the shore here, during which Man kindly introduced us to several of his new friends, who generously offered to share some bottles of the local wine, a sweet and delicious liquer. There was much jollity that night, dancing and singing and the like, but the next morning we awoke to find that sleep had not entirely cured us of the effects of this liquer, and many of us, on attempting to walk, found ourselves swaying and bobbing along as though we were making our way across the deck during a squall. Man in particular was afflicted in this way, and though to begin with he appeared eager to continue the jollity and amusements of the previous night, he soon became quite melancholy and morose, staring down at his shoes and muttering unintelligibly to himself. When it came time for us to return to the ship he had sunk into the deepest misery and refused to follow us, allowing tears to fall down his cheeks and saying that he didn't want to leave these fine people and that he wouldn't either, and that the Master and the mate could go to hell if they thought they could persuade him otherwise because the Devil himself couldn't shift him from this place. 'I have journeyed long enough, Valpo,' he said to me when I tried to reason with him, 'and I shall go no further.' He made a most pitiful sight, I can assure you, and I felt great sympathy towards him. Unfortunately our mate was not capable of such gentle feelings. When we were late returning to the ship he came ashore to find us, and approaching us set to cursing in a manner that I shall not offend your ears with. Poor Man bore the brunt of many of these curses and when he still refused to move the mate clobbered him about the head with the side of his hand and administered the most fearful kick to his behind, an operation he repeated several times on the way back to the ship, all the while continuing his stream of imprecations and calling on Man to 'stop his dago blubbering and behave like a proper man.' It was a sad conclusion to our stay on Madeira.

Forty-five days out we crossed the 'Line'. This is a day of good cheer and merriment on board of a ship. Even Merv was in high and agreeable spirits the day we crossed, and appeared on deck carrying a trident fashioned out of an old harpoon, and adorned in a long white beard and golden crown, and had us all address him reverently as 'Father Neptune'. His 'wife' for the day was a young lad from Liverpool named Neil, who had taken – even for an event like this – an unusual amount of care in preparing himself for his role. He was sporting a wig of curly blonde tresses and a dress of bright scarlet, and had carefully shaved and powdered his face before applying a thick, red lipstick. He seemed greatly pleased with his appearance and was a bit loath to relinquish it at the end of the day's ceremonies. These ceremonies themselves consisted, firstly, of all the seamen gathering themselves into a row on the deck while 'Neptune' and his 'wife' went from man to man asking, 'Have you ever crossed the Line before?' Those who answered in the negative – of which I was one – were then separated into a group and forced to undergo various trials and ordeals. Foremost among these, and reckoned the most essential of them, was being 'shaved'. For this, Neptune's supplicants were required to have their faces smeared with a paste made of paint and some other substance which we were mercifully unaware of, but whose obnoxious odour suggested an origin somewhere in either the cook's leftovers or the latrine. A good portion of this, I shudder to recollect, found its way into the mouths of those foolish enough to leave them agape. Afterwards, when this paste had hardened sufficiently, Neptune's barber, otherwise known as the ship's carpenter, would come around and 'shave' it off as vigorously as possible with a piece of wood. We were then allowed to turn our 'new' complexions to the Southern hemisphere, though this newness was quite figurative – it taking us several days to remove the paste completely from our skins. Once our shaving was done with we suffered a number of duckings and other trials, all presided over by Neptune, who gained much pleasure in devising them. With the ceremonies complete we were allowed to spent the rest of the day in celebration, with jigs and songs and other entertainments, and the Master, who was normally quite strict about enforcing temperance on board the ship, let us all enjoy a modest portion of 'grog', with which we warmly toasted Neptune and his dominions. As night began to fall Neil stood up and sang a beautiful and heartfelt Irish song, about the fields of a lost valley. When he finished there was scarce a dry eye to be found amongst us and we all applauded him as 'the true Queen of Cambria'.

The next weeks were uneventful, until we came in sight of Tristan da Cunha, an island some 2000 miles due west of Cape Town. We hove-to in the lee of this island, so that its male inhabitants could row out to us in their whaleboats and trade. Unfortunately their harvest appeared to have been a meagre one, consisting of a miscellaneous collection of withered vegatables, juiceless fruit, and unappetising lumps of meat. I can only conjecture that it had been a poor season for them, and that they had struggled to gather much from their salty earth, or that storms and gales had beset them. What they did have they were eager to barter for bottles of wine or other intoxicating liquers, claiming they were needed for 'invalid wives' and 'sick children', and seemed little interested in anything else, such as money or clothes. I can only conclude that this is a most dissolute, drunken and unproductive island. After we had set sail once more, I turned back for a final glimpse of the island and found its outline to be curiously indefinite, shifting here and there on the horizon as though it were not firmly fixed to the globe and liable at any moment to vanish. There were the rocky remains of an old volcano at its heart that resembled nothing so much as an ancient tower, which appears the finest thing this place has erected.

A hundred and five days after leaving the Thames we reached Sydney, considered a good-to-average passage for a ship such as ours, and during which we met with no other vessels or docked in any ports, which was a disappointment for me as I had been very hopeful of setting eyes on the famous 'Table Top' of Cape Town. Sydney, however, proved more than a consolation for this disappointment. We arrived in the small hours, and when it came time for my watch we had already come to anchor in one of the innumerable coves that distinguish this vast and magnificent harbour, which stretches some thousand miles round from one head to another. I stepped out onto the deck, just as the sun began to rise, and each of its strengthening beams disclosed some wonderful novelty to me. The beauty of the scenery was dazzling, and abounded with all manner of trees, flowers and birds, many of which I had never seen before, and scarce believed could exist at all, let alone in such a wonderful profusion. This truly was a new world to me, and, as I stood there in the perfect stillness of the morning, with only the unfamiliar yet lovely melody of the birds' singing to be heard, I half-imagined that I must have somehow passed through into Paradise during the night.

Later that day a doctor from the harbour came aboard our ship and had the entire crew line up for an examination, to ensure that we were free from plague or any other ailments. This required us to show our tongues and bare our chests, and would have required us to bare a deal more if it weren't the doctor's misfortune to find Merv first in the line, who, on hearing his request, was filled with consternation and told him in a loud bellow to go to the devil or find a whore to do his job, at which both Neil and Man, who were standing beside me, started giggling amongst themselves and whispering that the mate had little to worry about in this way, very little.

We were two weeks in Sydney, during which there were plenty of amusements to be had. I went to the Mission to Seamen's Hall on several occasions, where they held excellent concerts, and where I met with the Rev W Wynne Jones, the chaplain of the Welsh chapel here, who was a friend of my father. He kindly invited me for dinner at his house, where he described many things about this fascinating country to me. In particular he talked about the great desert in its centre, a vast and arid place full of red dirt and trackless wastes, and inhabited only by wandering bands of savages who were able to distill water from rocks. I could barely bring myself to imagine such a place, especially as the land about Sydney appeared so lush and green, but the Rev assured me of its reality and brought out a piece of red stone that he had kept as a souvenir of a trip he had made there, that he gave to me as a gift and which I have kept with me ever since. After these two weeks we travelled up the coast to Newcastle, a large coal shipping port, where we took on a cargo, and from where we embarked on our way across the Pacific ocean.

This was the first time, since my infancy, that I had been in these fabled waters, and I need not describe to you my excitement on entering a realm so imbued with the most colourful and picturesque of associations. Who, as a child, has not been thrilled by tales of this romantic ocean, with its myriad, palm-fringed Edens, its sparkling blue lagoons and forests of coral, its dancing houris and ferocious cannibals and hidden treasure. I was quite beside myself with the prospect of the adventures that I hoped lay before me. In my enthusiasm I communicated some of these expectations to Man, who instantly set about dampening them. He informed me, with a long and cynical sigh, that I should put these notions out of my head and back into the books where I had found them. He had been across this ocean many times, he said, and had found that the place I described did not exist, nor had it ever existed as far as he could tell. He said that I was more likely to find myself amongst lepers and decaying grass huts than surrounded by dancing beauties and strapping savages; and that any adventures I might come across would probably leave me not with a casket of gold coins, but a bad dose, an empty pocket, and a night in some French jail. He then added, a bit more gently, that perhaps it was better for me to keep to my childish imaginings and not have them spoilt by setting foot on any actual ground, concluding, rather philosophically, that if his many years of voyaging had taught him anything, it had taught him that the world was a more marvellous place if you didn't go about getting your hands dirty in it. As it was, however, I had no opportunity to test these claims and assertions. Our Master, it turned out, had no inclination towards any adventure other than getting his cargo safely over to South America, and had set a course that promised to take us past nothing more exciting than water.

The weeks of this passage were long and hard ones. On several occasions we found ourselves becalmed for days on end in the doldrums, with not the merest breath of wind to aid our headway. This was a most frustrating condition, as there were often signs of breezes no further than half a mile distant, yet around us the water would remain as smooth as glass. Once we even caught sight of another ship bowling merrily along in the near distance, with all its sails set and full, while we stood as still as a ship in a bottle. During these times the Master would stand on the quarter deck and search the horizon for traces of wind, and then have us lower the boats and attempt to tow the ship in their direction. I cannot fully describe the exhaustion and disappointment we suffered as a result of this futile, yet arduous, chasing after what appeared to be phantom breezes. Many of the men in the boats would come to cursing the Master and his eyes, a rare occurrence as our Captain was on the whole an unusually popular one among the crew. Some of this irritation was due as much to the effects of being caught in a calm as it was to the physical discomfort of towing the ship. For those of you at home who have never spent a stretch of time at sea, it will be hard to fathom the terrors of a calm, which many sailors fear almost as much as a storm. The best I can say on this matter is that a sailor, like his ship, is in most cases designed for motion; he is not fitted, constitutionally, for prolonged periods of stillness. During a calm irritations, bad tempers, grievances, begin to grow on him like the barnacles on the hull below; his mind starts to play tricks on him, making him fancy that the Captain has lost his way, or leading him to the awful conclusion that he will never escape this one tedious, watery waste and that this limbo will be his for eternity. I have heard of instances where sailors have purposely loaded their jackets with weights and thrown themselves into the ocean to escape this imagined prospect.

Yes, these calms affected us all badly. However, if I am to be quite honest, our entire passage across this ocean was a dull and uneventful one. There were times when I began to question my vocation, and many a moment that I dreamed of being home, forgetting entirely the strong, restless impulses and curiosity that had led me years before to follow in my father's boundless footsteps. But this is ever a sailor's lot I suppose: to dream of home abroad, and when at home to yearn for elsewhere. And there is no getting around it, because only the grave will release him from it, and even of that nobody can be certain.

We were sixty-one days in our crossing, during which, as I have noted, there was little of interest to report. There were two incidents though that provided us with some degree of excitement. The first was the capture of a shark. This fearful creature had taken to following the ship, and when caught in one of the aforementioned calms it was the cause of much perturbation amongst the crew, who let on that it was in possession of a mysterious foreknowledge as to our fate, and was waiting for us to meet with some unforeseen catastrophe or disaster. To the landsman this notion probably appears somewhat absurd, and no doubt he will pass it off as an example of the nigh-on proverbial superstition of sailors. However, if you had witnessed this creature, and moreover had witnessed it in the conditions we then suffered, you might have thought differently. There was indeed something portentous and unearthly in its constant circling of us, in particular on those nights – of which there were several – when the water was filled with phosphorescence and we could see it gliding about the ship shrouded in a ghostly covering of light. It was with a great deal of relief then that we finally took it on a baited hook. After bringing it up to the side of the ship we dropped a running bowline over its tail and hauled it onto the deck, an operation that took five men – it being in excess of three hundredweight and measuring some twelve and half feet. Once we had it on deck we ripped open its stomach and found nothing more appalling there than a tin can and a piece of rag. We then cut off its tail and nailed it to the end of our jib-boom, which is a tradition on ships and is said to ward off head winds.

The second incident was a more curious affair and took place one evening as Neil and I were on watch together. It was nearing twilight and I was watching as a beautiful sunset started to form itself in the west when suddenly, and quite unexpectedly, Neil called out that land was ahoy, pointing vigorously in a direction to the Northwest of us. At first I couldn't make out anything; but then, in the distance, I thought I could clearly discern the outline of an island. At one end it rose into a gentle hill, dotted here and there with patches of green, while at the other it fell away into a long, flat promontory. I was delighted at the sighting, and instantly joined with Neil in calling it out. Unfortunately, at this time, our mate was below decks and our Master in his cabin, so that it was some minutes before either of them was able to come on deck. When they did our island had faded from immediate sight, and despite repeated efforts neither of them was able to make it out, either with the naked eye or the glass. Meanwhile the sunset had deepened in the direction it had once been, burnishing the horizon into shades of rich copper and crimson, and making it difficult to properly apprehend what lay beyond it. Neil and I were asked if it were not possible that we had mistaken a cloud bank for land, to which we both replied no, although this question did raise certain doubts in our minds which may have shown on our faces. At this the mate, who had been catching a nap when we disturbed him, set to cursing the pair of us for our greenness and blindness. Our Master, however, simply scratched his head and said that as far as he knew there was no land to be found anywhere within three hundred miles of our current position, but that he would keep a careful watch himself for a few hours just in case. Afterwards Neil and I discussed this incident at length between ourselves and other members of the crew, remaining adamant that we had certainly seen something. Man suggested that sometimes, after a period at sea, the desire for setting eyes on land of some sort could lead men's minds to conjure it out of an empty horizon; that oftentimes men were inclined to invent, even unwittingly, what they wanted and needed most. Nevertheless, later that night I sat down with a candle and made a sketch of this island, jotting down the position from which we had spotted it, and naming it Ynys Llanysgerbwd, in the fancy that perhaps one day it would actually be discovered and that hence we would, in some measure, be immortalised on future charts of this great ocean.

Our arrival in the harbour of Valparaiso was the cause of much relief amongst the crew, and most especially for me, who at last was able to set eyes upon the place of my birth. It was with a strange combination of feelings that I entered this harbour. Part of me, like everyone else, was simply happy to have arrived safely after a long passage, and yet my mind quickly turned to the tales my mother and father had related to me about my first arrival here, in the cabin of the *Western Monarch*. I remembered being told how this harbour, being exposed to the North, was open to the full fury of "Northers" – which are strong gales that occasionally sweep over these latitudes – and that on the day of my birth one of these had blown up, requiring the sailors to fix extra cables to the ship in order to keep it from running aground, at the very moment those inside the cabin were trying to cast off those others that held me to my mother. And of how the ship's cook, a hardened old tar, had walked in to find me only halfway into this world, and had gone instantly pale and fainted onto the floorboards. I also remembered my mother telling me that seconds after my birth the church bells in the town had started pealing – as part of some saint's day or other – an occurrence which all those on board the ship took as an auspicious sign for me and a guarantee of a happy and prosperous future. And yet alongside these recollections I could raise no actual memories that I myself had of this place. I searched my surroundings for a particular object or view or scene that might strike me as familiar, or at least spark the faintest of reminiscences from my infancy, but could find none. The place was as new to me now as it had been then, which left a cold and empty feeling in my heart. Maybe it was because I had drawn my name from here, or had half-believed the prophesy of those bells, but I'd often wondered if some destiny had not marked out this place for my advent, had chosen it above any other and connected us together for ever after. And only now, as I stood on deck in full view of it, did it begin to occur to me that perhaps it was merely chance and coincidence, a vagary of time and tide and season; a thought which inexplicably filled me with sadness and the lonely sense of being adrift in the world. It was while sunk in this despondent mood that I spotted the remains of a wreck in the harbour, the victim, I supposed, of one of those same Northers that had rocked me during my birth. For several hours I surveyed its mouldering planks, watching the gulls wink through its shattered masts, and all the while thoughts of its sad ending mixed with thoughts of my beginning, until eventually I was led to the melancholy reflection that our fates were somehow commensurate; that I had not been born here but rather beached, that I had arrived in this world a scuttled carcass, to lie forever abandoned in the unfamiliar waters of a foreign port.

It was not until we departed Valparaiso that my spirits finally lifted. We were headed for the port of San Francisco, and everyone in the crew was excited at the prospect of a visit there. Neil especially was thrilled at the opportunity, for he had long been fascinated, he told me, with tales of the American West. For the whole of our journey he entertained me with bloodcurdling accounts of the savage Indians who inhabited there; of their ferocious habits and customs, their colourful costumes and strange dances, until after a few weeks my mind was quite awash with scalpings, war whoops, totems and arrows. However, when we did eventually come in sight of land – a thickly forested shore before the entrance to the harbour – I did not associate them with these lurid pictures, but instead thought of my taid, who had once travelled through the interior of this wide continent. I tried to picture his footsteps through its strange and alien landscapes, which I had only ever seen in the crude illustrations of books, but in the end could only picture the back room of my house in Llanysgerbwd and the portrait of him that hangs there, dressed all in furs and leather, holding a pipe in one hand and a tomahawk in the other.

And thus it was with thoughts of home that I entered this harbour, where we are currently anchored and where I must now conclude this account and prepare to post it to you. Of course, if our return is blessed with good winds and an easy passage around the Horn, then I may well arrive back before it does. In which case I will happily be able to offer you my greetings and best wishes in person.

Yours

Valpo Jones
San Francisco 1904

Johnny went on, 'So it was by no means the first time she'd seen him, or even heard from him I suppose, but it was the first time she'd noticed him. And later that same day she noticed him for a second time, walking up the path to her front door with a bag of herrings in his hand, which he'd given to her father before asking if it would be alright if he spoke to his daughter.'

And whatever his father said that day, Johnny told me, it must have been good, because they were married within the year.

6

I saw her next on the verge of the New Year – two days before
to be exact. Maybe it was the time of year, with everyone
exhausted after Christmas, or perhaps it was the ugly wet
darkness of the night, but nobody else was on the village
street as I walked home from the Dragon. Usually there was
at least a sprinkling of moody, sullen-looking children lurking
in the shadows of the bus shelter, or on the strip of concrete
in front of the chapel – anywhere to escape the insides of their
homes and the expanses of grass and mud that surrounded
them. I saw them almost every night, gathered together in thin
circles, marooned under billowing clouds of Lambert & Butler
smoke. But not this night. She and I were the sole inhabitants
of the street, as far as I could tell.

I'd caught her in the corner of my eye, leaning against the
village's solitary working street light, a figure smudged under

its wan orange glow. For a second, I thought she might be waiting for something, or someone, but the time of night was wrong: there were no buses due, and it was still too early for other people to be coming out of the pub. I couldn't tell whether she'd seen me go by, but I was more or less sure she hadn't: she didn't seem to be looking in front of her, but up at the light itself. And so I stopped walking and crouched down behind the wall of the house next to me. Why I did this I'm not sure, only that I didn't want to leave her alone. And I waited too, for minutes, maybe longer, it was hard to tell. I had my hands on the wall and I could feel the coldness and the dampness of the stones seep into me.

By the time she moved, my legs were so cramped I could barely follow her. I tried stamping them gently on the ground to get the blood running, and fortunately the wind – which had not stopped blowing for a month – drowned out the sound. She walked slowly up the street, through the lower part of the village, flanked on either side by the terraced houses that slanted down the hill. It was easy following her here. She never once looked back.

It became more difficult when she reached the upper part, where the terraces merged into a small council estate. The street veered away towards the fields and turned into a road, and was replaced by winding drives and cul-de-sacs. In the darkness I scrambled after her, making my way past little square gardens with rickety wooden fences and no flowers, strewn here and there with the shapes of toys abandoned to the winter. Hiding behind corners I scraped my hands on the rash of pebble-dash that infected the skin of all these houses. Occasionally a piece of moonlight would filter through the clouds and glint off one of these cheap, white bits of gravel; and I began to imagine that they were the whites of eyes and that they were pointed at me. Becoming furtive and nervous I kept myself in the deepest shadows. Somewhere I could hear a dog snarling.

But she never once looked back.

The door she finally arrived at looked like all the other doors, and so I memorised the number. There was a light coming from the downstairs room and no curtains covering the window. There were gaps everywhere in the fence and it took no effort to slip between them. I huddled myself in a corner of the garden, away from the wind and with the best view through the window, and then just waited – for what, I didn't know.

There was a TV set on in the room and it cast out a flickering, bluish-grey light. I could make out the contours of a settee and in front of it a table covered in crumpled, oily, chip-paper blossoms. Sometimes the light would flare out strongly enough to illuminate the walls, which were all bare. There was a tense, knotted feeling in my stomach and, when she came into the room, it seemed to squeeze still further. With her coat off you could see the bare flesh of her neck and chest and arms; the TV light made it look pallid and bloodless and dead. She sat down on the settee and stared at the moving pictures without moving, and I searched out her eyes through the glass of the window. I couldn't tell at that moment whether I'd rather be inside with her or outside watching her, wanting to be inside.

The coldness and dampness of the stones had stuck to my hands. When I reached below to touch myself it shocked me.

133

I flinched, but then I got used to it. It seems strange but it wasn't as though my hand warmed up, so much as everything else cooled down, was eased into coolness by the chilly, clammy friction. The skin on my hand felt cold and smooth like marble. Afterwards I fell into a kind of stupor and thought that now we could share a moment of perfect stillness and contentedness. I felt that I would be with her then, that neither of us would really be alone, and that it was somehow better this way, less difficult, less messy. And then we weren't alone.

They were barely footsteps at first, just faint sounds that filled the occasional intervals between gusts. But they quickly became louder, until eventually they were impossible to mistake. As they came closer I pushed myself up against the boards of the fence and tried to hide, and would have succeeded too if the boards hadn't given way and tumbled me onto the pavement.

'Good evening, Jonathon,' he said, with a voice as flat and thin as paper.

7

I don't know how far away you can feel earthquakes, but they say the tremors can travel much further than you think. A house can shake apart in Turkey say, and you can reach across the table right here and find the salt trembling ever so slightly. I don't know, I really don't. So maybe, on August 16th, 1906, my mother might have felt or seen something without knowing it: a mysterious quivering in the handle of her hairbrush; a shudder in her windowpane, with not a breath of wind about; a vibration that wobbled the surface of her tea. For certain though, two weeks afterwards she browsed the back pages of a newspaper, passing quickly over a paragraph that would have seemed, at the time, just as inconsequential. It was barely a paragraph really, only a couple of sentences, belatedly informing the reader that the South American city of Valparaiso had been devastated by an earthquake. No more than that. If it hadn't reminded her of her new husband's name she wouldn't even have read it. On the page before there was a long feature about the Amlwch brass band and their recent tour through the South of England, and on the next a lengthy report on Holyhead FC's 6–1 triumph over a hapless and disorganised Newborough eleven. The world only took up one page of the paper back then, and there was a lot to cram in. In fact, my mother's thoughts quickly skipped over Valparaiso's tragedy, and returned to the brass brand's tour, which one of her cousins had gone on. She made a note of it, she said, so she'd remember to ask him about the trip the next time they saw each other.

It was only some days later, after a chat with a neighbour who'd asked about Valpo's current whereabouts, that she'd gone and fetched the paper from the outhouse and looked over those sentences again. August 16th, 1906, they said. The city devastated. Number of victims as yet unknown. It seemed ridiculous, of course it did, but just in case she'd also fetched out her last letter from Valpo. She checked the date and place first. May 1st, Sydney. Yes, it was ridiculous. He was safely on another continent, as she'd known all along. And she'd sat there thinking how difficult it sometimes was for sailors' wives, having to keep half an eye on all the world's disasters, just on the off-chance, just on the one-in-a-million chance. She'd mention this to my nain, she'd thought, which would give them something to talk about together – it having been quite hard for her since moving into Valpo's parents' house after the wedding. And she was still in the middle of thinking this as she scanned the rest of the letter, which she was already quite familiar with, having read it four or five times at least: a visit to the botanical gardens; a trip to the Owain Glyndwr, a tavern owned by a man originally from Llangefni (which she hadn't liked); a night of hymns at the Seamen's Chapel (which she'd liked a bit more); and some sweet stuff about him missing her, including a few lines of poetry (which she had liked – the sentiments that is, not the poetry). She'd gone over pretty much the whole of it, including the poetry, before she came across the one line that she'd never really taken notice of: 'Our Master has decided on our course, and will let us know of it tomorrow.' A line very easily not noticed, I suppose, even under the scrutiny of a young wife.

So where had tomorrow pointed him?

She wasn't even that anxious about the answer, not at first, because she had seen so many unfamiliar names of places in his letters that she had begun to think of his world as an endless succession of unaccustomed syllables, an inexhaustible alphabet rather than a blunt, finite, physical space, somewhere you arrived and departed and actually passed through, over and about. And this had always comforted her somehow. Because how could letters and words harm him? How could things and places which didn't exist for her until she awkwardly shaped them with her tongue and breath break his bones and body? So she wasn't anxious, not in those first few moments, because the only place tomorrow could take him then was a name.

It wasn't until the next week that it became a destination.

My taid was the one who found that out. Captain Idris Jones, who'd retired from the sea years before, but who now, probably for the first time, was to feel the apprehension of waiting, of not knowing, of being stuck on the shore. To begin with, he told my mother not to be silly. But as the days went by she said she could see him start to get fretful and uneasy. He was suddenly unable to spend too long inland, setting out in the morning on long walks that took him to, and around, the coast, and which he'd often not return from until night had begun to fall. He was an old man then, and these walks would exhaust him, leaving him, my mother remembered, terribly pale and worn. But he was unable to stay still. It was as though this worry had resurrected in him the desire, the need, for movement. For his whole life, I suppose, the necessity for action had meant embarkation; if something needed to be done you hoisted the sails and got going. It was the only thing he knew how to do. Until finally, one evening, as he sat slumped and fatigued in the sitting room, my nain had gone to him and said: 'You'll have to go and ask, Idris.' And so the next morning he set off for Caernarfon, to the house of Llewelyn Williams – the owner of the *Queen of Cambria* – to ask for the ship's sailing instructions.

He didn't return till late in the night. And when he did he simply opened the door, gave a single nod to my mother and nain, and then traipsed wearily up to his room. My father had had, a destination then, and all of them knew where it was.

Nobody was surprised when the letter came from Liverpool. It was like the Fates had already cut the strings and left them to pick away at the frayed ends. Her Majesty's Consul in Valparaiso, it informed them, was sorry to relate that, during the recent disaster, the *Queen of Cambria*, together with four other foreign craft, had been sunk in the harbour. The Consul was currently endeavouring to gather information as to possible survivors, a process that might take some weeks.

But Valpo Jones was dead the moment they read this – if he hadn't already been partly dead before, since the night my taid got back from Caernarfon. Later, years later, my mother would wonder what status he had had in those previous weeks, whether in that time, before they had known, he'd continued to exist, like a ship on the very furthest edge of the horizon, half-seen and half-hallucinated into existence, at once there and not there. And had wondered if, with each signal, each clue, of his demise, that life had ebbed away, had receded out of view, until he was no more alive than the piece of paper that told them he wasn't.

For weeks after that letter arrived, my mother became obsessed with the article which had first chipped him away, going over and over it until, in her mind, my father had become the earthquake and the city. She could see his limbs twist and shake apart; his skin rent open in bloody fissures, disclosing twitching sinews that split and snapped before her eyes. His face became a rubble of shattered bone, hung with rags of torn, ripped flesh that flapped and fluttered on the Andean breeze. Stray dogs crept through his ruins, gnawing on his innards, pissing into his blood, while orphans huddled in the wreckage of his ribs and a million flies feasted on his open, overflowing veins. She could not see her husband, only the diseased and suppurating plain of his body, oozing with the strewn ranks of the homeless, the hopeless, the displaced and the dead. Valparaiso, August 16th 1906. And this was what he would remain until my taid went to fetch him back.

8

I was feeling my way through a box of mushrooms, trying to find the least rotten ones, when I next heard his voice.

'Good afternoon, Jonathon,' he said.

I recognised it without turning around, remembering how I had run away from it that night, had jumped to my feet and scuttled off into the dark, like a crab exposed in the shallows racing for the deep. And I would have run again if there had been anywhere to hide. But the village Spar was small and horribly intimate; there was no option of escape.

'Hello, Goronwy,' I replied, slowly wheeling myself around, knowing he was close behind me, so close I could almost smell the dust on his old, papery breath.

He was a dry stick of a man, Goronwy, a whittled-down collection of lank bones wrapped in tweed. Even as near as this I struggled not to lose his outline against the background of the winter vegetable stand. The skin on his face was taut and desiccated, a calcified extension of his skull rather than a covering; his wrinkles looked like cracks and fractures. The only moisture in his body was pooled in his eyes, which always seemed to be on the verge of crying.

We stood awkwardly together for a few seconds before he remarked, 'They're not very good, are they.' Good I thought, what does good have to do with it? Did what I did make me bad? And who are you to judge me? I didn't hurt her, I didn't even touch... and then I realised he was gesturing towards the mushrooms.

'I suppose not,' I admitted.

When I got outside onto the pavement I contemplated running again, but before I had time to decide he'd sidled up beside me like an emaciated shadow. Usually I'd have been happy to talk to him – there were things I wanted to ask him about Johnny – but now we were trapped together in the as-yet unspoken memory of that night. It was only about four o'clock but already it was almost dark. In the weeks since we'd last met I could hardly recall there being any light, just a kind of sodden, wind-blown grey that tried to pass for day. The island had begun to feel increasingly enclosed, until the mainland and the mountains were no more than the rumour of an outline on an invisible horizon. I wished he would bring it up, that he would just say it, and then we could walk away and leave it behind. But he didn't. Instead he asked me about Johnny.

I was glad of the distraction and told him that Johnny had been telling me about Llanysgerbwd and his ancestor's travels. He didn't reply at first. I saw him lift an eyebrow and then begin to nod in a thoughtful, judicious way; and was reminded that Nut had told me he was a retired professor, though of what, he didn't know. And there was certainly something scholarly in his look now, as though he were carefully weighing up a tricky and contentious proposition. Across the road a kid, huddled up like a monk in a hooded top, gave us a bored glance, took a drag on his cigarette, and then spat onto the ground.

'Oh yes,' he suddenly said, as though he'd come at last to an adequate conclusion, 'he's very interested in travel.'

'He's not very interested in mine,' I replied, half-joking but also, rather unexpectedly, irritated with Johnny for never asking me anything. Goronwy didn't appear to hear me.

'We learnt a lot about travel in school,' he continued, looking at a space just above my head as if he was addressing a lecture hall. And, to tell the truth, there was a stiff formality in his speech that made it seem exactly like he was.

'I remember learning about it in the cold stone schoolroom in town, which was somehow always cold, even in May and June. As though learning was meant to be an arctic endeavour, was meant to imbue its shivering devotees with the fortitude of a Scott, someone our teacher was greatly enamoured of and who he cited continually as an example of how great actions were always the result of those with great character. "Only great men," he would say, "do great things," looking all the time doubtful as to whether this maxim could possibly apply to the ragtag collection of boys assembled in front of him. We, in our turn, were equally doubtful as to whether Dr Lovelock had any more than an academic involvement in his theory. He certainly bore little resemblance to the collection of rugged explorers whom he eulogised and whose pictures adorned the walls, making it look as though all their strenuous efforts to cross deserts and icy wastelands and thick forests were no more than attempts to find their way into the frosty precincts of a provincial schoolroom. Of course, maybe their august Victorian portraitists had beefed them up a bit, put a covering of good imperial muscle onto their limbs and enlarged the territory of their jawlines. Perhaps Stanley and Livingstone had never quite been the Herculean figures that strode the walls of our grammar, but, nevertheless, they certainly could never have been mistaken for Lovelock.

'I can see him now, you know. He was short, and alarmingly spindly, with two blue eyes that were so crossed that sometimes they looked as though they might suddenly jump out of their sockets and change places. They made it tremendously difficult for him to navigate the narrow channels between the boys' desks, and most of his speeches were punctuated by him clattering into some unfortunate pupil. If he had, by some miracle, found the source of the Nile or some great inland sea or some untraversed ocean, he would have without doubt fallen into it.'

I wasn't certain where Goronwy's recollection was going, or what exactly it had to do with Johnny, but by this time I'd become an all-too-good listener. Besides, it was better listening to this than having to explain that other night. As he talked Goronwy had begun walking down the pavement, and, almost unconsciously, I followed him. Occasionally we'd pause, usually at the end of what I took to be breaks in the flow of Goronwy's meticulous speech, as though his footsteps themselves were a kind of physical grammar. We passed several cars parked on the edge of the pavement, out of which drifted a muffled, thumping music, and into which various hooded children leaned, as if whispering benedictions; they were cars used as shelters, with nowhere to go; miniature cathedrals of boredom. I didn't know where we were going.

'So you could call it compensation I suppose, an imaginative make-do for all the places our teacher's spindly legs would never take him. And, as he made the circuit of that room, crammed in between its slate floor and slate roof, with its single window whose view was blocked by the walls of the castle, you could almost see him bask in the extent of the landscapes he had conjured and taken possession of. You see, for a Welshman, Dr Lovelock had an unhealthy appetite for empires, or at least their beginnings. They seemed to dazzle and entrance him, and I wonder if it was the contemplation of them that'd made his eyes squint. As for us, well there were times I think he simply didn't see us; that we were like natives pushed into the corners and peripheries of his doubled vision. Occasionally he'd rouse himself to punish us, to cane a bit of "character" into our frozen backsides, but apart from that we were just the baggage carriers and lackeys of his grand expeditions.

'Still, there were some dubious benefits to all of this. I doubt there were any children in Wales – or adults for that matter – who knew as much as us about Columbus, Cortes and the Conquistadors, about De Salle, La Perouse, Bougainville, Wallis, Cook, Park, Lewis and Clarke – the list of names has never left me – although what good this knowledge did us I don't know. It certainly never prepared me for my own travels, which turned out to be nothing like as glorious as the ones I'd learned about.

145

'But Johnny loved hearing about them. I remember how he never took his eyes off Lovelock when he described them, though at other times his attention was as hard as an eel to hold. He used to borrow books from him too, which was unprecedented really as Lovelock was usually scrupulous in paying no attention whatsoever to our extra-curricular lives. I'd see him handing them to Johnny after classes, surreptitiously, as though this was some special favour that he didn't want the other children to know about. And, occasionally, I'd come across Johnny – at the top of the quarry mostly, where he spent much of his free time, even then – copying things out of these books, scribbling frantically onto notebooks or scraps of paper, anything he could get his hands on, stopping only now and then to look out across the sea as though, if he looked hard and long enough, the sails of ships would appear. They spoke about these books as well, Lovelock and Johnny, holding secret discussions during breaktimes; confabs about longitudes and latitudes, about flora and fauna, about worlds that neither of them had or would see, and that perhaps already no longer existed.'

By this time, in our staccato fashion, we'd reached the far end of the village, where the houses gave way to fields. It was almost completely dark now and I was a little loath to leave the lights in the windows behind me. It was hard to tell, but I think at some point Goronwy had lowered his gaze by a few degrees and was now looking directly at me; I could just about make out the moist glimmer of his eyes. Then we veered to the right and started up a narrow lane, one I'd never noticed before.

'He made up a map once, did Johnny, of an island. I saw him showing it to Lovelock one morning, before class, and later on I opened up his desk and sneaked a look at it. It was very convincing. The land was formed in the shape of an egg, with a stubby, wide promontory jutting out from its south-eastern shore, making it look a bit like a fat L. He'd drawn contour lines over its surface, quite close together in the north and then widening out towards the centre and around the sides. The details was impressive: the coast was notched with coves and bays; the beaches were coloured a tawny brown; he'd even shaded areas off the shore to show shoals and reefs. It was as if he was eager – were you to find such a place – that you'd be able to safely navigate your way around it. The only ambiguities were around the edges: a set of indecipherable squiggles in the sea which might have indicated currents and tides, but could just as well have been dragons. It must have taken a while to draw, and back then I wondered why he'd wasted so much energy on it, invested so much in something that wasn't even real. But, when I think about it now, the time he must have spent poring over charts and pictures in those books, rambling with dead men across paper topographies, that fake map was just about as real as anything else in his life.'

And then we reached a full stop, or the end of a paragraph, or the end of a page, I'm not sure which, because at that moment he halted abruptly and turned and left me, disappearing through a small gate that led only, as far as I could see, into an even deeper darkness. At the time I was somewhat relieved, because he'd not once mentioned her, and only later did I begin to wonder what had provoked Goronwy's sudden bout of reminiscence.

9

He set out two months later, my taid, on the first ship that was going and that would take him. Captain Idris Jones, a tired old sailor who'd hoped never to have to cross the world again, having to beg one final passage to retrieve his son. He'd taken it badly, my mother told me, convincing himself that, in some inexplicable way, it was his fault; that by having his child born in the place, by naming him after it, he'd somehow conspired in tweaking and shaping a destiny for him. He was inconsolable, my taid, and the single thing he thought could make amends for his tragic mistake was to ensure his son ended up where he should have begun. My nain was terrified that he wouldn't survive his last journey. She pleaded with him, told him that it was God's will and Design, and that if He saw fit to have their child rest abroad, then who were they to interfere? But my nain's God was not my taid's

God. Though they came from the same church they had learned to see Him from divergent angles. And from the deck of a ship, under a thousand different skies, He had become more difficult for my taid to apprehend; an elusive, capricious, fleeting figure, whose will and Design were at best a half-drawn chart, full of blanks and ellipses, beneath which lurked countless reefs and shoals and wrecks. These were dangerous waters, and he had learned that it was safest to keep one foot, at least, on the ground. Or if not on it, then in it.

'His body belongs in Llanysgerbwd,' he said, and that for him was final, was the only thing to be said.

And so they waved him off from the Liverpool docks, a frail, heartbroken old man whom neither my nain nor my mother was certain they would see again. But he made it there, into the harbour, in sight of a ruined city that limped up from its centre in the lee of a range of high hills, towards the crest of those hills, as though the buildings themselves had made one last, abortive effort to escape. The devastation was visible even from his anchored ship, but my taid never described it, not to my mother anyway, and I somehow doubt he ever properly looked at it: he had come there to exhume the remnants of one disaster, one sliver of one, and probably couldn't bear to set eyes on the whole of it.

For two days he searched for Valpo, asking around among the crews and captains of the ships, none of whom could help him. And then on the third day he met a sailor ashore who had survived the earthquake itself. How many had lived, he asked him? Not many, the sailor replied. How many, he asked? Ten, said the sailor, including himself, and that from five ships. And any from a Welsh ship, the *Queen of Cambria*? None, replied the sailor. And how had they died? asked my taid. So the sailor had told him.

It had begun just before morning, he said, in the greyness of the preceding dawn. It was his watch, and he'd been drowsing on deck. There was barely any reason to be awake, he said, because the sea was as flat and calm as a duck-pond and there had been no whisper of wind for days. And then, through his half-shut eyes, he'd seen the rigging shake, ever so slightly, and had waited for the breeze that shook it to waft across his face and wake him up. Except it never came. For a few seconds he was uncertain if he'd not dreamed this movement, or blinked it into being, because when he looked out at the water it was still as smooth and steady as treacle. And then the rigging had shaken again, more violently this time, and the whole ship had begun, unmistakably, to shudder and creak. But there was still no wind and not a single ripple to be seen on the entire visible surface of the ocean. He could feel the ship straining on her cables, and shouted frantically for the mate to come on deck. He was terrified, he said, and of what he didn't know. It seemed like something supernatural, like something he had never heard of apart from in the whispered stories traded at night on the fo'csle and only ever half-believed. But this was real. By the time the mate and captain, and the other sailors, had got on deck the ship was trembling like a man in the final spasms of a fever. Nobody could stay on their feet, and in the murk the men careered and collided against each other, scared out of their wits, searching desperately for something, anything, to grasp hold of. And then suddenly it was over and the ship was left gently rocking on the placid surface of a flat and deathly calm.

It wasn't until he looked towards the shore, which was about half a mile distant, that it started to dawn on him what had happened. At first, he said, all he could see were the fires that had begun to blossom sporadically through the shadows that still covered the city. He had watched as, one by one, they sprang up and multiplied, dancing their way through the darkened streets and across the roofs of the houses, until the whole place had seemed a lurid carnival of flames. And out of this had emerged the mingled cries of people and children and animals; a caterwauling, bawling, barking, screaming din that swept towards the ship over the calm water, sending a shiver down the spine of every man among them. And as the light of the fires faded into the light of the morning sun the shapes of people had appeared along the shore, jostling frantically like bees around the edges of a broken hive. There were hundreds, thousands. Some of them were clambering madly into boats, rafts, anything that would float, while others, in their panic, were simply leaping into the harbour. Those fortunate enough to get into the boats made their way towards the ships, the sailor said, and, as they approached his, he could hear them calling out to be allowed to shelter on board. His Captain, seeing their numbers, would not allow this; but this did not stop them. They pulled up beside the ship, trying to attach themselves to it with ropes, while all the time their shouts and cries grew louder and more fearful. Many of them had been terribly burned, and he could see the blisters forming on their skin; while others had been injured by falling walls and ceilings. All of them, he said, were covered in a pale, grey dust.

Those that didn't reach the ships had carried on past them. He remembered watching them head out towards the

152

open sea in their flimsy craft, thinking how for them anywhere was better than the horror that they'd left behind. Because at that moment nobody, not him, not these people, not even the Captain, was to know that it was from this sea, and not the land, that the next horror would arrive.

To begin with it was a line on the horizon, he said, a single line. And then it had grown into a shallow bank of cloud, nothing more than that. The sea had not changed. There was still no wind. It had remained a cloudbank for at least two or three minutes, long enough, certainly, for him to think that a change in the weather might be coming. By the time it became a wave it was already too late. He'd never seen anything like it, he said, not in all his years as a sailor: one sheer wall of water, rising twenty, thirty, maybe forty feet into the air out of a flat sea. He'd watched it grow on the horizon, they all had, watched it looming into the windless, birdless sky. And nobody had moved. He said it was those moments that he'd never forget, that had somehow congealed and frozen themselves into his mind, those moments when they had all stood like statues watching and nobody had moved, nothing had moved, as if all movement, all capacity for movement, had been drained out of the world and drawn, ineluctably, into the momentum of the wave itself. After this he remembered very little. He'd seen the ships anchored beyond his, lifted up like toys and hung above him, and then he'd woken up on the streets of the city in a clump of seaweed. Only ten survivors from the ships, and him one of them.

And what about the others, my taid had asked? Over there, replied the sailor, pointing to the base of a hill some mile or two from where they stood. And will you take me

153

there, said my taid? And the sailor had said yes, explaining that he had taken four of his friends there to begin with and should like to pay them his respects.

Although the mound of earth had been dug only seven months before, there were already plants and grass beginning to grow on it. In other circumstances it would not have been an unattractive place. There was a pleasant copse of willows behind it, and a fine view of the town and harbour in front of it. To the left someone had hammered a white wooden cross into the ground. There were forty men below this earth, the sailor informed him, all of those whose bodies had been found. But finding one of them, my taid had thought, beneath all this dirt, how was he supposed to go about that? The sailor refused to help him dig, saying that he had filled up this grave once and would not do it twice. Nor would he stay and watch while another man did. He did not wish to risk seeing his friends again, not like this. But before he left he told my taid that, as much as possible (depending on who had recognized them), they had placed the bodies of each crew together in the grave, and indicated that those from the *Queen of Cambria* were in a spot at the far edge. My taid thanked him for this and then began to dig the ground above this spot with his bare hands, which were all he'd brought with him.

It took him four hours to unearth the first body, or the first part of one, and when he did the stench was so powerful that he was forced to pull away and retch. What he'd found was an arm, and after he'd followed it up to its shoulder, and then neck, and then face, he discovered that the maggots and worms had eaten away most of its features. He tried to turn the head sideways, cradling it, hoping to find a profile that he could recognise, but when he did the creatures slid out of its mouth and sockets onto his arms and all he could see was a flat, blackened, noseless blank. He had no idea then how he would ever find his son.

Beneath this first body he uncovered a tangled mess of limbs and torsos; a charnel, Gordian knot of them. Extricating them seemed nigh on impossible, so instead he rooted among them for the heads, which, when he found them, seemed to resemble the pods, or eggs, of one writhing, composite, underground insect. Some of them cracked and split in his fingers, but he searched each one, nevertheless, for anything that might be familiar, that could remind him of something that might once have been his son's face. Eventually he came across two heads pushed against each other, almost in a kiss, and saw that one was still covered with blonde hair. He remembered then how Valpo's letters had mentioned a friend of his, a cabin boy from Norway with blonde, nearly white, hair; and so this must be him he'd thought. And then he'd looked at the other head and seen the jaw.

It was unmistakeable. It was exactly the same as his own, except with the skin partially rotted, partially eaten, away. Whether it was the emotion of finding Valpo, or the effects of the heat and the smell, my taid didn't know, but at that moment he began to feel his mind cloud over and his knees wobble. He became terribly afraid that he'd faint, and that if he fainted some passer-by would mistake him for a corpse and re-fill the grave with him inside of it. What a prospect, he'd thought, to end up with two Joneses buried here. And so, hastily, he grabbed hold of the jaw and pulled it towards him, only to have it come off in his hand. He fell backwards, still clutching it, and could barely summon the energy to get back on his feet. He knew he was running out of time now. He shoved the jaw into his pocket and started desperately trying to disentangle his son's body from the others. The trouble was, he couldn't tell which parts were his and which belonged to the others. Pieces of them kept twisting off when he tugged at them, until eventually, with his last ounce of strength, he'd gathered together these fragments – the jaw, a leg, some ribs and half a pelvis – and carried them out of the grave and back down to the city.

His plan was to rest for a bit and then return to collect the rest of Valpo. And to make sure the pieces he already had were properly his. But by the time he was able to, his ship was preparing to leave. He begged the captain to wait another day, but he wouldn't. He even refused to let my taid take what he had got on the ship, saying that the stench was too awful and that besides it was unhygienic – and not a little morbid – to have such things on a ship. And so my taid's last hours in Valparaiso were spent boiling the flesh off his cargo and concealing it in a wooden box.

As his ship lifted its anchor and embarked, my taid had stood on the deck, looking disconsolately back at the city and the harbour, pondering the destiny he had inadvertently made for his son. To travel here three times: once to be born, once to be disappointed, and once more to die. And the final part of that destiny he now held in his hands: a box of boiled and dubious bones that he would return, once and for all, to Llanysgerbwd.

10

I looked out of the window and counted them. One for sorrow, two for joy, three for a girl, four for a boy; and what was for five. Now that I thought about it I realised I'd never really got past four. There hadn't been any need: in the places we'd lived there'd never been more than four to count. 'You're supposed to salute them,' she'd said, interrupting the rhyme she was teaching me. 'To bring good luck.' How a bunch of magpies was supposed to bring luck was beyond me, though it did occur to me that luck was something we were sorely deficient in. 'Why?' I'd ask.

'Well I don't know, do I. It just does.' And whenever my mother told me 'it just does', I'd know better than to carry on questioning her.

I'd then tried to work out for myself the association between magpies and good fortune, perhaps imagining that if

I could figure it out, and then make sure I saw more of them, things would change, would get better. But I couldn't figure it out at all. In my eyes they were just vermin, who picked at our bins in the same way rats and stray cats did. And you didn't hear rhymes about them, did you. And nobody claimed they brought you luck, or joy – though maybe a little sorrow, when the bin bags were ripped open. At the time I simply couldn't understand where my mother had got these strange ideas from. It was no wonder things never got better.

But now, as I watched them from my cottage window, I realised that it hadn't ever occurred to me back then that these birds lived in fields and hedgerows like this. It wasn't the landscape I'd grown to know them in; it wasn't a landscape I knew. And seeing them hopping and darting across the churned and sodden grass, searching for the shrivelled remains of hawthorn berries in the hedges, it suddenly struck me that maybe they could be lucky; or at least that here the proposition that they were seemed more feasible. At that moment I saw a small tree in the corner of the field move and they scattered, and I saw that the tree had turned into Bub, who often appeared so blended in with the topography of his fields as to be at times indistinguishable from it. And then it dawned on me that saluting magpies was something it wouldn't seem at all strange for *him* to do.

This was the first time that I suspected my mother might have actually been here. As each day her image receded further and further from me, it had left behind the revelation of how little I'd known about her. It was as if I had only ever apprehended her in a series of shifting presents, one after the other after the other, and never linked them together, never fitted them onto a past, so that now, when her image was lost to me, there was nothing left of her.

What did I really know of her history? The grandparents we'd not talked about, the uncle the solicitor had informed me of. In my father's houses we were not allowed to have histories; they were surplus baggage, what you got away from, what you left behind. At the age of fourteen he'd fled from the orphanage with nothing but a bit of cash and the clothes he was wearing, a flight *he* recalled endlessly: the full moon that had lit the front yard; his climb over the heavy iron gates; the teacher who'd run out and called after him; how he'd stood out in the road giving him the finger, calling back fuck you, fuck all of you. He loved telling people about it, becoming bold and defiant once more as he did, as though you were that teacher and there was nothing he needed to explain or justify. It was the only story about his past he really told, though. His Exodus. Genesis didn't interest him, while the Promised Land was everywhere he hadn't got to yet. And God forbid that my mother should mention her parents, or where she'd grown up, or what she'd done before she met him. It sent him into terrible sulks and rages, and so she'd ended up hiding that too.

With the magpies gone and Bub vanished back into the hedgerow, I left the window and set about searching the cottage for evidence of my mother's presence. In the back of my mind I knew this was hopeless. If she had been here it would have been at least thirty years ago. Besides, how would I know if anything I did find would have actually belonged to her: crowded between me and this possible her were all those legions of summer visitors whose cheery, satisfied spectres, despite all my efforts, still lingered about the place. In the end the best I could come up with was an old porcelain plate that I found on a shelf beneath the sink. I put it on the empty table beside my bed. Sometimes it helped me to remember her, but at others it just sat there like the mute relic of a lost civilisation; a temple crumbling away in a pathless jungle. And sometimes it was just a plate, that had probably belonged to someone else.

Later that afternoon I walked over to Johnny's. The search through my cottage had left me despondent and restless. My thoughts and questions and attempts to remember had all seemed to trail away into a distant and irretrievable nowhere, drifting through it like luckless satellites lost in space. And this had translated itself into a physical discomfort, a yearning ache in my belly, an inability to sit still, the compulsion to move with them on foot, and almost automatically I'd begun heading towards Johnny's.

The journey there was a blur. I was so preoccupied that I hardly noticed the ground under my feet. I was dimly aware of the wind gusting around my ears and, in the brief lulls between, the forlorn sound of a plane rumbling somewhere above. But apart from that I was almost entirely insensate of the world around me until I'd reached a point about two hundred yards away from the top of Johnny's track, where, for a second, I looked up – just in time to glimpse a figure emerge from it and disappear down the road ahead. For a while I stood there and blinked, wondering if I'd actually seen anything at all, if perhaps this figure had merely been the hallucinated shadow of my own thoughts. But I quickly dismissed the idea: because this shadow appeared to know exactly where it was going and my thoughts most certainly didn't. I went through some other possibilities. A ghost? I doubted it. There'd been nothing ghostlike about it; it hadn't been floating or gliding or anything, it had been walking, and walking in a particularly matter-of-fact and industrious manner at that. Or maybe Bub or Nut? But I knew how Bub walked, and Nut hardly walked anywhere. And besides, I was sure it had had a decidedly feminine shape. I pondered this as I made my way down Johnny's track, confused because I was sure that, with the rare exception of Goronwy, I was Johnny's only visitor. But by the time I got to his door my mind had strayed back to my thoughts of before.

'I think she might have stayed here once,' I said.

Johnny was looking down at the table. There was a freshly ironed white cloth spread over it and he appeared rather bemused as to how it had ended up there beneath his eyes.

'In my house, Tŷ Gwynt,' I continued, beginning to realise that I was really clutching at straws if it had come to this. 'I think my mother might have stayed there. Years ago – thirty at least.'

'Who?' he abruptly asked, not shifting his gaze. And I couldn't work out if he was asking who I was talking about or who'd put this cloth on the table.

'My mother.'

'Why would she come here?' Over by the fireplace there was a towel hung out to dry and he now turned his attention towards it.

'I'm not sure why. But I've got a feeling she did and I was wondering if maybe you remembered...'

'Why?'

Because she talked about magpies when I was a child, I thought. Because she told me it was good luck to salute them.

'Well I'm not that certain why, but....' Johnny had got up from the table. He walked over to the towel and took it off the

161

nail on which it was hanging. He held it up to his face for a second and sniffed it. I already knew it was clean because you could smell the soap that had steamed out of it into the room, but he looked surprised to find this out. Then he put it back on the nail and returned to his chair, continuing to eye it suspiciously as though it had somehow fallen out of the sky. I tried again.

'You see, I was wondering if maybe you might remember her visiting here, perhaps even living around here. It would've been thirty years ago at least, probably more.'

'Who?'

'My mother.'

Why on earth was I trying to talk to him? I must have been getting a little desperate. She was almost entirely gone and I had only the plate.

Every conversation I'd attempted to have with Johnny had ended like this. He'd pretend to be distracted whenever I mentioned something about myself, or else he'd take what I was trying to say and use it as a prompt for another of his stories, an opportunity to get back to what he seemed to need to tell me. He didn't want a conversation. All he wanted was a listener. I was the guest at the wedding and the only difference between us was that I'd gone looking for him.

'My mother never liked it here, you know!' he suddenly spat out, as though in direct response to what I'd been saying. 'She hated it!' There was a vehemence, a violence almost, in his voice when he told me this that I'd never heard before.

Directly beside Johnny's cottage there are the remains of a garden. You can guess it was a garden once because of the wall that encircles it, but apart from this there are few signs that it has ever been anything other than the tangle of brambles and blackthorns and nettles it is now. Johnny told me it was in this garden that he'd begun to realise that his mother hated the place they lived in. He was five years old then. He said it was the first thing he clearly remembered.

It was in the Spring and he was playing in the garden. The brambles and nettles had already started to grow there, creeping up the walls and spreading across the grass, while the blackthorns, like him, were barely beyond their infancy; no more than the thorny beginnings of trees. He must have played in this garden often, he said, because although he had no single, definite memory of being in it prior to that Spring afternoon, he was conscious of a familiarity that must have pre-dated this moment, a vague blur of recollection, of Winter mud and puddles, of Autumn leaves and slugs, which adhered to it like a dark, damp, second skin. He was also conscious of its enticing unfamiliarity. There always seemed to be something new about it, some corner he hadn't yet explored, some object he hadn't found: a nest between the stones of the wall, a mound of earth, a hole in the ground that promised something, somewhere, else. It was his favourite spot to play. And as he'd played there that afternoon, surrounded by fresh growths of nettles and the unaccustomed colours of bramble blossoms, he'd looked up to catch another unexpected sight edging its way into his view.

It was his grandfather. He was making his way down the steep and treacherous descent that led from the lane to the cottage, treading carefully (as I'd woefully neglected to do that first time) on the slabs of slate that served for steps. Even when he'd got safely to the bottom his footsteps had remained tentative, chary, as though he half expected the ground beneath him to suddenly tilt or sway, and occasionally he'd put his stick out in front of him and lean on it, just in case. In this manner he'd got almost to the door, and was about to knock on it when a thought appeared to cross his mind and he stopped with his fist raised just inches away from the wood. And instead of knocking he'd made a sly detour towards the garden, ducking beneath the kitchen window as he went, only to come face to face with the boy who'd been watching him all along.

'Well, if it isn't Johnny Bach,' he'd called out, louder than he needed to, loud enough for anyone inside to hear and so not think he was sneaking about. 'And so how's my little one then,' he'd continued, entering the garden through a rickety gate and threading his way around the new clumps of nettles, pausing now and then to take a swishing blow at them with his stick.

'So look at you,' he said, arriving beside Johnny and reaching down to pat him on his shoulder. 'Three inches bigger at least.'

Johnny had looked up at him, fascinated immediately by a face he must have seen many times before but couldn't clearly recall. A remarkable face – to Johnny anyway – creased and cross-hatched with long wrinkled lines that looked like something, but not something he knew yet. A face that he noticed was not quite looking at him, but instead was shifting subtly from side to side as his grandfather surveyed the corners of the garden.

'Three inches at least,' he said, aiming a concerned glance towards the shoots of a nearby blackthorn tree. 'Wait till I tell your nain, won't she be proud of you.'

'Dad!' came his mother's voice, from the gate, where she was suddenly standing. She didn't sound altogether overjoyed to see him.

'Hello, cariad,' he replied, adding quickly, almost apologetically, 'I was just telling Johnny how his nain would be proud of him. Three inches he's grown, I swear.'

'I wasn't expecting you,' she said, like it was a question.

And then Johnny had stopped listening to their voices and turned his attention to a length of discarded skin that he'd found in the grass. It looked like the shell of a worm, or a long, thin sausage with its insides taken out. He didn't know what it was or where it had come from. There were some ants creeping inside it and he squeezed them out before putting it in his pocket. Later on, in his room, he'd take it out and put it on the floor and imagine it had been left behind by a snake or a dragon or a sea monster, and wonder if he kept it whether this creature would come back to collect it. In the end his mother found it and threw it away.

And then he could hear their voices again.

'She worries about you,' his grandfather said. 'And the boy too. If you'd just visit once or twice, just bring him over. It's not a lot to ask.'

'There's nothing to worry about, is there. I'm fine. He's fine.'

'But still, cariad, once or twice, it couldn't hurt, could it. For his nain's sake.'

'I won't go back there. You know that, Dad, you know that.'

With the skin safely in his pocket, Johnny had turned his curiosity back towards his grandfather. Like the garden, Johnny's grandfather was familiar to him without him having any definite memories of the man before this moment. Three things about him were lodged in his mind, although how they had got there was as mysterious to him as how certain rocks ended up in certain places. They came, he supposed, from his own pre-history. He knew that he was fascinated by his face. He knew that he loved him visiting. He knew that he came from somewhere else that was close enough for him to walk from, but that he (Johnny) had never been. This was the substratum classified in his young brain as Grandfather. But now, as he listened to his mother talking to her father-in-law, he began to speculate what lay beneath, or above, this thin layering. Where was the 'there' that his mother wouldn't visit, which he was sure was the somewhere his grandfather came from? Why she wouldn't visit was as yet beyond him, even as a question. How come his grandfather's face appeared so much older and weathered than the other grandfathers' faces he'd seen? There were other things too, but thinking about them made him a little dizzy. And besides, the voices had already moved on to other topics.

'So if you won't come back for a visit, then why can't you at least let me help you with this garden? I mean, really, cariad, it's turning into a jungle. And it wouldn't take me more than an afternoon or two to clear it.'

'You'll leave this garden well alone, Idris,' said his mother's voice, in the steady, low-pitched tone that he knew meant she was angry. His grandfather appeared unaware of this.

'But you haven't touched it since you came here. How's the boy going to play in it if it gets any worse?'

'That's none of your business. It's not your garden.' As she said this Johnny had looked up at his mother and found her staring not, as he'd expected, at his grandfather, but past him at the garden. There was no doubt she was angry. Her lips were pulled thinly shut, her nostrils were slightly flared, her eyes were dark and ominously shiny, the irises enlarged, the colours almost invisible. There was no doubt. It was anger, an outraged and defiant anger, and it was directed not at his grandfather, who was leaning silently on his stick, cowed and uncomfortable, but at the garden which, as far as Johnny knew, had never done anything wrong or bad to deserve such a look. This first memory ended with his grandfather walking back up the track and a strange feeling, which was entirely new to him, of being alone in a place where he'd never felt alone. It was like his mother had squeezed something living out of it. It was as though it were shrinking and fading in front of his eyes, becoming, as it would ever after remain, no more than a small, mean, familiar patch of weeds.

'Because I was beginning to learn then,' Johnny said. 'I was beginning to learn that she hated it here. There I was, only a boy, beginning to learn that her refusal to touch our garden, and even the way she bloody looked at it, meant something. But I didn't know what yet, how could I – I was five years old. And I didn't know why. How could I have? I didn't know anything yet. I was just a boy who lived in a house with a mother, and a father who was nothing more than the name of a city. It didn't seem unusual.'

Johnny had a way of talking as if everything was a story, as if he were reading everything he told me out of a book. It was all a bit too rehearsed. He never faltered mid-sentence, he never forgot what was coming next. Sometimes I wondered if his relatives were only characters. Sometimes I wondered if this younger version of himself was as well. Sometimes I wondered if I believed a word he said or even the words he showed me. I still do.

But that afternoon, as he told me about his mother and his disenchanted garden, he became unusually agitated. He kept getting up out of his chair and moving around the room. Twice he paused, as though he might forget exactly what he was going to say. At one point he went over to the oak cabinet and rearranged some of the crockery. Or perhaps rearranged is the wrong way to put it. What he did was move it around and leave pieces of it scattered randomly on its shelves. He disarranged it.

'I wish she'd let this stuff alone,' he said as he did this. 'I wish she'd not tidy it.' I wasn't certain who he was referring to, but when he'd finished he sat back down and described to me how inordinately, fussily, tidy his mother had been.

He said he couldn't remember her with a hair out of place. He said that in the picture of her that he'd die with she'd be standing over a table, or reaching up to a dresser, with a cloth in her hand and every inch of her clothing ironed and starched to a diamond perfection; a domestic silhouette cut with crystal razor blades. And as he described that picture you could almost catch the scent of soap and detergent emanating from it, bleaching its interiors, sterilising the synapses in which it was held, as though his mother would not allow him to leave a clutter behind, not even in his memory of her; as though at that very moment she was stalking through his cerebellum, brushing away cobwebs, dusting off dead cells, trying to polish all the windows there that had grimed and sooted over.

168

And she must have been doing a thorough job because Johnny was not only able to recall her easily, but the whole of his house as it had been then. Because it was something of a paradox, he told me; that, while his mother had left the outside of the house studiously untouched, she had kept the inside in an exact and Spartan order. It helped that there was so little of it. His mother didn't really go in for superfluous belongings, he said. Everything had a function as well as a place. The kitchen had one table to eat on, one counter to prepare food on, four knives and forks and spoons (the extra two were for his nain and taid in case they visited). In the cupboard there were the same number of plates and bowls, which, after they'd been used, were put back in exactly the same spot they always were: the plates in the far right-hand corner, the bowls to the left. Two pale circles remained on the wood of this cupboard, Johnny said, the scar tissue of her fussiness. There were two tea towels, one blue and one white, that were hung on a rail beside the stove. There was a single black pot for making stew, and when it wasn't on the stove it was sat on the second shelf below the counter. In the corner furthest away from the window there were three unmarked pots, one for flour, one for sugar, and one for barley. He never saw them with their lids off. In fact, as a child, it had amazed him that his mother would actually allow food into this kitchen. The sight of a chunk of salted pork for instance, with its jagged edges and asymmetric bulk, would lie like an affront on her table, and he'd almost expect her to chastise it rather than cook it. And the same went for any number of unruly vegetables that made their way over the doorstep: beets, with their wayward, flaring greens;

169

turnips, squat and misshapen like savage idols, freighted with treacherous ladings of earth; the riotous curls of cabbage leaves, all of them looked – the moment they came into his mother's house – like fugitives from an alien realm of chaos and messy profusion. Sometimes at night he'd dream of being there, caught in crazy, criss-crossed vines and heavy, grape-plump clusters, dream of it until he'd wake up to the austere surroundings of his room – the narrow bed with its polished brass frame, the single wooden dresser with a chilly white washbowl on top and mirror above, the one Shaker-plain chair, the chamber pot – wake up to find them subtly begrudging his presence amongst them, as though maybe the dream had contaminated him and he might pollute them, so that it seemed that the mirror didn't want his face in it, that the chamber pot flinched from his behind, that even his starch-smoothed pillows recoiled from his cheeks. Wake up and run downstairs to escape them, downstairs to this room with the cabinet and its carefully arranged and never-used porcelain cups and saucers and the table scrubbed clean after not being eaten on and the fireplace with no fire because that would leave ashes behind and the clock hands ticking cold through the pristine, untenanted Arctic.

There he was, Johnny said, a boy trapped in a house that didn't want him in it, that didn't want anybody in it. Because what his mother so scrupulously maintained was only the cruel simulacrum of a house, the immaculate, sloughed-off skin of one. His room was meant to be a room for a boy: it wasn't meant to be a room lived in by a boy. And the same was true of the rest of it. And it was what his mother had made it. Because she hated it, which he didn't quite know yet, but

170

which he was beginning to guess, slowly, not quite realising even then that anything about his life was unusual. And then one day, when he was eight, it came to him.

About a mile and a half from Johnny's, on the immediate outskirts of the village, there is an old manor house. It's not very grand, but it is big enough to set it apart from the other houses in the village, an apartness reinforced by a tree-lined drive that leads up to it from the main road. I've passed it many times. A few months ago some men arrived and began thinning out the trees. Goronwy told me a family from London had recently bought it and were planning to renovate it, which was a shame, he said, because up to then it had served as the village's haunted house, and every village around here used to have its own haunted house. It was good for the children he told me, it gave them something to be frightened of, something to do. And looking across the road from the Spar, where we were standing, I caught sight of a marauding group of them and agreed with him. A bit of fear might break up the boredom.

One afternoon when he was eight, Johnny told me, he'd dodged school with two other boys. They'd decided to break into the haunted house and made their way to the entrance to the track. It was a gloomy winter's day and as they began to walk towards the house it got more gloomy, as the tall pine trees that lined the track blocked out the already meagre light. Erratic gusts of wind scattered rooks off their branches and their blackness rose and faded into the grey slivers of visible sky. The canopy above them crackled and cackled and interspersed amongst it they could make out the dark, thick boughs of monkey-puzzle trees, crouched there like giant tarantula legs. With each step forward Johnny had noticed the other boys slowing down. They were getting frightened. But he wasn't frightened, he said. He had never been frightened of ghosts. The closer they got to the house the slower these boys became, until eventually they had fallen well behind Johnny, who was forced to tease and cajole them onwards. By the time they got to the front door they wanted to go back but Johnny wouldn't let them, and besides, he said, the house itself hadn't looked that haunted back then; the slates hadn't begun to fall from the roof, the ivy hadn't grown up the walls, its windows were still intact. It was Johnny who broke the first one, to get them in. Inside it was quiet and still and for a few minutes his companions seemed happy to be there, to be away from the trees and the wind. But the instant they began to explore the rooms their fear had returned twofold. They went into the kitchen, where spiders crept through the abandoned cupboards and spun homes in the stove; they rootled through a sitting room and found a picture frame with nothing inside and two chairs where some dust sat; in the hall there was a jacket on a hook. The boys visibly flinched from each object, as if something might lurk inside it, something left over and terrible that was just waiting for their touch to release it. And with each new room their unease grew, and Johnny could tell that the stillness and quietness and emptiness inside had become far more terrifying to them than the spooky, blustery, noisy outside. But not for him. To Johnny it seemed familiar. When, eventually, they came to one of the bedrooms and discovered a single bed there, small enough to be unmistakably the bed of a child, and a stationary rocking-horse with red glass eyes, their nerve finally broke altogether and despite Johnny's protestations they'd scuttled back to the window, climbed out

172

and run away. But Johnny had stayed inside, on his own, for almost an hour, searching on through the rest of the rooms until at last he returned to the child's room where he sat down on the bed, realising that not only did this place seem familiar but that it was almost exactly the same as his own. The horse he contemplated with envy.

Through Johnny's window I could see the light beginning to fail. There were shadows falling into the room. One of them had fallen across him and he sat in it looking momentarily distracted, a little lost. For a few seconds he was quiet, staring down at the surface of the table as though he were trying to find his bearings there, in the faint circles our mugs of tea had left behind. And then he lifted his head, as if whatever he'd needed to find he'd found, and now he knew where he was again.

In the journals and papers of some explorers, he told me, you would find places that they'd discovered, and then discovered they didn't like: a mangrove swamp, filled with crocodiles and fevers, a desert, an arid mountain range with valleys of stone. You could tell they didn't like them, he said, not only from what they wrote but from how they mapped them. Some just left them as a blank, a void on paper that marked their distaste through sheer neglect. But others made sure to chart them even more carefully than the places they liked. You could see the special attention they lavished on them, the added details and features, the accuracy of the proportions, the minuteness of the observations. And submerged beneath this meticulous care and attention was their dislike, as though instinctively they had realised that the best way to keep these places at arm's length, to blunt their distasteful reality, to make them exist less, was to arrange and order them as exactly as possible. Finding themselves somewhere they didn't want to be they set about reducing it to a cold and accurate transcription, a lifeless spectre of ink.

The day he sat on that bed in the haunted house, Johnny told me, was the day he first realised that he never had, and never would be, afraid of haunted houses. It was the day he realised that he'd grown up in a house that had always been haunted because his mother refused to truly live in it. And by that refusal she had turned it into a phantom house and had come to hate it. All of it, he said. All of it apart from one room. The one room where the real ghost lived, the ghost that had turned her into a ghost.

The one room he wasn't allowed into.

11

I was a lot more careful on my next visits to Tammy. First of all I made sure not to go until at least half eleven or midnight – when there remained a good chance that most of the older people in the village were in the Dragon, but less of a chance that Goronwy would be out for his evening walk. Of course there were still the perpetually loitering kids to avoid and so I worked out an alternative route to her house, one that circumvented the village street altogether. It wasn't difficult. I soon discovered that the maze of lanes that covered the island branched out all around the village, and that, by following one of its strands for a few hundred yards and then clambering back through a field, I could get almost directly to her door. Secondly, I made sure to pick the right place in her garden to hide. There was a spot in the far corner where a bramble bush had grown up over the fence, and I found that by nestling myself halfway beneath it I was almost entirely invisible both from the road and from the front window.

Freed, as I thought, from the anxiety of being seen, I began to notice Tammy's night-time habits. They were not that varied, consisting mainly of trips back and forth between the kitchen and sofa, but they had a certain soothing regularity to them, a grooved and satisfying constancy. Occasionally she'd stop suddenly, in the middle of these journeys, and stand and stare for a few seconds as though she didn't quite know where she was, but soon enough she'd fall back into her steps and complete them. These were just blips really and I'd quickly put them out of my mind. She tended to stay up late, often until three or four in the morning, and sometimes I'd find myself dozing in and out of sleep while I waited for her to go to bed. I tried to stop this happening because there were times, when it did, that I'd discover myself trapped in a panic, halfway towards consciousness, surrounded by figures in the near distance who were staring at me and continued to stare at me until eventually they recrudesced into the branches of trees and fence posts and the pole of a broken streetlight that stood on the corner of the road. And even afterwards, when I was fully awake again, a faint nimbus of unease would continue to hang about them, as if these benign and inanimate witnesses were concealing others who weren't.

Her preparations for bed were always the same. To start with she'd make one last trip into the kitchen, where she'd boil the kettle and prepare a cup of tea; then, after pausing for a few minutes while it cooled, she'd return to the living room as usual, except that this time she wouldn't sit back down on the sofa. Following this, and always in the same sequence, she'd place the cup on the coffee table, lean over to switch the television off, and then change out of her shirt or sweater and put on a black dressing-gown that was hanging up behind the living room door. Only then would she begin her slow walk up the stairs towards her bedroom. She always left the tea on the table. Unfortunately, there was a thick, red curtain drawn across her bedroom window so I could never follow her there, though on several occasions the light inside would linger on for hours.

My observations were also helped by an abrupt and unexpected change in the weather. January had frozen the wind into a temporary submission, leaving behind a chilly, crackling stillness. It lasted for about a fortnight, and imbued everything with a kind of hard-edged, icy clarity. The days now finally released and revealed the horizon. From the fields in front of my house I could look across to my right and see the mountains of the mainland cut like grey-blue diamonds against the sky; while, further over in front of me, the little island, named after some saint, lay stranded off the shore. And it was during these days that, down by the quarry, I first began to discover those other, uncertain hills and islands, wandering like crystal phantoms across the freezing, static sea.

The nights became startlingly, almost eerily, pellucid. A faint layering of frost covered everything, refracting and accentuating every point of light, while the still emptiness of the atmosphere seemed to ease its passage through the air, so that even the weakest stars appeared to shine right down onto the ground. The moon was like a white flashbulb.

On these nights I found that the faint glare from Tammy's window became ever more variegated and revealing. I started to play a game with myself, imagining that I was able to distinguish what was on her television by the different qualities of light that radiated from its screen and filtered out to blend with those that covered the garden. Take channels, for instance: if there was a sudden, intermittent jerking and flickering, a break in what had previously been a steadier, more rhythmic pulse, then I'd guess that these must be ads she was watching. And my interpretations became increasingly subtle and elaborate. I actually worked out a formula that I thought allowed me to identify particular types of programme: for nature documentaries I looked for long, looping effusions – tinctured with hints and motes of green – which suggested the sweep of a camera across verdant plains; for reality shows a dull, unmoving glow, punctuated only occasionally by the monotonous progress of a shadow through the light; for music videos a quick-fire refulgence, the breathless, epileptic dance of photons. I'd sometimes try to verify my conjectures by attempting to read Tammy's reactions to these programmes in her features. It was an almost impossible task. Her face was blank and indecipherable; it only reflected back what was shone upon it.

Nevertheless, I enjoyed this game because it gave us something to share; it brought us together in the same light. It also helped to distract me from the memory of other nights I had spent like this. When I was a child I used to sneak out at night to hide in the garden – and, though I use the singular here, the reality is plural: there were many gardens – and from there I'd spy through the windows at my parents. I spent countless nights like this – nobody appeared to notice – although my memory of them seems to have condensed into one lone tableau. In it, my father is seated in front of the television – we do not share its light – caught forever in a half-gesture of frustration and anger, his arm raised towards the screen, while my mother hovers somewhere in the background, at the far end of the room, or in another window, looking pensively in a direction I am unsure of, although sometimes her gaze is pointed out of the window, past the garden, and me, into the spaces beyond. It is a picture that disturbs me even now, filling me with an anxiety that I cannot quite put my finger on. There is an ambivalence that returns to ache inside me each time I recollect it. Because although, on the surface, it looks like the most settled of domestic scenes, a scene probably duplicated in every window on that street – on all the streets – I am aware of a certain fleetingness that plays about its edges, in the corners of my mother's eyes, in the curve of my father's hand, as though everything in it is implicitly poised on the point of movement, of flight, of elsewhere. Like a cafe in a Hopper print, it is an image haunted with intimations of dispersal. And at every moment (at this one in fact and all the others that will come when I remember it), I am terrified that they will disappear and leave me by myself in the garden, that I will look up to find the rooms deserted.

12

In all the time I knew Johnny I only saw him outside of his front room on four occasions. Perhaps this sounds a little strange. In fact, the more I think of it, it is a little strange: four times in almost a year. But the truth is I never expected to see him anywhere else. What seemed strange back then was seeing him outside.

I remember those four occasions quite vividly. The first was when I caught him washing his teeth. The third was much later, towards the end, when I found him sitting one afternoon on the cliffs above the quarry, staring out across the sea. The last was in his coffin; but perhaps this doesn't count, because although half of it was in his hallway, the other half was in his front room. As for the second, well that was in the very middle of the winter – in the very middle of everything, I suppose – when, unable to sleep after a night at Tammy's, I arrived at his cottage unusually early.

It was still almost dark and to begin with I couldn't work out what the shape was in his front yard. It looked like a hunched shadow and appeared to be brooding over a wooden stump. For a few seconds I imagined it might be the figure I'd thought I'd seen before, or else one of the plethora of ghosts that Bub and Nut had assured me continued to enjoy a rude health in these parts. I'd yet to witness any and, to be honest, was somewhat eager to: not having a ghost story around here marked you out as someone who the local ghosts wouldn't necessarily bother materialising for. Why go to the effort of haunting people who'd never pass down the story of their haunting, they must have reckoned; much better to think generationally: one visit would last for decades, would give a spot a reputation for centuries. Tourists hardly ever see ghosts – it's a waste of phantom labour.

So I was genuinely hopeful that this shadow would turn out to have no head, or no eyes, or, at the very least, no face. And adding to this expectation was the fact that Johnny's cottage seemed such a perfect place for ghosts. It was something about the way you had to walk down to it, to descend, as though this alteration in gradient augured a subtle alteration in dimension as well. Most other-worlds, to my knowledge anyway, tend to be underworlds. Coupled with this was the cottage itself. It didn't look – it never looked – like a building someone actually lived in. It looked like a building that had been left behind. The surprise of seeing Johnny come out of its door on that first visit had always stayed with me; it continued to astound me every time I found him sitting inside at his table. And yet there was a certain logic, or aptness, about this incongruity. It somehow seemed absolutely fitting that Johnny should inhabit a building that already appeared like a relic, and a relic of himself to boot.

When my spectre started chopping kindling with a rusty hatchet I was a bit disappointed. But since I'd barely ever seen Johnny do anything other than talk, there was an undeniable fascination to be had in watching him engaged in a different activity. I was shocked he looked so normal. I don't know why this was. I think that maybe I'd come to know him too much as other things, as a voice, as a mysterious hermit, as some sort of a guide, as a way into the island I wanted to be my home; and that the one thing he unambiguously was – an old, rather lonely, man, with very little else to cling on to apart from his past – had quite passed me by. And yet this was the man whom I now found weakly hacking at a pile of sticks in his yard. His arms were thin and frail and trembled pathetically under the weight of the hatchet; his back was stooped; his trousers drooped below the fleshless absence of his buttocks and fell away down the feeble length of his legs. It was difficult for me to register this Johnny, almost to believe in him. Perhaps I would have preferred a ghost.

As I approached him Johnny looked up. Yet, although I was directly in his line of vision, he made no sign or gesture to acknowledge my presence. I called out a greeting but still he ignored me.

'Morning, Johnny,' I said, no more than two feet from him.

He said nothing. Picking up his sticks in one hand and holding the hatchet in the other, he stared right past me and, without uttering a word, walked into his cottage.

The odd thing was that as soon as I'd followed him into the front room he'd started talking. There was no mention of what had happened a few minutes previously. The sticks he'd carried in were now failing to ignite in his fireplace and the hatchet was laid out on the table.

'This belonged to my great-grandfather,' he informed me, 'Medicine Jones.'

In the laws of physics it's theoretically possible to exist in two places at once. In the laws of Johnny I seemed allowed only to exist in one.

13

Bub and Nut had been cool with me since the night in the Dragon, so I was relieved when one day, towards the end of January, I heard the familiar droning of Nut's tractor approaching the entrance to my yard. Within minutes he was knocking on my door. My first reaction was a sudden pang of nerves and guilt. I thought he might have spotted me on my nocturnal forays to Tammy's. Bub and Nut, I'd realised, both had the unsettling capacity to be simultaneously nowhere and everywhere. I'd often find myself walking past their farm and glancing through the gate, only to discover it entirely untenanted: the yard empty, the cottage unlit and silent, even the dogs gone. It would look as though no one lived there, or had done for some time; an appearance reinforced by the collection of rusty and apparently long-worn-out metal objects that lay strewn about the place, which to my eye looked about as useful and functional as a clump of dinosaur bones. And yet, seconds after I'd gone past, I'd catch a glimpse through the hawthorn branches of some figure moving about, or hear an engine splutter into life. The same was true of just about every other part of the landscape around my house. You could be walking through a vacant field, or looking out of the window at an uninhabited horizon, when suddenly one of them would materialise out of a hedge or step out of a wall. It was impossible ever to be certain that you were alone, that there wasn't some hidden pair of eyes in your vicinity.

But my misgivings were eased the moment I opened the door and found Nut smiling, somewhat mischievously, on the other side. He was wearing a new bright red baseball cap, with Ferrari embossed above its peak, and looked altogether pleased with himself.

'A-right,' he said.

'Fine,' I replied, 'and you?'

'A-right.'

'Yu busy today?' he asked, and when I said no he grinned again and started shuffling his weight impatiently from foot to foot.

'Yu wouldn't fancy givin' us a hand then would yu?'

'With what?' I asked.

'With some bullocks,' he said.

As we walked over to the farm I asked him several times what exactly we had to do with the bullocks, which seemed to amuse him greatly even though he didn't offer any answers. I didn't mind. I was secretly pleased that he had come to me for help. It made me feel as though I'd reached a certain higher status of neighbourliness, that I was being ushered further into the authentic life of the island. I could also feel my anxiety about Tammy recede with every step. The night in the George appeared to be long forgotten, and as we approached the entrance to the farm I recalled that neither Bub or Nut had ever actually warned me off her, or not exactly anyway. Perhaps I had mis-read their annoyance, had blown it out of proportion.

It looked a bit like a Caesarian – or what I'd guess one would look like. First, he made a short cut through the smooth, pink skin of the bag, and then reached down to squeeze its contents until gradually one of them would protrude through the incision. You'd think that the cut was too small, that there was no way it would fit through, but it did every time. Out they would slip, one after the other, flopping with a soft, moist thud onto the dung-encrusted wooden slats at the bottom of the crush. They looked so vulnerable there, so exposed, that to begin with I wanted to cover them, to protect them from the harsh coldness of the January air, from the cruel brightness of the light. They didn't belong in this world of filth and dirt, and lying there on the slats, wreathed in gossamer threads of steam, they looked almost astonished to have been forced into it. There was something alien and beautiful about them. They were shaped like hearts, and had a milky, silken texture, like liquid ivory. If you looked closely you could see delicate purple veins forking across their skin like streaks of amethyst through quartz. I watched them gather into small piles, filled with a sense of pity and revulsion and wincing, eye-watering empathy, before Nut eventually kicked them out into the yard towards the hungrily waiting dogs.

I'd never seen a castration before, and I'm not certain if this was the way it was usually done. On arriving at the farm

Nut had led me over to a shed made of corrugated iron, out of which emanated an agitated lowing, and left me there while he and Bub manoeuvered a decrepit, complicated-looking metal contraption across the yard and pushed it against the door. Once it was in place Bub turned around and nodded hello to me.

'What's this then?' I had asked with an awkward smile.

'U-crush,' he'd replied somewhat tentatively, barely able to conceal his surprise at my ignorance.

'Oh,' I'd said, thinking it might be best to leave it at that, but unable to stop myself adding, 'and what's that for?' At this he looked incredulous, as though not knowing the function of a crush was like not knowing how to breathe.

'It's fu thu cuttle,' he'd eventually answered, staring suspiciously at me now as if my ignorance might be some kind of joke. Behind him Nut's grin had spread uncontrollably across his face.

I quickly learned the function of the crush: it was a kind of iron cage designed to trap and restrain the bullocks as they bolted out of the shed. It was open at one end and had a gap wide enough for a cow's head and shoulders to fit through at the other. My job was to wait until each unfortunate bullock had tried to push its head through this gap, and then yank on a piece of rope attached to a metal lever, pull it tight against the bullock's neck, and lock it into place. Once this was done it couldn't move forwards or backwards. Bub would then squat down precariously beneath the animal's stomach, holding a razorblade between his teeth and what looked like an elaborate pair of pliers in his hands. The bullocks would jolt and lurch forward when he used the razor, their eyes filling momentarily with an unseeing panic, but soon afterwards relaxed into a thoughtful, bovine resignation. Some of them started chewing their cud as their testicles lolled about on the ground beneath them. After he'd finished Bub would place the razor carefully back between his teeth, stopping only occasionally to wipe away the droplets of blood that had gathered about his lips.

We went for tea in the kitchen afterwards, and as Bub put the kettle on to boil I glanced out of the window towards the field where the bullocks had been released. They appeared unfazed by their sudden loss, calm even; but it was a stunned, befuddled kind of calmness, as though they were drowsily trying to recall what they were missing, like someone reaching hopelessly backwards towards a dream from which they'd just awoken. I was used to seeing them running about in the fields about my house, playfully butting each other, jumping up onto each others' backs, but now they just quietly munched on the sparse, infertile remains of January grass. They didn't look all that eager to go anywhere or do anything. Most of them would be killed by Autumn.

Nut was still terribly amused with himself, and started sniggering when he called over to Bub and asked for two lumps in his tea please. But after a few minutes his face straightened and became more serious, which disconcerted me for some reason.

'So, what yu been up to?' he asked me.

'Not that much really,' I replied, with a casualness that I instantly realised was forced.

'Yeh,' he said, 'I've seen yu about, like.'

At the sink Bub was washing the last remnants of bullocks' blood from his face.

14

It looked like a hatchet to me, an old one admittedly, with a palm-smoothed handle and a rusted head, but an ordinary hatchet nevertheless; the kind you might buy in your average garden supplies centre. Yet Johnny assured me it was his great-grandfather's tomahawk. Yes, it had lost most of its trimmings, been shorn of its once bright drapery of scalps and beads, had its engravings rubbed away, but that didn't make it one iota less a tomahawk, according to Johnny anyhow. And, whatever scepticism I harboured about its authenticity I quickly decided to keep to myself when he picked it up and held it in his fist, brandishing it with all the ferocity his liver-spotted hands could muster, and looking very much like he was on the point of leaping up from the table to start whooping and dancing.

'I think of him every time I touch it,' he said, 'out there in the wilderness, with a thousand miles of nothing on every side.'

191

Medicine Jones had not always been Medicine. Once upon a time he had just been plain Gwilym. But Johnny didn't seem that interested in Gwilym. Before his transformation he'd led a modest, island life, trading pigs and trinkets across the four corners of Ynys Môn, occasionally writing a poem or two, but rarely venturing across the straits. All of which Johnny informed me in an impatient, perfunctory way, like a lepidopterist describing a chrysalis. He wasn't even that good with his pigs and trinkets apparently, and it was while down on his luck and down to his last few sows and a final pocketful of glass beads that he'd stumbled upon the scene that would propel him over an ocean, up a river, across a continent and into a new name.

'They said it was a sermon that set him on his way,' Johnny told me, happier and more at home with this part of the story; vivified, as he always was, by embarkations.

One of those hillside sermons that the Methodists used to deliver; with the preacher standing outside on any piece of higher ground he could find on the island and his congregation gathered below, dressed in every piece of black clothing they could muster. They had them right up to my mother's time, you know, and she remembered being dragged to them and watching these preachers shouting from the hillsides, probably thinking they were mountaintops, and the people beneath spread out like a shroud, listening rapt and spellbound and maybe just a little bored. Well, my great-grandfather, he came across one of these sermons, you see, and though he wasn't that religious he stayed to watch, maybe thinking it'd be good to hang around because one or two of these preachers, so they say, were such good speakers that they'd get people so passionate and hot under the collar and corset about God and Jesus that they'd lose control of themselves a bit, and you'd catch quite a few going off together into the fields and woods to celebrate Their glory in a different, more ancient, kind of way. But for some reason, as he waited around for the action to begin, he got sucked into the sermon instead.

It wasn't the subject that got him; it was the gloss, the illustration. The minister was talking about a revival that hadn't quite revived his flock enough. Although the darkness, the blackness, of ignorance had been lifted and lightened in no small degree, he proclaimed, although the first tendrils of dawn had crept over the horizon and illuminated one corner of the sky, there was still a great swathe of night pressing down on them, a heavy, sooty mass of it that the Son had yet to raise up and disperse. And in the version that was passed down to me, it was at this moment that Gwilym tried to make his exit, feeling quite content with the crippling heft of his ignorance, and pretty thirsty too, except that the crowd around him – and back then there were hundreds, thousands that went to these things – suddenly began to surge upwards towards the preacher, gravitating towards him, as though he personally might be able to alleviate the burden he'd just placed upon them. And poor Gwilym was swept along with them until he found himself nigh on face to face with him, staring straight at the sweat on his bald head and the veins popping out on his neck and his green eyes that wobbled like seaweed behind the thick lenses of his glasses. There were men and women living right now, on this very island, the preacher spat out, who were as far away from God as their long lost brethren who wandered the plains of the far

193

West. And imagine, he said, what a distance that was; a distance not to be computed in miles and fathoms and furlongs, but in the sheer, incalculable depths and gulfs of depravity. How far they had fallen! Far enough to roam the land as savages, naked and murderous and unashamed, far enough to feast on the raw flesh of beasts and pluck the bloodied scalps of their enemies, far enough to live in the gross and lascivious embrace of a harem of wives. How far indeed! And you might think them unfortunate, he continued, and much deserving of your pity. And so you should. Because were they not stranded by their Prince, Madoc, a thousand miles from home; stranded in a howling, shrieking, inhospitable wilderness, a thousand miles from home but a million, no millions, of miles from His Word, and left to crawl and skulk and sink into the horrid mire of heathenism. Yes, pity them, weep for them, pray for them. But remember this too: they are not only your brethren in blood, but your brethren in sin. The darkness upon them is no more than the darkness upon you. For if you have fallen, then you have fallen just as far as them. Do not think for a minute, for a second, that God deals in petty measurements, that He reckons by degrees. All sin is the self-same thing in his eyes, it has no gradients or circumferences or densities, and looks as ugly and terrible on the banks of the Menai as it does on those of the Missouri.

Afterwards, as the crowd slowly melted away, Gwilym had stood on the hillside, looking down across the flat distances that were spread out beneath him. For maybe the first time in his life they did not seem that far, not so very far at all. He thought of Caergybi to his north and Porthaethwy out of sight in the south; he thought of Aberffraw and Cemais

194

and the sandy shores of the west, of Penmon, Amlwch, Pentraeth, Benllech and the east, the whole round of the island, which until half an hour before it had hurt his feet just to contemplate. And now, in his mind, he imagined them as no more than a few strides apart. He blinked and wondered. Had he grown, or had it shrunk? It was hard to tell. One thing alone appeared certain: where once these places had been far-flung they were now tight-knit, knotted, the pinching, painful links of a chain that engirdled him.

From that day onwards a continent began to form in Gwilym's head. Out of what exactly I can't be certain, because he had no real knowledge of anywhere beyond Chester. But form it did. I can only guess it was forged out of imagined space, out of those abstract vistas of yearning that all men seem to carry inside them, which he piled together in vast, tectonic slabs to create his continent, and to fill it with rivers and mountains and plains and everything he thought a continent should have. And across it all roamed Madoc's people, not lost now but liberated, set free to wander the whole pristine extent of his creation. How he envied them.

And how he dreamed of them too.

15

In February the wind and cloud returned and I was glad of them. The cold, empty lull of January had been too revealing. I needed the camouflage of this winter tumult to obscure what had by now become a troubling need, an ever more urgent obsession. I could hardly get by without seeing her. I found that without the sight of Tammy at night my days became purposeless intervals of time. I couldn't bring myself to visit Johnny, or help out at Bub and Nut's farm, but instead would sit for long hours in my kitchen looking at nothing, or else on the rocks of Chwarel Wen, tracing patterns in the sea and stones which would eventually all become swirling and tumbling circles, with no circumference and me in their centre.

Besides, the constant sight of the mainland, the too-clear horizon, had begun to haunt me with memories of other places.

In one I am looking through the window of a train as it slides through the outskirts of Delhi. It is early in the morning and I have watched as a flat landscape of fields and tall, solitary trees has turned, in the thin grey light, into a rubble of shacks and derelict houses. There is a covering of wire mesh across the window, to stop beggars' hands getting through, and it segments the view into little pieces. To begin with I cannot see a single soul and don't imagine that I will: this sprawl of hot dust and bricks appears utterly deserted, the tumbled down relic of a city rather than the purlieus of a living one. But, as the light thickens and brightens, I start to catch glimpses of movement. At first I can't make out what they are, whether they might not just be ripples of heat rising up into the air, but soon they have begun to take on shapes and substance, like phantoms condensing into flesh and bone. Suddenly there are hundreds of them, legions of spare brown bodies resurrected almost miraculously out of these vistas of dust and debris. They move silently towards me as the train gradually slows, slipping further into focus, gathering faces and features in the intensifying light. Some of them are carrying tins in their hands, others are brushing their teeth with bits of twig. I press my face against the wire, so that its strands will not break up my vision, and then I see them come right up to the edge of the tracks, turn their backs to me, and then squat down. The sun has risen on a hundred moons.

In another I am lying on a bed in a hotel in Toronto, watching as the fan on the ceiling spins uselessly round, failing to move one inch of the stagnant, humid air that fills the room. It is the cheapest hotel I could find, and the rooms are rented out by the hour to the whores who flock the streets around it. I have only paid for one hour, but have stayed for six and am now frightened that the owner, a vicious looking man with tattoos of flames creeping up his thick neck, will come in and find me. I am waiting nervously for the first hint of light to arrive in the tiny sliver of sky visible through the filthy windowpane. There is a peephole in the door, to let others look in, and the wall beside my pillow is covered with sticky, inky finger smudges. All night I have been kept awake by pimps and girls bickering in the hallway, and at one point I have heard the sound of a fist slapping against someone's skin. Every inch of my own skin is sweating, even the air seems to sweat. I am desperate to leave but am somehow unable to move until the light comes. When it finally does I grab my backpack and dart out into the corridor, passing a man in a crumpled suit who smells like onions, and then rush down into the lobby which is full of plastic palm plants. But the man with flames on his neck is standing by the doors, smoking a cigarette, and there is no way for me to get out without him seeing me. For a few seconds I wait behind one of the palms, and spot that the sand in which it is planted has become an ashtray, and then I make my way back into the corridor. I am frantic to escape now; my shirt is so drenched that it has become another colour. At last I find a fire exit, but it is closed, and so I kick it open. Suddenly the street is in front of me and the high, piercing noise of the fire alarm has burst through the wet air. It is unbelievably, terrifyingly loud. I sprint away from it, rushing down the street with my eyes fixed firmly on the ground, and keep sprinting until its wailing has receded into a distant clamour. Only then do I look up. The street is wide and empty – there is not a single car in sight – and on each side of it there are rows of tall glass skyscrapers, stretching out almost as far as I can see. In the delicate, premonitory light that comes just before morning it has become an avenue of mirrors, and as I catch my breath I find myself walking through the refracted sky. It reminds me of the first time I looked out of the window of a plane and was filled with the desire to step out into the landscape of clouds below me, and it seems, for those few minutes, the most beautiful place I have been.

The last is less distinct, less specific, and came to me only in snatches and shards. I am standing in a bus shelter, somewhere in a northern city, watching the tail-lights of my mother's car disappear behind a corner. The houses around me are made of red brick and a heavy drizzle has stained them into a dark, foreboding crimson. There are children waiting around beside me and we are all dressed in black jumpers and white shirts, though none of them speaks to me. Eventually a bus arrives and everybody clambers aboard. As it pulls away some of the children, who have run down to the back of the bus and started lighting cigarettes, begin gesturing to me through the window. I barely know their faces and am unsure what the gestures mean, although I can see that they are laughing as they make them. When the bus is out of sight I begin walking and after a few hundred yards the street has become unfamiliar; I don't know where to go, but I do know that I can't go back to where I've been, and so I keep walking until I come to the entrance of an arcade. Inside there are rows of slot machines with nobody playing on them. I reach into my pocket to take out the small handful of coins my mother pressed into my palm before she left me, and am about to put them into one of the machines, when a man wearing a black teeshirt suddenly appears from out of a glass booth at the back of the room.

'Not one of you lot again,' he says, and I realise he must be referring to me because there is no one else here. I don't say anything.

'Look, mate, I've told you lot before, you can't come in here during school hours. I've had enough fucking hassle about it, alright.' But he hasn't told me anything before and so I continue standing there without saying anything.

'I mean you could at least make some kind of effort, change your clothes or something, anything to stop yourself looking so bloody obvious. I'd think about letting you stay then, I honestly would mate, but you're a fucking liability like this, you really are. It's more than my job's worth having you in here, I'm telling you.' But I don't have anything I can change into, except the gym kit which is in my bag, and so I walk back out into the grey morning.

And I didn't know why it was these memories that came back to me and not others, the ones I wanted to come back. I hated them. I could see very clearly now how they were all false dawns, beginnings without endings, and in none of them could I trace, or recall, what happened afterwards; they were like the streams of water that cascaded over the cliffs of Chwarel Wen, flowing off the island into the restless oblivion of the ocean. And all I wanted was for this island to be my everywhere, a full stop. If I could I would have stretched out the straits, made them a thousand miles wide, and banished the horizon. Tammy's window was three feet high and two feet wide. That was enough for me.

16

And continued dreaming of them. Until one day it was the people he met on the island who seemed like the dream and Madoc's tribe who seemed most real. It was like he'd been born in the wrong place, in the wrong time – had missed the boat that'd left a thousand years before. So he went and found a map of America and tried to find them there. But they weren't on it, not anywhere.

On the Eastside there were some towns and cities, a few borders, the squiggle of a river or two, and on the West the odd Spanish name hugging the coast, but in the middle there was almost nothing. The blankness of it must have entranced him. Because of course here it was, the continent in his head, and it was obvious that it was pointless trying to find it on a map. Until he went there it wouldn't exist. He wasn't to know – even though the bottom right-hand corner told him clearly that it was drawn in 1815 and hence twenty years out of date – that it existed a whole lot more than he thought. And who could blame him for that oversight? Who could blame him for not knowing that history was moving so quickly over there, was filling up all the blanks he thought were his. How could he have known, coming from a place where it hardly seemed to move at all, and, where it did, moved as slowly as the lichen that spread over its monuments. Twenty years out of date! I've looked at maps of Ynys Môn from five hundred years ago and could have found my way about the island quite happily with them.

The last of his pigs secured him a passage. In fact Gwilym became a lot more resourceful without his pigs. On the boat over, apparently, he managed to meet some German Count, or Baron – I'm not sure which – a natural historian of sorts who was on his way to record 'the as-yet unfallen savages of the West'. Which must have confused my great-grandfather a little at first, because the one thing he thought he knew was that these savages were well and truly fallen – and though he would've never admitted it, that was part of their attraction. But he was getting smart enough to keep his mouth shut by then, was Gwilym – a talent he'd never had before – and started listening and watching instead. And, for the next seven weeks, as their boat made its slow way across the Atlantic, he did nothing but watch and listen. He learned a great deal during those weeks: how scientific gentlemen spoke, how they kept journals, learned that he was to be curious about customs, clothing, habits and beliefs, however benighted and outlandish they should seem. He even read some books that the Count kindly lent him. And so well did the Count teach him, or so well did my great-grandfather ape him, that by the time he got off the boat in Philadelphia, to be dazzled and surprised by the biggest city he'd ever seen, he was halfway able to pass himself off as a man of science in search of a subject to record. He spent the last of his pig money on some pens and a notebook.

How he got the rest of the way is a mystery to me. It never got into that new notebook. I can only guess that his own ingenuity grew along the way, or else he imbibed some of the native, Yankee variety the further he went. But, nevertheless, within six months or so he was a fair distance up the Missouri, headed right on up and across into the blank spaces that had filled his mind before. And from then on he wrote it all down.

Leaving the tomahawk on the table, Johnny then went upstairs and fetched an old bundle of paper. It was still partly glued together at the spine, and had what looked like the remains of a red-leather binding. When he passed it to me I found it was surprisingly slim and alarmingly fragile. I was afraid at first that the pages would disintegrate in my hands. I lifted open the front cover and found, written awkwardly in ink, the title:

The Journal Of Gwilym Jones; Concerning the Manners, Customs and Condition of the Mandan Indians, During the Year 1837, Observed in the Course of the Author's Journey to, and Residence Amongst, these People.

But when I began to turn over the pages, which were all covered in the same cramped and clumsy hand, I found there were substantial chunks of it torn out. Gwilym's journal was at best a half, maybe only a third, of its original size.

'What happened to the rest of it?' I asked Johnny.

'I don't really know,' Johnny replied. 'He never let anyone look at it and nobody did when he was still alive. But before he died he must have ripped out some parts of it, although what they contained, and why he destroyed them, well, your guess is as good as mine.'

So I began on the first page, which wasn't the first page:

...and having said my farewells to Mr Laidlaw and the rest at Fort Leavenworth I once more boarded our steamer, the *St Peter*, and heard Mr Laidlaw joke, as I ascended onto the deck, that he was in no wise certain whether our craft would guide me into heaven but that with luck it would fetch me upon many novel and unusual scenes. Our company upon the *St Peter* is thus much diminished, comprised as it is of myself, the two fur trappers, Joseph Joyaille and Bonaventure Lebrun, who are both originally from the Canadas, and two Indian agents headed for the mouth of the Yellowstone, together of course with the crew itself.

Today is the one-month anniversary of our departure from St Louis, and our progress thus far has been slow and treacherous to say the least. This is due – as I have mentioned before – in no small measure to the peculiar character of this river. Its muddy and yellow waters are in a perpetual tumult, boiling and churning their way around the bow of our boat as though there were a continual freshet upon them. Added to this impediment are the many trees which these currents have sucked from the banks into their embrace; either whirling them around on the surface, or else pulling them down onto the bed of the river, where they crowd and sway beneath the turbid waters like a submarine forest. Each day the poor *St Peter* toils its way from snag to snare, accompanied by the shouts and curses of its crew, while us others wait patiently on its deck and watch the seething progress of what, some weeks into our journey, Mr Laidlaw humourously referred to as a veritable River Styx.

I think I should be most grateful for these trees if only they were planted on the land above rather than the river below. They would surely help vary a landscape which has settled of late into a wearisome sameness. For the first few hundred miles after departing, the banks on either side of us were often covered with a thick and luxuriant growth of timber, mostly cottonwoods, that winked the pale undersides of their leaves at us in the breeze as we passed by. But for some distance since these pleasant forests have dwindled away, confined to the occasional river bottom and the flat areas of land which surround the mouths of tributary streams. In their place there is now spread an endless succession of low, sweeping hills and dales, denuded of all but a blanket of grass. The river itself makes a seemingly infinite meander through these hills, cutting deep into them to produce a valley or channel edged on either side with high bluffs and headlands. In places where the river has overflowed its banks it has left behind wide, flat meadows, that stretch on occasion to many miles. Such are the regularity of these features that there have been several instances where I have fallen asleep on deck and, on waking, found that we had not apparently moved an inch. And then, imagining that I had not slept at all but merely blinked, have inquired of the others as to our circumstances, only to discover that I had indeed slumbered for many hours and that the boat had travelled a very considerable distance. I have never before encountered a landscape with this capacity for baffling one's senses; there are moments when I feel time and progress to be mere notions in this place – conceits that we have packed away with our luggage but which have no use nor function here. And yet, in other ways, this is the most beguiling of terrains....

June 5th

We have seen this day several bands of Indians, circling the bluffs upon their horses. Joseph, who was with me on deck when I spotted them, informed me that they were most probably of the Pawnees; a powerful tribe that, he says, inhabits this area, together with several others – among them the Ioways, Konzas and Omahas.

The sight of them thrilled me. For some time I have waited in keen anticipation of glimpsing these people in their original and natural condition. Those who I have come across in Philadelphia and St Louis were – I am sorry to relate – extremely poor representatives of Indian life. Many I found to have fallen into the most lamentable of states, ravaged both by drink and poverty, and often reduced to begging on the street. How well, alas, do I recall the first such specimen of degraded savagery that I came across in this country. I stumbled upon him on the wharves at Philadelphia, with my feet barely five minutes on the American main. There he was, slumped against some casks, and I would have quite passed him by if it had not been for an embroidery of once colourful beads that lined the front of his filthy shirt; which caught my eye and led me to inquire of him if he was from Indian stock and, if so, to what nation he belonged. Lifting his head from his chest he cast a wary, yellowed and bloodshot look at me, replying, as far as I could decipher it, with the word 'ugh', before returning his head back onto his chest. Seeing it was useless to continue with this interview I then carried on my way, taking with me the image of his dreadfully pocked and pitted visage, framed by a matted tangle of black hair. I can scarce describe the feelings of pity and disappointment that gathered in my bosom immediately after this episode. Is this what the famous red men of the West have been reduced to, I thought? And if so then to what purpose have I journeyed so far? There I stood, ignorant of all around me, uncertain of even my destination, dejectedly contemplating the possibility that I had given up everything in search of a chimera. It was only some time later that this mood dispersed, when, during a conversation I overheard between the Count and several of his learned contacts in the city, I discovered that in almost every case those Indians who fell into continuous contact with civilisation had been corrupted and ruined by the experience. The true Indians, these men explained, were only to be found in the West; and the true West, they added, had moved on apace in the last few years, and was moving on further even as they spoke. They advised the Count to get on his way as quickly as possible, before it was gone entirely, or before, they mused, it had been pushed right off the edge of the continent and into the waters of the Pacific.

The sight of these Pawnees has thus done much to reassure me. I would have wished to examine them at closer quarters, but they would not approach any nearer than the tops of the bluffs. Nevertheless, I shall carry the apparition of their splendid silhouettes with me as proof both of the continued existence of what I came here to seek and the promise of that which I have yet to find.

June 28th

I write this entry with a hand so fatigued that my pen seems a great burden on my fingers. This past week I have crossed, on foot, almost one hundred and fifty miles of the plains; though it has felt, oddly, like both many more and many less. I was presented with this opportunity for an overland excursion when our boat went aground on a sand bar, and our captain informed us we should have to wait some ten days for the river to rise and free it. The two agents, one of who had developed a slight fever, were quite content to wait out this delay aboard; but Joseph and Bon decided they would go ahead by land and meet the boat at a trading fort up the river. I was extremely eager to join them in this expedition, affording me, as it did, the chance to explore further the land beyond the river's banks. And I mounted the bluffs with the keenest anticipation of what lay before me.

What I had not anticipated was a monotony almost beyond description. I set out light of foot and buoyant in spirit, happy to have the soft ground beneath me; which, on examination, I found to be covered with the most delightful array of wild flowers. And for some miles, keeping my eyes fixed upon these flowers and the ground, I made my gentle way; seemingly floating over them like the cooling breezes that gusted us on. It was only when I lifted my head to survey the upper world, that a different prospect, or should I say a prospect without prospect, began to unfold around me. For an uncertain distance in every direction the prairies undulated away from my eyes, falling and then rising and then stretching towards a horizon that tapered finally into a continuous and perfect straight line. Here all I could see was absence – before and behind – a boundless green ocean of it; without a landmark, without a hill or mountain, without a single bush or shrub or tree, without a wall or house, without an ending, without anything. It is difficult to put into words the appalling nature of this vast nothingness. You must think of a flatness and emptiness magnified beyond any expanse of it you have ever seen; then expand that flatness and emptiness a thousand-fold, ten thousand-fold, and keep on expanding it until even your imagination begins to creak and shake and shudder at its edges in the effort to contain it, until it splinters those edges and overflows them, augmenting, increasing, 'til it has spilt quite outside the confines of comprehension. Think of this. And then think of being a pedestrian through it. For days I walked, not knowing how far I went, or how far I had to go, with nothing to measure distance by except more distance. At night we slept on the ground where the darkness caught us up, kindling fires with buffalo dung beneath a firmament wider and brighter than I had ever seen. And when I slept the sight of it would filter through my eyelids into my dreams, mixing with the day's visions there to produce nightmares of space, of the infinity above reflected in the infinity below, and me drifting helplessly and hopelessly across the invisible interface between them. On waking the spot where I lay would look exactly like the spot I

211

had woken on the morning before and the morning before that; the view would be unchanged, unaltered: the sky the same, the ground the same, even the flowers that had first charmed me the same flowers, a tedium of colour in an interminable round of green and blue. Hours of walking were like minutes and seconds, taking you nowhere, making you wonder if, like a squirrel in his cage, all your toil and movement had left you standing still. The only intimation of progress was the pain in my feet and legs. Mirages began to fill my irises, soothing, tantalising, and tormenting me as I went. I saw lakes and lawns and copses emerge on the horizon and then vapourise back into its dreadful vacuity; I saw the gardens of Penrhyn and the low, stony hills of Llanysgerbwd; I saw the slow rise of Ynys Seiriol, topped with its lonely tower, and the looming outline of the Orme; I saw the banks of the Menai and the ribbed, sparkling of sands of Traeth Coch. And I almost wept for them to be real, wept for the folly that had led me here and turned them into a memory on the tortured surface of my eye.

I have yet to recover from the peculiar terrors of this journey. Sitting here in the welcome comfort of Fort Pierre, whose wooden ramparts I had to touch when we arrived this evening, to test their substantiality, it feels like I have come a million miles and hardly travelled at all. Tomorrow, however, promises the arrival of a band of the Sioux or Dahcotas, whose country we are now in and which extends from the mouth of the Teton river right across to the Rocky Mountains in the West. I am very curious to see them and the head of the fort – who they call the Bourgeois – has promised to introduce me to several of their chiefs.

June 29th

This morning I awoke in a much improved state of mind. In full daylight the fort appears a fine and tidy place, enclosing about three hundred square feet, wherein there are built some eight to ten houses and stores. The place is run by the American Fur Company, and the chief article of trade is the hide of the buffalo, which they gather in immense numbers from the Indians and sell on to New York and other Eastern markets. I was anxious as to the arrival of the Sioux, for our boat had anchored off the shore the night before and is planning to embark tomorrow morning, but the Bourgeois assured me they would come in the afternoon.

He is a Scotsman by birth, this Bourgeois, a large, burly man with angry red hair. He told me he had come here as a young boy, and made his way ever further into the West because, he said, it was the only place a man could live as he liked without being bothered and put upon by others. But I can scarce imagine anyone daring to bother this man. When he asked me what my purpose was in travelling through these regions I told him I had come in the hope of seeing a portion of the great untenented reaches of the West, and in the course of this to search for a tribe of Indians who were fabled to be descendants of my own countrymen and who I wished to observe. At this he laughed heartily, slapping me on the back, and said I should take a stroll beyond the ramparts and take a good look around me, because this is what I was likely to see from here all the way to the Rockies. As for the Mandans he said, well I was not the first who had come this way to find them, and that in each case these men had arrived with such improbable notions as myself, thinking them to speak the Welsh tongue and other nonsense, only to be disappointed. He knew this tribe very well, he informed me, and they were as Indian as any other tribe on the plains. And besides, he added scornfully, were there not enough of my own people living next door to me at home that I should have to journey this far on the off chance of finding more of them? After this outburst, however, he softened somewhat, and asked me how I was supporting myself on this 'expedition' – as he archly referred to it. I said I was uncertain about this, for I had almost no money left and nigh on nothing in the way of possessions apart from my notebook. In response to this information a look of concern spread across his features. I was likely to find myself in a very perilous position, he told me, if I were to run out of money in this country; and then, leaving me to ponder this a minute, he continued, saying that since we both originated in the old country he was willing to take pity on my predicament and suggest some means whereby I could save myself. Showing me to one of his stores he then opened its door, revealing the most curious of contents.

Inside was heaped a considerable collection of Indian goods and artifacts. There were shields and spears, pipes and papooses, and even an ornate headdress, plumed with eagle feathers. But strangest of all, and most startling, was a great profusion of skulls, some of which lay scattered on the floor, while others were packed onto a row of shelves, from where they seemed to stare at us with ghoulish outrage through their empty, shadowy sockets. This, said the Bourgeois, was a part of his own private business, and was a venture that he vehemently enjoined me not to speak of to the others in the fort. I was dumbfounded as to what this business could be, and from where – and for what reason – these skulls had been obtained. Seeing my evident confusion he smiled and, picking up one of the skulls in his hand, held it toward me, telling me not to be afraid of old Yorick and his pals for they were all just savage remains. He said there was a lucrative trade in these artifacts – in particular the skulls – and that there were men in the East willing to pay a high price for them; mostly scientific gentlemen, who were loath to suffer the efforts and dangers necessary to fetch them. In the East they preferred their Indians in museums, the Bourgeois concluded, and if possible without the encumbrance of flesh and blood. He then offered to pay me a fair price for any objects such as these that I could get my hands on. After this he left me and joined Bon and Joseph, with whom he already seemed to be well acquainted, and spent the day drinking whisky while I loitered by the ramparts, considering his proposal and waiting for the arrival of the Sioux.

They did not come till late in the afternoon, and the sight of their advent will linger long in my memory. It was nearing dusk when I first spotted the out-runners, a group of braves, wending their way through a gap between the bluffs down onto the river plain where the fort was situated. There were some thirty to forty of them, and as they approached nearer I could see that they were dressed in the full regalia of the savage warrior. The feathers of their headdresses waved above them, matching the slow and stately movements of their horses, while in their hands they held bright spears and shields decorated with hieroglyphic insignia. The seams of their hide tunics and leggings were fringed with a drapery of porcupine quills and tresses of black hair, gathered from the scalps of their slain enemies, which now gleamed elegantly under the beams of the dying sun. They looked like a retinue of olden knights, or barbarous kings, and I was still marveling at their costumes and appearance when behind them the rest of their band hove into view. This consisted of up to three hundred horses, many of which were heavily freighted with women and children, either upon their backs or on a sled of sorts, made of long poles, that they dragged behind them. And interspersed around and about and often beneath the feet of these horses was an innumerable swarm of dogs, some of which ran free, while others – which I supposed to be the slower and less cunning beasts – struggled with burdens attached to them in a similar fashion to those the horses pulled. They soon half-filled the plain, and even from a distance I could hear the accompanying refrains of this yipping, barking, bellowing cavalcade.

It took them no more than half an hour to gather themselves about the fort, where I thought night would surely overtake them before they had an opportunity to set up their camp. But in this I was much mistaken. In the time it would take most of us to make up our beds, their tents sprouted up upon the plain – a tall, conical forest of them, whose floor was just as quickly bedecked with blossoms of flame, as they prepared fires for their evening meal. I am told the Sioux drift almost constantly across their lands in the West, following the great herds of buffalo on which they rely for their livelihood, and I could not help but admire the speed and grace and ease with which these Ishmaelites of the prairie both carried and assembled their homes.

When night had fallen proper I was treated to another quite extraordinary scene. Much of this I witnessed but incompletely, by the light of their fires and from a distance – I did not get a chance to enter the camp itself, the Bourgeois having reneged on his promise of an introduction and fallen into deep and drunken slumber. But from what I could see it appeared to be some kind of dance or celebration. It took place on a piece of vacant ground in the centre of the camp, surrounded by a ring of torches. In the midst of this circle of flame I gradually made out the outline of limbs and torsos, flailing madly through the firelight like shadows gone berserk. I witnessed the shapes of spears and knives and clubs brandished ferociously in half-seen hands, slicing and bludgeoning the darkness; heard the noise of moccasined feet thumping and stamping the earth, and rising above this the frightful sound of wild yelps and whoops. Distorted faces, bulging eyeballs, and gnashing teeth flickered into and out of view. Every grimace and mask of the battlefield flashed before me! Whatever dance this was, I thought, it was none that I had ever seen or heard of.

I say dance, but at first I could discern no pattern in the apparent chaos of this movement, and thought it a frenzy, a savage Bacchanal. It was only by degrees that I apprehended a certain choreography at work in it. The dancers, all of whom were warriors, were following a circular route, around what I now dimly perceived to be a group of young women. And this group of women, who remained utterly still throughout, were holding poles in their hands, each one of which was gruesomely topped by a human scalp.

Even as I write the purpose of this wild revelry eludes me. I can only conclude it commemorates some victory in a recent

217

skirmish or battle. The sight of it, however, has left a vivid impress upon my mind; the candles, which at this very minute light my pen, bring instantly back to me that tableau of flame and fury, whose fires yet blaze beyond the ramparts of the fort. And my ears are still haunted by the faint strains of those fierce and terrifying voices.

July 13th

Every hour now we approach closer to the Mandan village. Bon and Joseph, who know the banks of this river as well as any men, have told me we are only days away from them, and I eagerly survey the shores for signs of their presence. I have of late become more accustomed to this landscape, and in the stead of that dreadful emptiness I saw before, I have taken to seeing its unbroken series of grass-covered bluffs and knolls as a picturesque equivalent of an older, more cultivated country like my own, albeit with the walls, houses and hedges removed. This is a world before the beginning, so to speak: before the hands of men have had time to shape and sculpt it, or indeed to divide it. This thought has given me a new appreciation of its beauty, although when I mentioned this to Bon and Joseph they scoffed at me, and informed me in no uncertain terms that this land was quite as cultivated as my own shaved chin. They said the Indians were careful to ensure that each season the top growth of these prairies was burned off, often by their own hands, in huge conflagrations that spread for miles. They also said that each inch of this land was absolutely accounted for, belonging to any number of tribes, and that the earth here had been drenched in blood for generations in order to establish borders and boundaries that were not less present because my untutored eye could not see them.

None of us has seen either of the agents for a considerable time, due to a fever that has laid them low for much of the voyage thus far. One of them, a young army man named Parkman, did come on deck for a few hours last week, but quickly returned below deck after an altercation with Joseph. Both Joseph and Bon hold these men in utter contempt. This is due, as far as I can tell, to their lack of experience of the people and country they are meant to supervise. Neither of them has been stationed beyond the Missisippi before, and I have heard both trappers comment, on more than one occasion, that the only West they had seen was on a compass. The altercation I spoke of took place when this Parkman remarked to Joseph, in the midst of a long speech he gave concerning the hopes he had of introducing various improvements and modes of civilisation amongst the Indians in his charge, that 'is not the Indian mind a beautiful blank on which anything can be written if the proper means be taken'. To which Joseph angrily replied that he would think them less blank when they were conspiring how to scalp him – which he heartily hoped they succeeded in doing – and that his wife, a Mandan women, had given him several children, and if the agent was inclined to write on those beautiful blanks then he'd happily scalp him himself. I was surprised on hearing this and afterwards brought it up with Joseph, asking why he had never told me of it, to which he replied that I had never asked.

July 17th

How should I describe the scene that is spread before me? For months I have thought of little else, and yet the reality of the place, in its strangeness and novelty, far surpasses anything that my mind was capable of invoking. Each turn of my head reveals some new spectacle to me, and with every one of these all the miles I have travelled, with their attendant deprivations and discomforts, seem to melt away into nothing. To think, if I had not left Môn this would never have passed before my eyes; I would still be making my beggarly round of the island, as closed in my horizons as my pigs in their pen, with nothing to lift my imagination but the strait-jacket of my metres. But here is the subject of a thousand books and poems!

Look to one side and see the great circle of earth-covered lodges, their ceilings domed above the ground like a fleet of giant coracles overturned upon the shore; see the scalp-poles that wave above them, a dread forest of human hair, and in their centre the high-hoisted effigies of men, made of cloth and beads and the skins of white buffaloes; and below these the parade of the living, the sachems, warriors, and priests, dressed in all the savage finery of their office, the squaws with their babies attached like pupae onto their breasts, the children with their miniature bows and arrows, the young braves wooing in the shadows, the multitudes of dogs. See this and then look again to the other side, beyond the wooden piquets of the village, towards the surround of verdant plains where the men practise their feats of arms and horsemanship, or search the distance for buffalo, or simply saunter about in

the perfect freedom their primitive condition has vouchsafed
them. Or again once more, to where the Missouri winds its
way past, and the women gather its waters and frolic in its
shallows. This is the panorama that now encompasses me, and
there is a thrilling newness to every view that it discloses. I
would that my pen were more capable of conveying something
of its colour and variety, but for the time being it is as much
as my eye can do to take it all in.

July 24th

It has been several days since I last visited the pages of this
journal and that time has been too crowded to fit into words.
The *St Peter* has departed, leaving Joseph and I here for the
foreseeable future. Bon has gone on to the mouth of the
Yellowstone. Parkman made a brief appearance in the village,
hoping to discuss matters with some of the chiefs, but his
fever had left him too debilitated to stay long; and besides,
Joseph, who is fluent in the tongue of the Mandans, had cast
so many aspersions about him that the chiefs would not deign
to receive him. I have been given a place to live in the lodge
of the Four Bears – or Mah-to-toh-pa as he is called in his own
language – to which Joseph is attached through his wife. This
is a considerable honour I have found, for this man is a
renowned warrior and one of the highest chiefs in the tribe.

I must say a word here about the construction of these
lodges. I have been told they are almost unique to the
Mandans, who, unlike the other tribes in this region, live all
year-long in their villages. Why they do not share in the
roaming propensities of their neighbours I am as yet uncertain

of, though if their history is what it is fabled to be then I would guess this has not always been the case. The lodges are without exception perfectly circular, having been built over foundations sunk about two feet into the ground, around which are placed a wall of timbers some six feet in height. These are secured by a substantial embankment of earth that is raised against them on the outside. Above these are placed a second row of timbers – at least twenty feet in length – that rise upwards at an angle of forty-five degrees and come to rest at an apex, about four feet in diameter, which serves as both a chimney and skylight. The lodge is then completed by covering the entire surface of this roof first of all with willow-boughs and then with a thick carapace of clay, which after a time becomes quite hard and water-tight. The result is a dwelling of amazing comfort and spaciousness. On the inside it is divided into a ring of beds, curtained with buffalo or elk skins, spread around the fire-place in the centre, over which there is seemingly always a pot of buffalo meat boiling. In fine weather, as I have discovered, the roof itself also becomes a kind of parlour or livingroom. The inmates of the lodge will often retire outside to lounge upon it, and in most cases it is also festooned with other paraphernalia of Indian life, such as buffalo bones, canoes, pottery and sleds. These lodges thus provide a home both inside and out, and I cannot help but admire their appearance of strength and solidity. However these people arrived here, they have built houses fit to pass down through generations.

July 27th

I have today been given a new name. It was bestowed upon me by Mah-to-toh-pa himself and I am very happy with it. The circumstances through which I earned it are curious ones and owe much to my previous entry in this journal. Whilst composing it, in the corner of the lodge, Mah-to-toh-pa approached me and – through Joseph who was sat nearby – inquired what it was I was doing. I told him I was trying to write down my thoughts and impressions of the previous days; although, I added, this was extremely difficult as there were so many of them that they quite over-filled my head. The Mandans have no word for writing – it not being a craft they possess – and so I guess Joseph must have made the best approximation he could in his translation. What picture had I drawn, the chief asked – holding his hand upon his tunic on which were inscribed various hieroglyphic renderings of warriors and horses – to which I replied, looking into these pages, that I had tried to describe his lodge. He seemed most pleased by this information and requested that I show him my picture. He was less pleased when I did. What was this he demanded angrily to know. Was his lodge, in my eyes, no more substantial than a bundle of twigs fallen in the snow! I hastily answered that this was not the case at all; that I had not the skill to draw a lodge as grand as his was, and so I was forced to reduce it to these marks, which stood for words, and though they were not pictures themselves they could hopefully produce them in a man's mind. Mah-to-toh-pa contemplated this answer for a considerable time, and then reflected that the priests of his tribe sometimes used words in songs to create

223

visions and that this must be similar. I said it was and that in my homeland I had often attempted something like this. He then smiled at me and inquired why, if I had this power, did I use it to conjure such an ordinary object as his lodge. To which I replied that it was not ordinary to me. He was much taken by this and concluded our conversation by pointing at me and uttering some words that Joseph translated for me as the White Medicine – which is what everyone now refers to me as. After this interview my new name and supposed powers became, and continue to be, a cause of great hilarity in Mah-to-toh-pa's lodge. Only this afternoon one of his wives came through the entrance struggling under the burden of a huge pot, a sight which prompted Mah-to-toh-pa to make a remark that had everyone burst into laughter. Afterwards Joseph told me that what he had said to this wife was: 'Don't worry about the weight of your burden. Show it to the White Medicine and he will make it small enough to fit into his little medicine-bag, and then he will be able to carry it about for you in his head.'

I have subsequently endeavoured to gain some understanding of my new appellation, but have found this idea of 'medicine' perplexing in the extreme. Joseph has tried his best to explain it to me; although his attempts have succeeded mostly in exhausting him and confusing me. As far as I can grasp it, 'medicine' is taken from the French word *Medecin*, used to denote a doctor or physician. Since, until recently, the majority of trappers and fur traders in this country were of French origin, it was the term naturally employed to describe the Indian doctors they encountered, who later became known by American traders as medicine-men. These doctors, however, are not doctors in the manner we commonly understand. In them is combined the role of healer, priest and magician. Their abilities as physicians they ascribe to their access to supernatural powers and spirits, an access only granted to those in possession of the secret lore and arcana of their craft. They are thus considered to deal in abstruse and esoteric knowledge, or mysteries; and hence all things that to the Indian mind appear mysterious and unaccountable they refer to as medicine, or at least to the word each tribe uses to mean mystery.

But, I assure you, this is only the least baffling meaning of medicine. In its widest application it seems to lie at the very heart of Indian custom and religion. For instance, each man carries with him his own medicine-bag, which is a kind of totem or good luck charm, made of that animal which he believes the Great Spirit has designated as his special protector in life and guide in death. However, I cannot as yet even pretend to comprehend these things and will therefore let them pass until I gain a greater understanding of them.

August 1st

Mah-to-toh-pa has proved to be the most generous and convivial of hosts. He is a tall and perfectly proportioned man, who holds himself with all the dignity and chiselled elegance of a prairie Apollo – although he has also shown himself to be an inveterate joker and humourist. Like the other men in the tribe he wears his hair extremely long, down almost to his hams, and plaits it in thick slabs filled with glue and red earth. The women also keep their hair long, though straight, and part it down the middle where they paint a line of vermilion. The lodge of Mah-to-toh-pa is a bustling, sociable household, made up of his three wives, his children, and several members of his extended family, including Joseph's wife – Om-pah (the Elk) – who is the sister of one of his wives. Every day they gather about the fire to eat and gossip and laugh, and are very curious about the new arrival in their home, who they are perpetually bombarding Joseph for information about. Mah-to-toh-pa himself is a good deal more reserved in his inquiries, although he remains slightly puzzled as to why I have come here. As for my own questions, which are just as numerous, he has taken it upon himself to answer them as best he can, and to act as an interpreter of Mandan history and life for me. Towards this object he has also enlisted the aid of one of the tribe's medicine-men – an office I spoke of earlier – an ancient and much-weathered man called Mah-to-he-hah, or the Old Bear.

I have also been granted the freedom to wander wherever I wish through the village and its environs, which I take at every opportunity, usually escorted by a populous entourage of dogs and children. Although I began by bringing my journal with me on these excursions, in order to jot down my observations of Indian life and manners, I have found that each time I open it it transports my companions into great outbursts of hilarity and exuberance, often resulting in me being playfully pelted with stones and toy arrows. So now I tend to sneak out without it, thinking it best to store away these observations in my mind until some later date when I have the leisure and privacy to record them all.

Yesterday, however, I did manage to shake off my attendants for a few hours and walk alone for a distance along the riverbank. It was early in the morning, near sunrise, and I had wandered about a mile when I came upon the most surprising and diverting of scenes. In the river below were gathered an assembly of the tribe's women and girls, some bathing in the eddying water of the stream, while others gambolled on the sands of a beautiful beach, and all of them dressed only in the costume nature had first provided them. Not wishing to disturb this scene with my presence I slipped behind a nearby hummock, where I could observe it unnoticed. The grace and ease with which these women swim is truly remarkable, and is a skill that I believe they must be initiated into at a very early age. The boiling currents of the Missouri held no terrors for them and they slid through its churning waters like so many otters, their glossy skins bright and glistening under the beams of the emerging sun. Those who were not in the river frolicked on the sands – a host of tawny Nereids – or else lay in innocent repose in the foam-flecked shallows, allowing the stream to gently sluice over their limbs. I wondered if this aquatic outing was a special, festive occasion, or a daily ritual, and was determining who I might ask in order to ascertain this when I caught sight of a familiar face among the group.

Ko-ka – the Antelope – is one of Om-pah's sisters and a member of Mah-to-toh-pa's lodge. She has lived there, apparently, for over a year, ever since her husband was killed in a skirmish between the Mandans and a marauding band of Sioux warriors. I had been struck soon after my arrival by the particular beauty and comeliness of her features, and was now slightly surprised to see them spring up, gasping and laughing, from beneath the waves. Even from a distance I could make

227

out the gleaming wet tresses of her hair, which was as soft and black as raven's wings, and the delicate outline of her shoulders, which bobbed up and down through the surface of the water with each stroke of her swimming. Never having witnessed her smile before – which I assumed to be due to her mourning – I was pleased to see a broad, instinctive grin spread across her face, that perfectly matched the playful abandon of her movements. And for a moment I fancied that grin was directed in the vicinity of my hiding-place.

Tomorrow I will set about gathering some information on the bathing habits of the Mandans, which is a subject....

August 6th

Ever since arriving I have looked for evidence to suggest the theory, widely held in my homeland, that these Mandans are in some way the descendants of Madoc and his followers. In this search, as the Bourgeois predicted, I have so far been disappointed. There is no resemblance between their language and ours that I can find, and their customs and habits are as different from those in Môn, Gwynedd and Powys as it is possible to imagine; in this respect I would do as well to search the moon for similarities. And yet in my heart I do feel a strong kinship with these people, which, if it is not the pull of a mutual, ancestral blood, is certainly derived from bonds of admiration and gratitude. I have rarely met with more generosity and kindness, and that extended to a stranger from, to all purposes, another world. Mah-to-toh-pa has treated me as nothing less than a member of his own family, and everywhere I have gone I have met only with curiosity and hospitality.

The other day I told Mah-to-toh-pa and Mah-to-he-hah the story of Madoc. I told them how he was reputed to have crossed over to this continent hundreds of years ago with twelve ships and, becoming stranded there, to have set up a colony. And how many of my countrymen, as well as others, believed the Mandans to be the distant progeny of this colony. This information produced an immediate effect. Mah-to-toh-pa was thrown into an uncontrollable fit of laughing and guffawing; and even Mah-to-he-hah, normally a studiously grave and serious man, had tears of mirth flow into his eyes. When eventually they could speak, they both conjectured that perhaps my peoples' minds had been addled somewhat by the white man's firewater. Their origins, they assured me, were both fixed and well-known; and had no mention of a Madoc, or a colony, or anything else so fanciful and ludicrous. Perhaps, Mah-to-toh-pa playfully suggested, my countrymen had got things all mixed up and the wrong way around: that it was the Mandans who had sailed East in twelve canoes, and set up a colony on my island. In which case, he added, my own costume, habits and beliefs evinced a pronounced decline from, and corruption of, our original ways.

After the general amusement that filled the lodge had subsided, Mah-to-he-hah earnestly set about correcting my faulty knowledge with a lengthy lecture on Mandan history and theology. But, if my theory appeared absurd to them, then the sketch he provided me of their genesis was almost equally bewildering. First of all he informed me that the earth was, in fact, a giant tortoise; and that it was on the back of this tortoise, which was covered in dirt, that we lived. He said that once upon a time the tortoise's back had been submerged beneath the waters of a great flood, and that nothing had been able to exist during this deluge, except for a figure named Nu-mohk-muck-a-nah – the First And Only Man – who, as far as I could tell, was not so much a man as a spirit or incarnated deity. This Nu-mohk-muck-a-nah had survived by building a giant canoe, which had floated over the flood and come to rest on a high mountain far to the North and West, where he apparently still dwelt.

As for the Mandans themselves, well they were, without doubt, the first people created on the earth. Or rather not on it but under it. For they had begun by living beneath the ground and had done so for some time, raising vines, until one of these vines had eventually grown up towards a hole in the earth above them, and a young brave had climbed the vine, gone through the hole, and set foot on the banks of the river where their village now stood. Returning to his people, he related tales of the wondrous sights he had beheld, the beautiful waters of the stream, the wide and bounteous prairies, the numberless buffaloes, and they had determined that they would follow him back up the vine and into this place. To start with, several chiefs made the ascent, taking with them several of the most beautiful women of the tribe; and more were preparing to follow when a particularly large and fat woman, whom these same chiefs had ordered to wait below until the last, had let her curiosity get the better of her and begun hauling herself up the vine. She succeeded in getting no further than halfway when it snapped under her weight, sending her tumbling back down, and forever severing the link between these upper and lower worlds. For there was no way of reversing this calamity, and due to her precipitate actions the Mandans had been sundered as a people, which they remained to this very day. Because, as Mah-to-he-hah assured me, those underground continued to exist; and, moreover, he professed to be able to hear them in certain places, where he would sometimes retire in order to seek their opinions and advice. He said the pain of their rupture still weighed heavily upon them, with those below lamenting the exile of those above, and those above grieving for the ones left beneath.

This was how the Mandans had come to live where they did, Mah-to-he-hah said, and soon after they arrived they had been visited by this Nu-mohk-muck-a-nah, who came down from his mountain in order to tell them of the flood, to whose subsidence they owed their lands and livelihood. It was he who had imparted to them the rituals and religious observances – many of which commemorated the subsidence of the floodwaters – that they still followed, and which they firmly believed favoured them in the eyes of the Great Spirit, thus ensuring their future survival and prosperity.

What exactly I was to make of this I don't know. In parts I was reminded of the Mosaic account of the flood, but if this is where this fantastical tale derives from, then it has been altered and mangled so much as to be a quite different species of story. But what of this I thought at the time, for in the genial surroundings of Mah-to-toh-pa's lodge, wreathed in the warm fellow feeling of my new companions and the pleasantly narcotic smoke of their pipes, what did it matter how we had all got here and where here was. It was more than enough that we were simply sat together, and who cared if it was by way of princes and ships, or vines and tortoises, that we had all arrived in this fine place.

August 12th

I have lately been much remiss in my entries to this journal. I confess that this is due, paradoxically, in no small part to my increasing familiarity with Mandan ways: so caught up have I been in the daily round of village life that I have scarcely made any effort to properly study and record it. Not that I have lacked materials. Over the past week I have, amongst other things, partaken in the thrills and excitement of a buffalo hunt, relaxed in a 'sweat lodge' and been initiated, by my band of infant warriors, into the skills of archery; all of which I shall, hopefully, on some later occasion, make a description of. In the meantime I will put down here an account of the excursion I made this morning to the singular precincts of what the Mandans call 'the village of the dead'.

On the plains adjacent to the Mandan's lodges, almost contiguous with the ramparts that surround them, are spread tens and maybe hundreds of wooden scaffolds, like a forest of truncated, leafless trees. On asking what function they served I was told that this was where, as they termed it, 'the dead lived'. For the Mandans, as I discovered, do not bury their dead, but instead mount them on these scaffolds where they are left to moulder and decay in the open air of the prairie. The scaffolds themselves are made of four posts, about six or seven feet in height – just high enough to keep their freight above the reach of wolves and dogs – which are driven into the ground and then topped with a platform of willow-rods. Upon this the body of the deceased is placed, dressed in his or her finest attire, with their feet pointed carefully in the vicinity of the rising sun, which is the direction that their spirit is expected to follow in order to reach those paradisiacal grounds where their ancestors abide. To aid in this final journey they are supplied with pipes, shields, tobacco, knives, and any other objects and provisions it is deemed will help them on their way.

Since arriving I had taken considerable pains to avoid passing through this village of the dead, making sure to plot courses that circumvented it, even if this necessitated long detours on my behalf. For though it held no terrors in the eyes of the Mandans – and was indeed a spot they happily wandered, stopping casually to meet and converse as they went – to me it seemed an eerie and unsettling place. There was something about a cemetery where the dead were visible that disturbed me in a way I cannot fully explain. I think the best I can say is that I was afraid of the witness of the dead: that though their eyes had most probably been pecked out by the crows and ravens I did not want them to see me – just as in another way I did not want to see them. And besides, there was such a haunting, strange aspect to this alternate village, this smokeless, lifeless, almost substanceless double of the one I resided in, that I unaccountably felt that if I were to visit it I myself might start to dwindle and waste away.

Yesterday I tried to describe this superstitious unease to Mah-toh-ta-pa, who became very concerned on hearing it, and told me that it was important for men to live in comfort and amity with the dead. As a means of remedying my discomfort he suggested that I visit the other village, and that in order to make this visit more tolerable I should go with Ko-ka, who went there every morning to see her husband. I instantly agreed to this, at which he smiled and remarked

233

that there were obviously some things I would go anywhere to look at.

And so this morning Ko-ka and I set out on our first expedition together, with me heartily desiring that we had some more cheerful destination in prospect. As we approached the outer row of scaffolds we were immediately met with a scene that seemed to confirm my worst trepidations. There in front of us was a newly erected example of their sepulchre, crowned with a corpse that I would swear had not been dead long enough to lose the flush on its cheeks. I could see these cheeks all too well, as well as the rest of the face, which was that of a young man of no more than twenty. Before I had time to properly avert my gaze I noted two things about this face: the first was that its eyelids were firmly sealed – for which I was grateful – the other was that its skin was pocked and swollen, which I thought unusual because in almost every case I have found the Mandans to be blessed with excellent and unblemished complexions. As for the rest of the scene, well I wish I had not seen it at all. Gathered beneath the scaffold were a collection of this young man's family, weeping and wailing in a frightful manner, several of whom had begun lacerating their own skin with stones and knives so that their faces and bodies were painted in a gruesome alloy of tears and blood. I did not know then which I feared most, the body or those that grieved so bitterly for it, and would have turned away at that very moment if Ko-ka had not taken my arm and led me further on.

As we continued on our way through this grisly copse of graves, Ko-ka did her best to appease my obvious distress by keeping up a constant, and incongruously light-hearted chattering, none of which I comprehended. Now and again she would stop us in front of a particular scaffold and point to it, letting me know – as far as I could tell – that its occupant was someone she had once been acquainted with, and making signs as if to introduce us; as though I might be expected to casually shake their bony hand and politely inquire about the weather. She seemed utterly at home here, and behaved just as she would have done in the actual village: calling out greetings, waving, and on one occasion even slowing down for what appeared a brief session of gossiping. We carried on like this until we had reached the centre of the site, which was a wide, open patch of ground.

What had been invisible from the village now became quite apparent. Spread in front of me were countless circles of human skulls, each one of which was gathered around a small mound of dirt in its centre, with two buffalo skulls placed on it and crowned by a tall pole decorated with skins and feathers. All around these circles extended, like earth-bound constellations, with each of the skulls positioned so as to face inwards and thus destined to stare across at each other for an eternity in the hidden inner sanctum of this Golgatha of the plains.

I tried my best to inquire of Ko-ka what the meaning of these circles was and, from what I understood of her energetic gesticulations, discovered that when one of the scaffolds decayed to the point of falling the relatives would remove the bones left on it and place the skull in one of these circles; which served, I suppose, the same purpose as a family plot in a graveyard. Ko-ka then left me to tend to her husband, who she indicated lived in a circle to my left. Thinking it an impropriety to intrude on such a private occasion I withdrew several yards, but Ko-ka appeared entirely unconcerned by my presence. She sat down on the ground beside her beloved and immediately commenced conversing with him in the most pleasant and endearing of tones, cooing sweet nothings in the proximity of where his ear would once have been, and looking delighted at what seemed to be his replies. This carried on for nearly an hour, when finally she took out a bunch of wild sage, placed it carefully beneath him, and bade him a sunny farewell.

On my return I found that I had been – just as Mah-to-toh-pa suggested – in some ways reconciled to the village of the dead by my visit; and looked on it with fewer misgivings than I had beforehand. In fact, the more I reflect on it, I cannot help but admire how having this other Mandan village extends the range and number of their intimates. For these skulls and bones are almost as close and important to them as their living kin.

August 20th

Today there were preparations afoot throughout the village for the chief ceremony in the Mandan calendar. This is the celebration of Mee-nee-ro-ka-ha-sha, or the sinking down of the waters, which I have previously mentioned. The day started with everyone bustling about, putting together costumes and the like, and readying the 'medicine lodge' in the village's centre – that serves as their church or chapel – around which much of this ceremony, I am told, will take place. However, though the day began full of high spirits and excitement, this afternoon it has taken on a darker and more sinister aspect. Four of the young braves who were meant to partake in the ceremony, where they were to be initiated into their manhood, have fallen gravely ill with fevers. All preparations have thus been halted in order that they be given time to recover.

August 21st

I must here sadly relate the deaths of the four braves, who did not survive the night. Mah-to-he-hah had accompanied them to their lodge, where for many hours he tried to administer his 'medicine' – which seemed to take the form of various elaborate chants – but did not succeed in saving them. What is more alarming is that several other members of their families have also taken ill in a similar fashion, and appear to be beyond all remedy. Mah-to-toh-pa has announced that the ceremony shall be cancelled for the foreseeable future.

August 26th

It pains me to write this, but I now believe the Mandans to be in the thrall of a widespread and deadly epidemic. There are today some fifty people infected with this fever, and all of those who came down with it previously have passed away. Joseph and I examined a collection of these bodies and found them all to be horribly swollen, and some of them to be covered with pocks and boils like those I had witnessed before on the young man's face in the cemetery. The sight of these utterly dismayed Joseph who told me that this was unquestionably a symptom of small-pox, and that in his experience the Indians had no defence against this disease. He has decided to take his family out of the village and attempt to lead them to a fort some four hundred miles to the North and West; which is a journey he is not confident of being successful in, due to the distance and the presence of hostile tribes, but that he says is probably his only chance of saving them. He offered to take me with him, but I have declined. It was these people that I came to this country to find and I will not leave them now. And so we shook hands and he wished me God's blessings, for he told me I would need them.

October 5th

I have seen this month and more what no man should see. I have lived these weeks as if in a dream so terrible that to call it nightmare would be to name a raindrop an ocean. To see a man die, *that* I could bear, have borne; to see many men die, that too; but to see a whole people die, who should bear that? Who can? I have prayed to God to erase these scenes from my memory forever, as he has cruelly taken them from his bitter creation, but they are now imprinted and seared and sealed. And if I do not put them down then who will? Because I alone am left here, where I wish I had never been.

For sixteen days I saw nothing but dying. Some by the disease itself, others – forewarned of its presence in their bodies and dreading the agonies to come – by their own hands; by knives pulled across their throats, by arrows pushed into their stomachs, by brains dashed on the rocks of the river banks below; by fire, by water, by steel, by anything. And all this time the only sound I heard was howling and weeping and wailing; days of it, nights of it, until there seemed no space, in all these multitudes of space, to hold it; until my ears bled with it, and my heart swelled and split with it like their bodies did. Sixteen days of dying, and on the seventeenth those still fit enough to stand, and those whom despair and dismay had not left prostrate and barely living, gathered themselves together and set out to scatter and save themselves on the plains. I remained, and with the others watched from the ramparts as they made their way, and watched as two Sioux war bands, who had also watched and waited for them, swept down from the prairie hills and cut them all to pieces. And those that were with me envied them. Some burst over the ramparts and ran after them, begging the Sioux to kill them, dragging themselves towards their spears, holding up their necks and scalps for their knives. Not one of them returned. So seventeen days of dying, and it was not done yet: there were seventeen more to finish it. I watched the village of the dead spread its dominion everywhere. I watched Ko-ka die, I watched Mah-to-toh-pa die, I watched Mah-to-he-hah die. I looked at corpses left abandoned on the thresh-holds of lodges, and looked at the hands that had perished dragging them. I saw the village swarm with flies, fattening themselves with dead blood, and the flocks of ravens descending to gorge themselves in charnal ecstasies. I saw lodges where whole families lay as if in pocked and bloated sleep, while their own dogs gnawed and feasted on their infected limbs. I saw innards dropped by buzzards and eyes robbed from sockets and mouths with no lips. And those who could speak to me while they lived I could not understand, only hear the frantic sounds of their voices as they prayed and pleaded and begged

239

me – for what I didn't know. At first I wept with them, but then I just watched and listened because that was all I could do; stand in mute, deaf witness until their words became their last words and then everything was quiet and still.

December 1st

Since my last entry I have passed unseeing back to the port where I first, unfortunately, disembarked. The Autumn has come and gone unnoticed; the forests, plains, towns and city have flitted by like the shadows of clouds over a sea. There is nothing left to record in this journal and when I put down my pen on this occasion I will leave it at that, wishing for the rest of my days that it was as blank and empty as when I began this ill-fated journey – when all before me did not yet exist.

For three weeks after the end I lived alone with the dead. And when they had almost been picked clean and turned to bones I saw a boat come up the river. It landed the Bourgeois and two of his men. They stood for a minute on the edge of the village, surveying the awful remains of the Mandans, and then set about gathering their possessions, and then them too. I did what I could to hinder them, but I was too weak to do much. I set what I could on fire, but they quickly dampened the flames and threw me down onto the ground. And so I did the only thing I could and joined these vultures, collecting in one box as many belongings from Mah-to-toh-pa's lodge as would fit, and in the other the heads of those I had known best, thinking that I would find some hidden place where I could lay them out together as they should have been. But I have yet to find one. The box of belongings I have regretfully sold to a gentleman here, because that is the sole means I have of getting home. A few items I kept, including Mah-to-toh-pa's treasured axe and a pipe made of soft, red stone that he once told me came from a sacred quarry in the West. As for the other box, well I will not part with that. Nor will I leave it here to be discovered. I have decided to take it back with me to Llanysgerbwd, which I will share with them as they once shared their own home with me.

17

'And did he make it back?' I asked Johnny.

'Oh yes, he made it back all right,' said Johnny, 'though I don't know how much of him actually made it back. They said he stepped off the ship looking about a hundred years older than when he'd stepped on it. And he was only really half there, they said. Not daft or cucu or anything like that, just missing something. And he never got it back either. For the next two years – which were his last two years – he sat in a room in his family's house in Llanysgerbwd; a room without a window and no candles. Sat there for days and weeks and months and finally years, hardly ever venturing out of it, and towards the end, never. It was a burden on our family because he didn't work or go back to his pigs, and showed no inclination towards any purpose, towards anything. No, he just sat there. And nobody would go into his room because he'd laid them out in it, in the circle he'd promised. And nobody outside the family would visit the house because they knew this; for twenty years afterwards children would hurry their steps past the door of the skull house. But Medicine didn't seem to care. He waited in that room for two whole years, waited for his mind and body to waste away, surrounded by the fleshless remnants of the only dream he'd ever really had.'

18

'Ynys Seiriol,' said Goronwy, referring to the small island off the shore, 'which means Seiriol's island; though they sometimes call it Puffin Island because they used to live on it once, before the rats came and stole their burrows and ate their eggs.' The lighthouse bell chimed, twice, and a wave broke over the black rocks at its base.

I had looked at this island almost every day for months and it was good to know its name.

'So who was Seiriol?' I asked.

'He was a saint,' said Goronwy, 'from the sixth century or thereabouts. One of the many who came evangelising through these parts back then. Most places around here have one of their own, and Seiriol's ours, I suppose.

In front of us two tourists, an elderly couple dressed in garishly coloured raincoats, had taken out their cameras and started to photograph the island. I could tell by the way they angled their cameras that were trying to get the lighthouse, which was planted about thirty yards off the shore, into their pictures. The island itself, I guessed, was not quite picturesque enough on its own.

'And what was that for?' I asked, pointing to the remains of a tiny stone building that sat on the slightly elevated summit of Seiriol's island.

'That was an anchorite cell,' he said. 'They used to build them in inaccessible places all down the West coast.'

'And so that's where Seiriol lived?'

'Well, not exactly, not as far as I know anyway. I'm sure Seiriol was busy converting us lot, which must have meant he had to get around a bit – you don't get beatified for sitting still. And the anchorites were an order of isolatos: once they settled in one of those cells there was no leaving.'

'You mean a bit like Johnny,' I joked.

He smiled.

'Yes, a bit like Johnny, but not quite, not really. You see the whole point of being an anchorite was that you abjured the world, or at least this one. You uncluttered your mind of everything and set out towards attaining a perfect and unobstructed contemplation of God. This world, being messy and intrusive, you kept to a minimum. And so they picked as small a portion of it as they could manage to live in and stayed there. These islands must have seemed like perfect homes to them – gifts of grace, blessings, places where they could forget everything except Him.'

'Which doesn't sound much like Johnny,' I said.

'No it doesn't, does it.'

As we spoke we made our way back from the shore towards the road. Although this spot was only three miles or so from my cottage I'd never visited it. It was hidden down the coast from Chwarel Wen, behind several jutting headlands, and apart from on clear days and nights when the chimes of the lighthouse became faintly audible, I'd been entirely ignorant of its existence.

It was Goronwy who'd suggested I might want to see it. Our encounter in Spar had been repeated on several occasions, and since I'd not got to know many people in the village apart from Bub and Nut, I was starting to welcome these meetings – however inauspiciously they'd begun. Thinking about it now it's odd how little I ever really found out about Goronwy during our time together. He hardly once spoke about himself. In fact he seemed supremely indifferent to, and bored by, this subject, and I quickly learnt to avoid it. I knew he'd gone to school with Johnny, I knew he'd not been married or had children, I knew that until about a decade before he'd worked and lived in England (though not where), I knew that after retiring he'd come back here to live, but apart from this, nothing. There was something pursed and spare about him, something that necessitated an economy of disclosure, of engagement, as if it was not just his body that had been whittled down by age but his entire self. Talking to him made you feel that you were taking from him. And more than this: that you were chipping away at a finite resource, that you were an active participant in his gradual diminishment. This is what I'd first thought of as cryptic. But it wasn't. At the most it was an essential ellipsis, a preservative thrift.

We'd walked about a mile down the road when we came

247

to an old stone dovecote and, opposite this, the fallen walls of a priory with a much newer and intact church nestled behind. Beyond this was yet another church, but there were only remnants of it still in place.

'They must have liked their churches here,' I laughed.

'Yes,' he said, stopping with me to look. 'But I think that's more to do with location than with any particular zeal. You see they always built new churches on pre-existing sites – so people wouldn't forget where they were I suppose. But also because some places were believed more holy than others, and people tend to remember that even longer than they remember churches. So if one fell down, well, as often as not, they'd just grab a few of the leftover stones and start over with them.'

'You mean there might be the remains of even more of them here, built into these ones?'

'I'm sure there are. If you'd like I'll show you what's rumoured to be the first one.'

We turned off the road, down a path that led beyond the churches' yard and through a thicket of hazel and blackthorn, until after about a hundred yards we came into a clearing. It was shaped in a rough circle, with slabs of grey-white limestone heaped around its perimeter. I couldn't tell whether these were natural outcrops, or if at some point they'd been planted here by human hands. It was almost impossible to tell, and Goronwy said that he wasn't that sure either. But whether it was by fortune or design, they formed a distinct enclosure. In places, behind the pale outlines of the stones, I could make out the thick dark green of yew leaves.

At the far side of this enclosure, nearly hidden beneath the branches of a solitary, overhanging oak, was a tiny stone building. It was barely big enough to hold two people and was so crudely put together – with three walls fashioned out of large, uneven rocks, and an open front – that it looked and felt more like a small cave. Inside the three walls protruded out into ledges, on which you could just about sit, and the floor was made up of four wedges of flat limestone, positioned carefully around a well of clear water.

'This is Seiriol's well,' said Goronwy. It was so hushed inside the building that even his voice boomed.

'And this was the first church then?' I asked.

'Yes. Well the first Christian one anyway. But I'm sure this place was sacred a long time before Seiriol ever set foot here.'

And at that moment I absolutely believed him. In the quietness of the air, in the pellucid stillness of the water, there was something that even I could tell antedated the stones and structures that were built in and around them.

As my eyes became accustomed to the shadows I began to make out objects that had been secreted in the gaps in the walls. One of them was a figure made of two twigs twisted together, though what it was meant to be I didn't know. Another was a piece of red ribbon. Then there was the stub of a candle with a photograph behind it, whose image had been turned by the damp into indistinct blotches of green and blue. I wondered what these all were, and Goronwy told me they were votive offerings of sorts, left behind by people who made secret pilgrimages here, or he assumed they were secret because he'd never seen them leave them. I asked him why they did this.

'The secret part,' he said, 'is because I guess some of them would be embarrassed to be known to do it. Like they

249

were superstitious or something, like it wasn't respectable, or rational. But to tell the truth there's a lot of people around here, church people and chapel people and others too, who still don't quite trust the newer places. And so when they want something or want to ask something or pray for something, they come here to do it.'

And with that he stood up and threw a penny into the well, whose bottom I now noticed was covered in copper coins.

Afterwards, as we made our way back down the road, I asked him what I'd been meaning to ask him for months.

'Why did Johnny never leave here?'

For a moment he glanced at me, with a tired, puzzled and exhausted look.

'That,' he said 'is something you'll probably have to ask him.'

Part Three

Part Three

1

It was springtime before I did.

March came and went and all I observed was the shortening of the nights and the light increasing behind Johnny's windowpane.

April was, if not the cruellest month, then a stingy, pusillanimous affair. Shivery breezes swept for weeks along the eastern shore – Siberian after-thoughts, chapping lips, chilling bones – until it seemed the winter would not let go of us. Outside my windows the fields lumbered down to the sea, amphibious beasts coated in the pale remains of December gales and January frosts, spotted here and there with hopeful, helpless tufts of new and gleaming green. Behind my cottage, where a small stream gurgled past, the tired willow trees huddled above the water, their leaves hanging half-curled from battered boughs. Everywhere I looked there were signs of an agonised evolution: the brilliant, azure smudge of bluebells tangled in rusty blankets of dead bracken; the nubbly tips of blackthorn blossoms hidden behind withered thorns.

And then one day, early in May, it was Spring.

The leaves and the flowers and the grass had won out, almost without me noticing, and I stepped out that morning into a triumphant blaze of colour, a glittering, vegetable mosaic of greens and yellows and whites and pinks. I felt the heat of the sun for the first time I could remember; the blue of the sky had thickened; even the air had filled up, and tasted of blossoms, and hummed and vibrated with the sound of insect wings and birdsong. And as I took this all in I was overwhelmed by a near inconsolable sense of dismay and disappointment and trepidation.

2

Because I knew now that the nights would not be long enough for me; that I would have to follow her into the days.

At first I couldn't work out how to go about this. For a start I had no idea what she did during the daylight, if she had a job, or a family, or a hobby – anything that might take her out of the house. Because the garden was no longer an option. I would have to wait for her to come out.

The problem was that there was nobody I could ask. I couldn't risk raising Bub and Nut's suspicions, and Goronwy was obviously out of the question. I very much doubted Johnny even knew who she was. So I was left with the other option of simply hanging around her place until she did go out, if she actually did at all. Which probably sounds a lot easier than it really was.

If you've ever tried waiting, unnoticed, for someone in a

small village then you'll get what I mean. Unless everybody knows you, and knows you well at that, then they're liable to take one look at you loitering and jump to all the worst conclusions: that you're a burglar, a perv, a stalker, or some other form of deviant that, because not homegrown, is infinitely more threatening. I've had to loiter in small towns and villages all over the world, sometimes because I was waiting to go somewhere else, others when I had nowhere else to go, and yet have never become inured to the discomfort produced in me by these suspicious glances. I become twitchingly self-conscious, I break out in nervy sweats, my eyes start wandering furtively in the wrong directions – down alleyways, towards schools, up at open windows – in fact I manage to behave in precisely the way that makes me look like the person they suspect I am. But I've never resented these people for this. Instead I've taken it as a proof and symptom of my condition: being nobody everywhere you have to expect to be perceived as anybody, and if that anybody always seems to turn out to be a weirdo, a criminal, or a menace, then so be it. But how demoralising, I thought, to have to face this here as well, where I had lived for months; and how dispiriting too when I was finally waiting around for a reason.

The first day I tried – a Monday – I went there early, which was a mistake. I arrived about eight, but after half an hour or so women started appearing everywhere on their doorsteps, pushing their kids out to school. I watched for a bit as they waved across at each other, and ran back to fetch school bags, but soon enough they'd spotted me and I beat a hasty retreat back to my cottage. The second time I tried was on a Wednesday afternoon, well after half past three, but this time I encountered the teenagers I'd so carefully managed to avoid through the winter. Some of the boys had picked up their young lovers from school, and were now sat in their cars, around which other kids quickly began to congregate. Through the growing clouds of cigarette smoke I could make out the drivers – who never seemed to actually drive anywhere – their hair gleaming and oozing with gel, their skin oily with it, lording it over their followers like juvenile patriarchs, with their thin, pasty-faced paramours clamped onto their knees. It was one of these, a redhead no more than fourteen, who noticed me. I heard her voice rise shrilly and screechingly over the throng:

'What yu looking at, yu fokking perv!'

And in the background the chorus:

'Wanker.'

So that was the afternoons done for as well. After about a fortnight I was getting desperate. I thought about getting a dog to walk, as cover. I wondered if it would seem strange and obvious if I took a paper delivery job. I even considered trying to join the village football team, whose ground was usefully close to her house, even though I'd not kicked a ball since my father told me about our name. And all the time the nights kept shortening; shrinking, attenuating, until they were the mere stub-ends of the days, derisory intermittences in the relentless, domineering light. In the end it was pure chance that saved me.

I'd seen the green bus go past Spar on several occasions, but had never been particularly curious about it. I knew the regular buses were a sickly purple colour, emblazoned with the absurdly misleading name Arriva, but whether or not the green ones were different in some way had not once passed my mind. It wouldn't have either, if one of the village boys hadn't driven his car into the bus stop.

It happened just as I was walking out of the shop. There wasn't much of a collision: he was barely moving when he hit it. The bumper crumpled against the stop's concrete side, a couple of old women came out and tut-tutted over their shopping bags, the boy and his girlfriend got out of the car and stood looking at the bumper. That was it. Nobody was hurt, though when I recognised the girl's red hair I sort of wished there'd been at least a few bruises – I took some comfort from the distraught and disconsolate look that filled her boyfriend's bloodshot and wildly dilated eyes. It was hardly even a crash. But it was enough to slow down the green bus.

I noticed the giant from the farmyard by Nut's place first. His face was pressed hard against the window, fogging up the glass and leaving a long slug-trail of saliva dripping below his chin. On the seat behind him there was a woman staring out, with a circle of deep crimson rouge on one cheek and nothing on the other. And then, at the very back, looking calmly across the road at the damaged car and the bus stop, was Tammy.

I almost ran after the bus. But I knew I wouldn't be able to follow it on foot and so I calmed myself and made a careful note of the time. It was half past two. Now I knew that she went out during the day, and when, all I had to do was find out where.

3

The fire that had hardly warmed an inch of the room for the whole winter had become a scorching furnace. How Johnny could stand it I didn't know. Why he kept the thing lit was quite beyond me. It'd been twenty degrees outside for a week.

The heat rose up into the already warm air like nausea. Each lump of coal, as it flared and spluttered smoke, seemed to release some stored residue of the carboniferous jungles out of which it had been formed, a condensed and clotted humidity that seeped directly into your skin and came back out instantly as sweat. I could feel it gathering on my forehead and dripping off the hair under my armpits. It didn't appear to affect Johnny at all. I wondered if he'd spent so long inside this house, inside this room, that he'd become immune to the shifts and turns of the seasons outside; that he'd somehow developed a kind of special recluse's metabolism,

259

which processed alteration into stasis. The Spring was only a conceit of light beyond the window, just as the Winter had only been a trick of the dark.

For the past week he'd been telling me about a family of farmers who'd owned the land behind Eglwys Fach, and the story of a schoolteacher who'd fallen in love with the baker's daughter and tried to elope with her to Aberystwyth. The elopement had turned out to be an unsuccessful one. In the end the daughter hadn't been able to go through with it, hadn't been able to leave. And so finally I asked him.

'Why did you never leave here Johnny? Why didn't you at least go to Llanysgerbwd?'

For a while he didn't say anything. I could hear the clock ticking but nothing else. A drop of sweat had fallen from my forehead onto the table and I watched it seep into the wood. Across from me I could see Johnny's hands resting on the table. There was not even a hint of moisture upon them. His liver spots looked like dead leaves lying on clumps of beached coral. In fact at that moment there didn't seem to be any life at all in him. His body was slumped back in his chair and his shoulders were drooped forward; he appeared crumpled, drained, inanimate, not a man but a marionette whose strings had been cut. When eventually he did speak his voice sounded thrown, ventriloquized.

'Not once in fourteen years,' it said. 'Not once. For fourteen years she kept it shut to me.'

Maybe everyone remembers best the places they were not allowed to go. Familiar rooms fade and disappear: living rooms, schoolrooms, nurseries – all the places you were permitted and supposed to be – they will slip away from you. But that shed at the end of the garden where your father kept his tools, or that derelict cottage that your mother worried would fall down on you, they remain, undiminished, perhaps augmented. Prohibition works like salt, it enhances and preserves.

And for me it's that room that looms largest in my memory, where it's not even a room yet but a locked door. I could walk upstairs right now and go into it, you know, it hasn't changed much, not at all really, but it wouldn't be the same room. I've seen it a thousand times now, ten thousand, I see it almost every day, and yet if I were to fall off a cliff tomorrow and my edited life was to flash before me, I'd see nothing but that locked door. It wouldn't open. I wouldn't be allowed in.

But perhaps I'd still hear her inside. Muffling those sobs that were as hidden from me as everything else was in there. I'd be a child come in from his ruined garden, standing with his ear pressed up against the rough wooden planks, listening, wanting to look, imagining her black hair pulled back straight from her forehead and her green eyes fringed with redness, wanting to come in, wanting to help, but not wanting to either because I know that that room makes her sad and I know that her sadness is something which frightens me and which I cannot understand. Or I'd be an older child, ten, maybe eleven, furious with that door, furious with what lies beyond it, because I am conscious now that what it conceals is something that has both been taken from me and is taking away from me.

When he was still alive, my taid used to take me for walks along the clifftops and tell me sailor stories. I loved these walks and tried to make them last as long as possible, too long for my taid I think, who was old and frail by then and needed a stick. Sometimes I'd see him wobble and stagger and plant his stick on the ground to stop himself from falling, but I was too greedy for his words to let him stop and would urge him further along. His face had collapsed into a thousand wrinkles that criss-crossed his brown and salt-shrunk skin like lines of latitude and longitude on a deflated, wizened globe, and I never tired of looking up at this face, endlessly fascinated by it as though it were somehow an illustration or map of his stories. His eyes he always kept averted from the sea itself, which puzzled me then but not later.

To begin with, he told me tales about pirates and cannibals and castaways. There were two I liked best and got him to repeat endlessly, and which each time he'd embroider and expand a little more, adding continents and characters as he went, to keep me happy. First, there was Connolly the Dancing Cannibal, who'd lived on an island in the South Seas. Connolly had got his name from an Irish sailor who'd had the misfortune to get washed up on his island and get eaten by him; a feast that not only gained Connolly a name but, rather miraculously, the ability to dance a wonderful selection of jigs and reels. And such were his newly digested talents that he was able to lure any number of other unfortunate mariners into his pot by dancing on the beach, where they'd come ashore to watch the show. Luckily for him, and me as well, as he pointed out, when my taid and his crew came to this island they weren't fooled by Connolly's ruse, and watched him cavorting from the safety of their ship. After a while, my taid told me, poor Connolly had quite worn himself out, and seeing he would not be able to entice anybody onto his beach he swam out to them instead, where they welcomed him onto the decks. And he became a firm favourite with my taid's crew, did Connolly, and danced for them every night until eventually, when it came time to hoist the anchor, they begged him to stay with the ship for a bit and share their journey, to which Connolly replied that he'd be happy to as he'd always wished to see the world. And see the world he did, according to my taid, who had him dance through all the most adventurous and exotic places a boy could dream of. He danced in India and China and Africa, he danced in the ports of the West Indies and on the shores of South America, and soon enough he'd danced all the way to America, where, in the city of New York, one Mr Barnum discovered him and hired him for his circus.

He quickly became a star of the circus. My taid described how he bounded into the ring with four fiddlers on either side of him, dressed in nothing but a skirt of grass and his tattoos, holding a spear in his hand, and how the audience would cheer and bang their feet on the floor to keep the beat as he jigged and reeled his way around. And this was how they left him, in all his pomp and glory, Connolly the Dancing Cannibal.

But I couldn't bring myself to leave him in the circus. I pestered and pestered my taid until finally he brought him back. By now he was very much down on his luck. The fickle circus crowds had tired of him, and he'd taken to lugging the old billboards with his name on them from tavern to tavern and dancing there for dimes, which had soon become pennies, and then just a meal and a drink. My taid said when they found him they hardly recognised him. The cold had frozen up his joints and the city soot had covered up his tattoos. So they took him back to the ship and washed him off and filled him with salted pork and rum, and then they sailed right round the

Horn and took him all the way back home. And the last time they saw him he was dancing on his beach again, waving them goodbye.

My other favourite had a hero with my name, or half of it at least. Johnny De Janeiro was a boy from Holyhead, about my age, who fell asleep in the hold of a ship one day and didn't wake up until it'd docked across the ocean in Rio. It was the first improbable step in a long and improbable journey that took Johnny as far as my taid's memory and experience would let him. Because when I look back now I can see that Johnny's adventures were my taid's way of telling me about himself and all the places he'd been, they were a form of recollection, and of sharing too. Because I think my taid wanted me to see what he had seen, wanted me to go where he had gone, but only in the safety of his mind where he could protect me from it. He wanted me to go with him, but he didn't want me to leave.

I followed Johnny across the world for two years. He had a penchant for turning up in ports in unusual ways. He made it to Sydney rowing in a whaleboat, after the ship he'd been on had sunk off the barrier reef. He arrived in Honolulu disguised as a missionary. He sailed into San Francisco in a yacht painted gold by its prospector owner. He also had an uncanny knack of being in the right place at the right time, or, more to the point, for being in the right place at the wrong time. You see many of Johnny's adventures seemed to revolve around disasters, and a good part of his travels were spent narrowly avoiding them. He only had to set foot in a place for a volcano to erupt or a hurricane to sweep in; if he stayed in a city you knew it might burn to the ground any minute; if he looked at a river then the floodwaters were probably already making their way down it. But he always escaped. When the flood arrived he'd be sleeping in a boat. When the flames came licking at the window he'd be outside on the street. The one spot the lava didn't flow through and burn – well you could bet he'd be standing on it. Johnny was an amazingly lucky boy who just kept turning up in places the moment they became unlucky.

Through Johnny and his travels I came to apprehend the world as a realm of imminent calamity and catastrophe. Whenever I thought about anywhere, whenever I saw the name of a foreign town, I'd always picture it on the point of bursting or exploding or drowning or blowing away. From my little corner of Môn I'd look out at the waves and imagine the ocean below them to be full of charred remains and floating debris. I was surprised the horizon was not constantly coated with plumes of smoke and ash. And yet through Johnny I also came to think of myself as charmed. When I climbed the cliffs in search of seagull eggs it never occurred to me I'd fall. I played without fear on the precarious and crumbling edges of the quarry. Nothing would hurt me. And secretly I longed to test my fortune, like Johnny, in the arena of disaster that lay beyond. And I think my taid began to notice this longing the stronger it grew in me, because one day, after two years of moving him about the globe, he brought Johnny back home.

It was an unspectacular return, on a normal ship, in normal circumstances, and since I knew that Holyhead was still standing I also knew that this was the end of his adventures. It was a bitter blow to me. I'd been happy for Connolly to be returned to his island, but with Johnny it was different because I could tell our fates were somehow more intimately entwined. I begged my taid to put him back to sea, to let him travel further, but he was adamant that this was it for his journeying, that Holyhead had been his real destination from the very beginning and now he'd reached it. And slowly, through my taid's repeated refusals, I realised that Johnny was as far as I was allowed to go.

Or not quite even that far. Because hadn't Johnny made it home? Intuitively I sensed there was something wrong with my taid's conclusion, something missing that pulled Johnny and me apart at the very last.

'Why can't we live with you in Llanysgerbwd?' I suddenly asked him. A question which he must have known would come, and that perhaps all his stories had been an attempt to delay. But once I'd asked it he didn't flinch from answering it. And it was only then that the door began to open. Just a little at first – barely enough for my young eyes to see into – but at least it was ajar, at least it was a beginning. And an ending too. A dead end.

4

'Yeh, right, yu mean the spaz bus,' Nut replied.

'So what does it do?' I asked.

Outside, through the living room window, I could see Bub in the yard struggling with a piece of machinery. He was hitting it with a wrench, and I could make out the contortions his lips went through as he swore at it.

'It don't really *do* anything matc, it jus takes 'em tu the hospital, like.'

'What for?' I asked, a little worried I might be showing too much interest.

'Tu be honest, mate, I couldn't tell yu. Never given it a thought. But I reckon some of 'em need help with stuff, therapy like. I know that Gwynfor Tros Marion's always trying tu hurt himself, not others yeh, jus' himself. An' there's a lad from down past the bridge who's always showing his nob tu people – kids, old bids, anyone really – an' I'm sure it's harmless cus he jus shows 'em it like, doesn't do anything with it, but it pisses some folk off an' so they must try tu do something with 'im. Fokk, that Villeneuve's a real prick.'

I wasn't too sure why Villeneuve was a prick, but I thought it'd be better if I didn't push my luck with the bus thing and so I turned my attention back to the race. I knew where the hospital was, which was all I really needed to know.

There were fifteen laps to go. I made a quick calculation. It was quarter past one and the fastest lap so far had been one minute forty-two seconds, which meant the average one would probably be one minute forty-five, and that meant with luck the race should be over in about twenty-five minutes. It took around fifteen minutes to get from Bub and Nut's to the village. If nothing went wrong I could catch the normal bus at two o'clock.

The outcome of the race, as it seemed to have been all season, was in no doubt. Schumacher was a lap and a half in front. The two cars behind him were both well ahead of the rest, and the commentator was trying his breathless best to make the battle for fourth place exciting.

'Yu know, Schumacher an Ferrari 'ave made it boring this year,' said Nut. But his voice didn't sound bored. He couldn't take his eyes off the television screen, and they followed each car as it growled and spat its way into, and out of, view. To me they looked flimsy and awkward, sliding and scuttling around the corners like careering insects with unnaturally huge and threatening voices.

'He's gonna 'ave tu change them tyres some time.'

I'd forgotten about this and added it into my calculation. Hopefully it would run smoothly and take only a few seconds.

I quite liked the excitement of the tyre change. The expectant approach, the stop, the sudden appearance of the clock and the frantic whirling of the seconds and the tenths and hundredths of seconds, the disciplined frenzy of the men around the car and, finally, the smoky screeching of the new tyres as they spun themselves desperately onto the track. I was beginning to recognise how racing was actually made up of these small concentrations of drama – the drama of the start (not the finish, not this season anyway), the drama of the pit stop, the occasional drama of overtaking, the high drama of the crash – and that the rest was just simple, repetitive, bounded motion. And I found something reassuring about this, because ultimately you knew that whatever happened the circuit would, in the end, contain it.

These Sunday afternoons had become a ritual of sorts for Nut and me. I'd come over by chance a few months before and found Nut in the living room, transfixed by the screen, and so I'd sat down and joined him. The next time I saw him he stopped his tractor and began telling me about qualifying laps. And, although it remained unspoken, I knew this was an invitation to watch the next race.

I think he was glad to have me there. Because I didn't know anything about racing, it gave him someone to guide through its intricacies. He explained how the points were allocated to drivers and manufacturers, how the positions on the starting grid were arranged, and other, more technical, details that I never understood. But he was happy to tell me about them anyway and became inordinately proud to discover he knew so much about something.

The moment the cars exploded off the grid a subtle transformation would come over Nut. You could see his normally taut body begin to relax. His shoulders fell back a few inches and his face seemed to unscrunch; his hands went still and rested on his slackened thighs. The speed of the race appeared to subsume his own impatience: it slowed him down. I never saw him so calm as when he had those cars whizzing hectically in front of him. You could sense this calmness filter out from him into the room where it gathered into an atmosphere, still, contemplative, intimate, lit up by the muted glow of the ever-moving pictures on the screen. And as we sat through those Sunday afternoons I think we became friends – or as close to friends as I had ever been used to.

The change took eight point two five seconds. The race was effectively over. I started to fidget during the last few laps and kept looking out of the window, where Bub had exchanged his wrench for an oily rag, apparently intent now on caressing rather than battering his machine into life. As they prepared the chequered flag I prepared my excuses. I got up as it came down.

'Where yu off tu?' Nut asked.

'Just into town,' I said, 'to get some videos.'

'Yer not stopping fer a panad?'

'I best not. I might miss the bus.'

'Right.'

And then I was out in the yard. I waved at Bub.

'Yu off?' he said.

'Got to dash,' I said.

'See yu.'

And then I was out on the lane and had started to panic slightly about the time. It might take longer than fifteen minutes to get to the bus shelter. I upped my strides into a jog, which became a run and eventually, as I came to the edge of the village, an outright sprint. I arrived at the bus shelter eight minutes early.

There were two old women in the bus shelter and they stopped talking when I went in and sat on the wooden bench. Outside it was hot and bright. There was sweat all over my forehead and the back of my neck from running, and out of the corner of their eyes I knew they were watching me. I was breathing heavily, like a pervert. Inside it was cooler and I gulped down the air, which smelt of cold urine. There were the remains of pools of it under the bench, in which fag butts had once swum, mixing their tar and ash with the liquid. Most of these pools had evaporated and left dark patterns on the concrete floor. You could make out strands of tobacco in these, lying around like pieces of tide-beached seaweed. When the bus arrived I waited for the two women to get on and then went and sat on the back seat where they couldn't see me.

We'd only gone about four miles when the bus turned off the main road and onto a narrow, winding one, that passed by fields and woods and ever smaller villages. We stopped in all of them, even if there wasn't anybody waiting there. And then we began to stop in places that weren't even villages, just collections of houses by the side of the road that didn't have bus shelters or Spars. Occasionally another old woman would materialise by the side of the road and get on, but mainly there was nobody and the bus would idle aimlessly for a second or two before moving on. After a while I could hardly bear to look out of the window. The high hedgerows, that the Spring had made dense and luxuriant, seemed to reach out and hold us back. The grey stone walls clutched at us like sphincter muscles. I thought I heard the engine slow each time I saw a house. Beyond the glass the island had become a topography of detour and delay. My watch told me it'd been half an hour already, and still there was no sign of the bridge or the sea or the mainland, and I imagined the green bus on a broad, straight road, speeding its way towards the hospital where I'd have no chance of finding it. When, eventually, the bridge did appear I'd almost given up hope, and the straits below looked wide and vast and full of whirlpools.

After we'd crossed the bridge and arrived at the hospital, the first thing I remember thinking was how long it'd been since I'd left the island. Without me noticing the months had accumulated and I'd settled into them; I'd hardly once even considered what lay beyond them. Stepping off the bus I became conscious of the feeling of being somewhere different, unaccustomed, and of the corresponding feeling – which was new and unusual to me – of being acutely aware of the place where I suddenly wasn't. I felt like one of the unlucky cars that spun off the track during a race, or the driver himself, climbing out onto the grass verge and staring bemusedly back towards the circuit he had just been roughly exiled from.

The hospital itself looked like it shouldn't be where it was, as if it too had skidded out of another landscape and come to rest somewhere that was not quite right for it. It was a sprawl of glass and concrete and car parks set plumb against a backdrop of green and empty mountains. It was a piece of city in the garden. And as I looked up from the revolving doors at its front, that rotated ashen-faced groups of people into the disinfected light within, and then others back out into the corrupted sunshine, I thought how unfeasible it seemed that these mountains should conceal so many – that the garden should be so populous, and sick – and imagined these verdant hills as a realm of profuse and perverse nature, where cancers sprouted and tumours grew and viral streams flooded the valleys.

The wards were named after the mountains. There was Tryfan for burns, and Aran for breaks and Craiglwyn for coronaries, and others too that I searched through for her. All of them were exactly the same and you could hardly tell when you'd left one and entered another, apart from the changing afflictions of the patients: some had plastic masks on their faces, some tubes in their bellies, others had their legs and arms bolted in plaster, their faces held in place with wires. But I didn't even know what was wrong with her, or what they would call it. For an hour I drifted from ward to ward, pretending to be a visitor, my own face held together in an unflinching mask of concern, until eventually I had drifted out of the main building of the hospital altogether. The outbuildings had no names. I went from one to the other, searching their windows ever more desperately, but there was no sign of her. And I'd almost given up when I came upon a building at the very edge of the hospital site – where it sheared abruptly into a field – that was shorter and narrower than the rest and reminded me of a mobile classroom from one of my schools, with its tarpaper wall and roof, and there she was, holding a piece of wood in her hands while a man with a name tag stood beside her.

They were making birdhouses. All the people I'd seen on the green bus – together with several others who I didn't recognise – were making them. They were different shapes and sizes, some bigger, some smaller, but all had the same basic and crude design: three walls made of pine boards with a slightly angled ceiling. The man with the name tag was helping them to make them, showing them where to hammer, and what boards to use, and I supposed that this exercise must be some kind of therapy, although what exactly its purpose might be eluded me. I could see that many of them were quite engrossed in their project, banging merrily away with their hammers and waving about the pieces of wood. And so was she. Except that while the others seemed intent on the process of building, on putting their houses together, she appeared content to let the man with the tag do this for her. Every time he showed her what to do she'd just wait until he was gone and then put down her hammer and stare at the boards, until eventually he'd return and put them together for her. In the end he built the whole thing.

I waited outside for half an hour before they came out. They were carrying their birdhouses and looked very happy with them. The giant boy was cradling his in his arms, making a soft moaning noise. But it was her that I watched most closely. I'd never seen her in this light, and as she walked past me – without once glancing in my direction – I knew that the window would no longer be enough for me, not anymore. I followed her with my eyes, and then with my feet, as she made her way towards the place where the buses stopped. The last thing she did before getting on the bus was to carefully drop her birdhouse into a rubbish bin beside the road.

5

One day around the end of May, Nut came over to collect me for the racing. I was upstairs and had left the front door open, so when he knocked I shouted down to him to let himself in.

'Put the kettle on,' I called when I heard the door open.

'Where's the kettle?' he called back.

'Over by the toaster,' I said.

'Yeh, found it.'

A few minutes later I came down into the kitchen and found him sitting beside the table.

'Fokking 'ell mate,' he said, 'yu've not got much in here av yu. I mean, if we're gonna 'ave a panad we'll 'ave to share a frigging cup, like.'

He was quite right: I only had one cup. In fact I only had one everything. And it suddenly dawned on me that Nut was the first person who'd come into my cottage.

I wonder how long it would have taken me to notice my cottage if Nut hadn't sat in my kitchen that day? I'd been staying in it for almost nine months and barely thought about it. And when I did think of it, it appeared in a series of negatives: it was where I'd hidden from the wind and rain; it was where I hid from the sun; it was where I was when I wasn't at Johnny's or Nut's; it was where I'd forgotten her; it was where I came back to sleep after Tammy's. Beyond this it was still almost as insubstantial to me as the syllables my mother's solicitor had struggled to get off his tongue all that time ago.

But the one thing I'd always learnt was how not to settle. Since the age of fourteen I've been able to keep my life in three boxes; never more than this, sometimes less. I suppose most people see the trajectory of their lives as accumulative, each step of the way you take more with you, but for me those boxes have represented a maximum volume, an absolute limit. Anything that didn't fit into them would have to be left behind. I've carted them into and out of a hundred Spartan interiors, which they've never really filled, which they've never really had to fill. And now here was Nut, more or less the only object in my house that hadn't arrived in one of these boxes, and it felt like I was seeing the place for the first time.

'Du-u fancy a smoke?' he asked.

Through the window a square of sunlight melted into the room. It mixed with the smoke and rose up towards the oak rafters, slowly, synaesthesically, tasting soft and buttery, sounding like cotton wool, hanging there above me in a cloud. For a minute I felt I could reach out and touch it, grab a handful of its golden warmth and hold it, swallow it, breathe it back into my lungs, but instead I let it fall into my eyes, where it gathered in red pools behind their lids. When I closed them the pools overflowed, upwards, dizzily cascading into the top of my head, until it felt like it couldn't hold anymore and so I opened them again and let it course out. The white-washed walls were smoothly flickering and Nut's hair was the colour of a weak-blooded moon.

'Nice gear this, innit,' I heard him say.

'It's good.'

'Some lad from Holyhead gets it. Says it's from Afghanistan or somewhere. Them mullahs or whatever they're called grow it.'

'It's good.'

And then talking felt difficult, treacherous, like our voices had become detached from our brains and left a rift between. The silence was incalculable. Seconds or minutes or maybe longer.

'Might as well go fer a wander before it starts,' I heard him say.

Outside the light was uncontainable. It was everywhere.

As we set off I looked at the cottage. The grass had grown tall around it and it appeared to have shrunk down into it. The two windows on either side of the front door stared back at me and I noticed that two wild rose bushes had climbed up the wall on each of its sides. It looked like a half-buried face with flowers behind its ears. And I wondered if it was smiling or scowling at me, but where its mouth would have been was below the ground.

'Might as well head down tu the beach,' said Nut, although there was no need to say so because we were already headed there, our feet instinctively following the slope of the land.

Everywhere the light touched had turned into colour. Everywhere the sun had unpacked the winter-hidden island. The green beneath my feet was dense and full of daisies; the green in the distance to my right and left was achingly bright; the green on the trees was more gentle and fluttered and flowed as a warm breeze swept across it. In front the sea was the blue of spilled ink, and there were white sails on it and the rocks of the quarry were silver against it and the sky was solid cobalt and Ynys Sieriol was an emerald and then all the colours were suddenly fluttering like the green on the trees only not as gentle now but with the quivering winking trembling intensity of hallucinations. My eyes began to flood my head again and I tried to blink it clear. I could hear Nut talking:

'...an so this lad says tu me he can get us a ticket fer almost nothin and I'd like tu go, I'm dead keen like, been wantin' tu fer ages, but I can't leave Bub on his own tu do the silage can I 'an so I've gotta tell him no yeh...'

The rift had got wider and deeper. I wasn't sure what he was saying. I felt a long way away from the words.

'...but fuk I wanted tu yu know 'cus yu can't hear 'em right on the telly or see how fast they really are. An' I've tried tu get Bub tu go with us before like but it's a bastard tu get 'im tu go anywhere cus he gets all awkward an' nervy an' stuff about having tu talk yeh, an' it's fine round here cus everyone knows an' they understand 'im a-right but when 'e's away they don't an' he gets all embarrassed yeh and so I've had tu tell this lad no but fuk I wanted tu go, I really fokking did.'

And still I wasn't sure. What I could tell was that Nut was disappointed, in a way I'd never seen him before. I tried to understand then because I wanted to make him feel better.

'Go where?' I asked.

'What?'

'Where did you want to go?'

'Tu the race mate – that's what I've just been telling yu!' And as he said this he looked at me warily, suspiciously, as though he wasn't sure what I was saying either, as though my questions might mean something else. His eyes narrowed. They were greener out here. His hair was redder too.

'But where's the race?' I asked.

'A-fokking-broad mate, in Monaco, like I jus been tellin yu. An I really wanted tu go an I fokking would've too if it weren't fer Bub, but I aven't got a choice like, 'ave I cus I can't jus leave 'im here, an' he's not gonna go. He never goes nowhere!'

Nut's head was rocking slightly in frustration, like a child's who's not been allowed to go to the toilet. As we got closer to the sea I could see the sails of the boats swinging back and forth to catch the wind. I tried to concentrate on Nut.

'Well, there's always next year.'

'Fokk next year, I wanted tu go this year. I been wanting tu go fer ages.'

'You know Nut, I've travelled around a lot and it's not what it's cracked up to be. Some places aren't as good as you think they're going to be. Sometimes it's best to just stay where you are and imagine them because then you won't be disappointed with them and they'll keep on seeming different

279

in your mind and you won't have to get there and then start thinking you want to be somewhere else. I mean think of Johnny, he never goes anywhere...'

'What yu talking about?' And suddenly I wasn't certain what I was talking about. The words were trailing out of my mouth but once they got out into the air and I heard them they sounded different to the ones I'd formed in my mind, and I wasn't in control of them and I was forgetting what they'd meant to say, what they'd meant to do. The light and the colours were hurting my eyes; they were filling my head again and I couldn't clear them out.

'I mean what *are* yu fokking talking about. Imagine what? All I wanted tu do was go tu Monaco an' see the race, see it really like, not on telly. S'a-right fer yu innit, yu've been about yeh, but I've never been, I never been fukking anywhere but stuck 'ere. An what's all this Johnny crap? Yu don't even really know Johnny, 'cept fer sitting around with 'im all day swapping stories. I've grown up beside 'im an I cun tell yu he's a bitter an' twisted old cunt who doesn't do fuk all but sit in 'is house; an' he pretends to know all sorts but how's he know anything if he doesn't do nothing or see nothing, yeh?'

Nut's face was as red as his hair now. I tried to think of things to say to calm him down but they all got confused before I could say them. The rift was getting wider and deeper and it was frightening us both I think, and Nut's fright was making him angry. I watched helplessly as some of the sailing boats veered around and began to head back towards Ynys Seiriol. The sea was so blue it was making me sick.

'Look, I don't know what I was trying to say, Nut. I'm a little fucked at the moment. All I meant was that maybe it's not worth being too disappointed about not being able to go.'

But he couldn't hear me now and went all quiet and I knew his anger was shifting dangerously in another direction.

'Yu'a bit of a weird fukker Jon, d'yu know that. I dunno why yu came 'ere or why yu hang about or why yu spend so much time listening tu Johnny or what, but I always reckoned yu were harmless like, jus a bit of a hippie yeh. But then I start seeing yu coming home at all hours an' I'm thinking what the frig are yu doing and so I follow yu one night an' I see yu outside Tammy's. An' I watch yu and yu don't do nothin' so I think yer a perv but not a bad un, not a dangerous un like, jus a strange un, an' apart from that yer a-right, sound yeh; a bit sad an' that, but a-right. An then I hear yer following 'er tu the hospital and I'm thinking yu must be a bit fukked upstairs, but I leave it out, I giv yu the benefit of the doubt, because yer a mate like. But I'm tellin yu now tu leave 'er alone. I like Tammy, she's a-right. I used tu see 'er a bit before 'er head got crocked an she's a decent bird, she's nice yeh, an I don't want yu following 'er an staring at 'er an' behaving like a fokking freak. So I'm tellin yu now to leave 'er a-fukking-lone, right!'

I could see the whites of his eyes as he was telling me this and they'd turned red as well. And then he'd walked off and I was left there in the unbearable light and colours, watching the space in the sea that the boats had left behind.

After a few minutes I made my way back to my cottage. I wasn't sure how long ago we'd set out from it, but it seemed a long while and the cottage again appeared as though I was looking at it for the first time. And as I approached it I suddenly began to wonder what it would have been like to live here twenty years before, and I pictured myself as a child running around outside until it was getting dark and I was too tired to run anymore, and then seeing the lights in the kitchen come on and the door opening and more light coming out and then my mother's frame appearing in that light and beckoning me in.

But when I did go in it was as empty as I'd left it. I sat down and tried to remember her face; but it was gone now, utterly gone. In my mind's eye I saw a plate crack and then shatter.

6

My taid told me that I became visible at about the same time my mother stopped looking at things.

He'd not been there himself to witness my first appearance as a bulge beneath my mother's dress, but my nain said I'd swelled into view about two weeks after he'd set out to collect my father. I was late showing up. My father had left six months before.

The clock in this room used to belong to my taid. He went out and bought it the day he was made a captain. He was taken by the aptness of its face and told my nain that whenever she wondered where he was she could just look at the time and know that he was somewhere there. It became a family tradition. 'So where do you think your father is,' my nain would ask my father when he was a child, and my father would glance up at the clock and say, 'He's at half past three,' or 'Ten past six' or whatever time it was. And it was the last thing my father said to my mother: 'If you want to know where I am look at the clock.' And for those six months she had. For a few hours each day she'd sit in the front room and watch the hands as they made their circumnavigations, watched them passionately and intently as though each elapsed and inched second were gradually ticking him back to her. But of course they weren't. They were headed for Valparaiso and then to nowhere. And when he'd arrived, and when she knew he'd gone, she stopped looking at it, knowing that the time would not bring him back, that it would only take him further away. Knowing that he'd fallen off the clockface. And then I appeared, a skewed and inverted chronology – the time gone wrong. I was the past come literally to life, as well as the future that had just died.

My nain began to worry about me when my mother moved into the back room of the house, the one without windows, and refused to come out. For two months I grew bigger in the darkness of that room; a second womb in which I lay curled and hidden like a flower in the night. My nain called the doctor but he said there was nothing he could do with my mother, nothing he could treat. As for me, well I was fine as far as he could tell, and would be coming out soon enough. But he couldn't get her to come out. Nobody could.

And then one day she did. At first my nain thought she'd got her senses back, that she'd suffered through the worst of it, but the truth was she'd only just started. She began by packing my father's belongings into boxes, everything he'd ever owned. She took his clothes, his books, his souvenirs; she even took his letters home, not just those to her but the ones he'd sent to his parents before he'd even met her. She went to the newspaper offices in town and asked for the one he'd sent them. Then she began to pack things that didn't belong to him, but which he must have told her about. She took Medicine's journal and his tomahawk; she took some of my taid's maps; she took my great-grandfather's compass. Everything he might have touched or admired or held in his hands as a child when he started to imagine the world, she sealed away in boxes where she wouldn't have to look at them. Until the only thing left was Llanysgerbwd itself. It was too big to go in a box so for two more weeks she packed herself back into the room where she wouldn't have to see it.

The next time she came out it was to tell my nain I can't live here anymore. And my nain said fine, she didn't have to, there were other places in the village she could live. And my mother said no, that's not what she meant, that it was in Llanysgerbwd she couldn't live. And my nain said what about your baby, you'll have to wait until it's born. And my mother had looked down at her belly then and it was like she'd just that second noticed I was there.

I disembarked reluctantly in Tŷ Carreg the day after my father came home. I didn't much want to arrive here apparently, and made an awful fuss about it. They poked me and prodded me and pulled me, until finally Dr Williams lost his patience and yanked me out with his forceps. Everyone was worried that he'd dented my head.

They buried my father when I turned four days old. My mother refused to go back to Llanysgerbwd for the funeral and so my taid brought a piece of him to live in our new house.

There was sweat all over my shirt. It was dripping from my neck and forehead. Every day Johnny's room was getting hotter, as though he'd finally reached the point where he wouldn't even let the heat escape.

I'd visited every morning for a week. Mainly because now there was really nowhere else for me to safely go, but also because I'd begun to detect an increased urgency to Johnny's recollections. You could read it in his hands. Their movements had become more and more jerky and impatient, as if he was conducting some frantic symphony. And you could hear it in his voice, which had taken on a croaky, breathless quality. He was hurrying along, you could tell. He was speeding up. He wanted this to be over. And it almost was.

And the more my taid told me the more the door opened. Until eventually, even without seeing inside, I came to know that room: it was the room where my father lived.

When I was fourteen I at last broke in. I kicked the door off its hinges one afternoon and walked straight through. Seeing it actually, physically, didn't surprise me at all. I already knew who my father was and what he looked like: he was a pile of boxes – some open, some sealed – he was a heap of old newspapers and cuttings, he was a bundle of long-sent letters, a journal or two, a collection of photographs, a hoard of souvenirs. He was a keepsake, a token, a memento, a relic – and he was the only person who truly lived in our house.

My mother, who kept everything else in the house in such strict order, was entirely haphazard with my father. He was strewn messily around, lying here and there on the floor, falling off chairs, gathering dust on the table, protruding out from half-shut drawers. And that first time I saw him I couldn't bring myself to touch him; I stood in the room for hours, looking, wondering, until my mother arrived back and found me and slapped my face and pushed me out. It was only later, when the door was back on its hinges, and I was back outside of it – forced once more to listen to them together in there, whispering, sobbing, shuffling paper – that I decided that the next time I went in I would touch it all, I would rummage through the lot of him, because I wanted to be together with them.

But I never was.

You see, whoever it was that my mother kept locked up in that room, it wasn't the same person that I slowly pieced together. If we'd ever sat down together in there – which we never did – we would've sat down with different men. Whenever she was away I snuck in – the hinges never held as fast as she thought they did – and page by page, bit by bit, began to assemble him. I remember quite clearly all those secret afternoons and mornings and evenings, listening carefully for her footsteps outside, while inside I picked my way through the mausoleum she was married to. I found him out by stealth, beneath her nose; I slyly fashioned him; I stole him.

And once I'd found my father I started to look for him everywhere. And because he was made out of paper and objects, that's where I searched for him. In school I followed his tracks in books of travels, across paragraphs where he'd never been and continents he'd never known and sentences he'd never walked through and seas he'd never sailed. I traced his journeys with a pencil. I drew his discoveries on a map. I hunted him through a world made of ink and escaped with only smudges on my fingers. I began to see him in other dead men: in Cook flailing on the beach; in Park crouched naked in the jungle; in Scott wrapped frost-bitten in furs; in Lewis by a riverside, thinking of the gun he'd later put to his head; in Medicine in his darkened room. I saw him in engravings and lithographs and paintings, half-hero, half-corpse, hiding beneath patterned surfaces and etched palms. I rooted him out of numbers, notations of longitude and latitude, wind speeds, soundings, dates, distances, hours, minutes, miles, leagues, knots and inches.

When I was a child there used to be a circus that came to town once a year and decamped on the green in front of the castle. It was one of the few excursions I was allowed, and I'd walk there with my taid who was very fond of the acrobats. The circus itself was a paltry affair really. The main tent was old and threadbare and always appeared dwarfed by the castle behind it. Its ribbons had faded and the white of the canvas had turned a yellowy brown, the same nicotine-stained colour as the fingers of the sullen men who put it up. They had an elephant who they kept miserably chained to a stake on the green, where he trampled disconsolate circles on the grass, and a herd of blank-eyed, ground-gazing horses and donkeys, who never looked up, even when the laughing children prodded their ribs with sticks. It was a tired and exhausted circus, frayed and worn and huddled out here on the windblown edge of the continent, where its only thought must have been to get back over the bridge as soon as possible.

The main performance was as cracked and stale as the make-up on the performer's faces. I don't remember much of it, only the elephant being whipped around the ring, and the desultory flips and tumbles of the acrobats, and their rictus smiles as they landed on their feet. What I do remember is the look on my taid's face as he watched it. He was entranced by every movement the acrobats made, and you could see his face scrunch with pleasure as they swung above us on the ropes and clasped hands in mid-air and wrapped their legs around the bar of the trapeze. And I couldn't imagine why he liked them so much, unless they somehow reminded him of dancing along the sails and through the rigging of those ships which existed now only in his childhood; that through them he saw his apprentice self, cavorting loose-limbed and carefree above the oceans which he barely knew yet and which had taken nothing from him. And you could tell that for the minutes their performance lasted he was with them in mid-air, outside of his ancient, striated skin and his arthritic, unstable body, hanging suspended in a tranced and spellbound world where he could defy time and gravity and everything else that was pulling him inexorably down. But I was always impatient for it to be over. I almost wished they'd fall.

Because the performance wasn't what I was interested in. Outside the main tent there were several smaller ones, where you could look at aborted foetuses bottled in formaldehyde called Two-Headed Children, and a woman with a false beard, and a shivering dwarf named Tom Thumb who warmed his hands with the ends of his cigarettes. And in the last of these was a collection of exotic knick-knacks that you could buy for a penny. I loved it in there. There was a table covered in 'Bornean Heads', that I knew were shrivelled oranges with tufts of horse hair glued on them, and a pile of straw figures advertised as 'Genuine Haitian Voodoo Charms'. In another corner they had a collection of crudely carved pieces of pine, dyed black, which were 'African Idols', and beside them a rack hung with pieces of horse hide, with a few glass beads sewn on, called 'Indian Scalps'. And even though I knew they were cheap fabrications, ersatz circus bric-a-brac as false as the smiles in the ring, I was thrilled by them. I'd stay in the tent until my taid would have to drag me out; but not before I'd nagged him into buying me at least a couple of these items. He never appeared to mind. It must have seemed harmless to him and he indulged me with them, like other taids indulged their grandchildren with toffee apples and goldfish.

Over the years my collection grew and grew. Each time the circus came they'd have one or two new pieces, and I'd lie awake the night before trying to picture what they'd be, what part of the globe they'd pretend to come from. Because half, maybe all, of the thrill of them was in their names and the make-believe origins they pointed to. It didn't matter to me that they'd been thrown together in Rhyl or Prestatyn or Blackpool or anywhere else the circus passed through to get to us, the important thing was that they conjured new places for me to search and imagine. I kept them hidden in a cache at the bottom of my garden, where my mother wouldn't discover them (the first ones I'd got she'd found in my room and thrown out – she didn't want such 'rubbish' in her house she told me after), and carefully wrote down their names in a blue notebook, half of which was already filled with a description of Cook's first journey to Tahiti and some drawings of a breadfruit that I'd copied. And when she was out I'd bring them into the house and put them in a circle around me, checking their names on my list, calling them out like a schoolmaster checking his register, until my recitation became like an incantation, Borneo, Brazil, Africa, America, Fiji, Haiti, Hindustan, until suddenly he had become them too, incarnated in glass and straw and horsehair and dried fruit and dead skin; and to keep him there, to make him present longer, I went beyond my list and carried on with places that weren't even on it, Rajistan, Rio, Rangoon, Burma, Brittany, Bahamas, Da Cunha, Cape Town, thinking that as long as I carried on he would stay here with me and not go back into the room with her, that my alternative hoard would hold him, would prolong him, would make him mine as well, Sydney, Newcastle, New South Wales, Valparaiso, Old Wales, Ynys Môn, Llanysgerbwd. And the moment I stopped I knew he was gone again.

7

She was sitting beside the well when I spotted her, half-covered in stone shadows, staring down into the copper-coin-tinted water. It was late in June and the grass had grown high and brushed against the back of my thighs as I crouched near the entrance to the enclosure. The air smelt of honeysuckle and in the stillness of the afternoon it gathered and thickened into an almost cloying sweetness. In the near distance, through the hazel and blackthorn boughs that overhung the path, you could see the road and the occasional tourist making their way towards the sea, where you could hear the lighthouse chiming for ships that weren't there. Having looked from the road myself I knew they couldn't see me, that this whole place was nearly invisible behind the leaves and there was no sign to guide them here. I knew I was safe – from them at least.

I think she dropped a penny into the well. I was near enough to hear a faint splash. And then she turned away from the water and towards the wall. I hadn't noticed the small black bag beside her, but she now reached across and opened it, taking out a bundle of freshly-picked flowers and a handful of paper. A shard of sun had fallen through the entrance and into the well; it sent ripples of light up across the slabs of stone and one of these caught the edge of the paper which refracted it off its shiny surface. It wasn't paper, it was a photograph. I watched as she carefully separated the flowers, lining them up on the ledge where she sat, and then separated the photographs too, putting them each beside one of the flowers. There were five photographs and five flowers. When she'd finished she picked them up, one by one, and placed them in the gaps in the wall. And as she did this she began to make a soft moaning noise, a low, barely discernible, almost animal whimpering, that initially I struggled to pick up through the static, pollen-clotted air, but which, when I did, I found shocking, startling, incomprehensible. It was the first time I'd heard her make a sound.

And I guess that sound must have broken something inside me, have shattered like glass the inhibitions that had kept me securely distant from her for all this time, and left the window jaggedly, dangerously, open. When I stood up I could feel the tempers begin to circle and swirl again, uncontrollably, and there seemed no other way to stop them but to walk on forward towards her. They were rushing through my blood and I was sick and dizzy and tired with them. I wanted them to stop. I wanted her to stop them.

By the time she turned around I was only a few feet away.

She didn't look surprised to see me. She didn't look like she recognised me either. Her eyes were puffed and swollen about their edges, and I could tell she'd been crying, but the moment she'd seen me in front of her whatever it was that had made her cry had been hidden away behind the same glazed and serene stare that I'd first noticed in the Dragon. Only now it was directed at me.

She didn't move when I sat down next to her. She didn't even stop looking at me. And as long as I could see her stare nothing had felt wrong; we were just two people comforting each other, distracting each other, sharing a bit of peace and companionship in an old saint's cell where nobody would find us. I was helping her to forget for a second whatever it was that hurt her. And the worst thing was that at that moment I think I was. She didn't move when I touched her.

The honeysuckle was everywhere. The air was thick and heavy with it. And as I moved my fingers beneath Tammy's shirt the fold of her belly felt like honeysuckle too, a warm, gelatinous deposit of scent, like pulped flowers. For a while I just left them lying there, four questions and a thumb, but I couldn't read any answer in her face and so I took her stillness as assent and moved my hand gently up and down across the soft rolls of her stomach. I was looking at her, and she was looking back at me, but I wasn't seeing her now; her face had become a pattern of shapes and colours almost indistinguishable from the blur of rippled light and shadow around it; and my eyes weren't bothering to process them because all my attention was channeled into my hand and the rest of my senses, the rest of myself, had become temporarily peripheral. I was nothing but the cool feeling of the buttons on her jeans and the coarse fabric of the denim, the pliant elastic and smooth cotton of her knickers, the curling fronds of her hair and the delicate skin underneath, the constricting, inward bulge of her thighs, the searching push of my fingers.

And when I'd reached there, there didn't seem anywhere else to go and so I stayed exactly as I was, afraid that to go further would break the sudden calm and contentment that had fallen over me. I don't know how long this lasted, but for those few seconds or minutes or more there was no before or after, no arriving or leaving, no remembering, nothing but my cramped hand. And then it began to tingle and throb and feel bigger than it was, and there were pin-pricks shooting through it, and I realised that the top of her jeans were cutting off my blood. The moment I started to wrench my hand out she came back into focus, everything did.

Her expression hadn't changed at all, except that maybe there was a confused, expectant quality in it that I hadn't seen there before. I think she wanted something, not me perhaps, but something. I'd never thought about her wanting anything, I'd only thought of wanting her. And having her here, so close to me that I could feel her breath and the faint moistness of her that was already drying off my fingers, made me uneasy and I found that I couldn't think about her properly like I was used to doing in her garden, or even picture her properly like I'd been able to do through her window, and her lips were slightly open and I was terrified that she might actually speak or say something to me and the walls around the well suddenly felt too small and narrow and the roof was too near to my head and I could smell the aroma of her sweat and see slight patches of it on her face and then I could see the faces on the photographs behind her as well and they were young and smiling and I knew they were them. And then I was running back down the path and the hazel and blackthorn were getting in my way and the honeysuckle was everywhere and it was clogging my nostrils and lungs and it was stinging my eyes and it was clinging to my skin and I was coughing and gagging on it and trying desperately to spit it out.

8

At first he looked like one of the stones. Like one of the stranded stones that had been blown off and never taken. They were strewn all along the surface of Chwarel Wen, abandoned in different attitudes and postures: some teetering on the very edge, looking down into the ocean; some standing more squarely and firmly on the upper shore, so that you could hardly tell they were separate; some at odd angles, jutting sideways like fallen obelisks; some bolt upright, like unsculpted Easter Island gods staring eyeless out to sea, (or maybe landward, it was hard to know).

He was sitting near the water with his back to me, and even from a distance I could make out the forlorn hunch of his shoulders and the curve of his neck, beneath which his head was hanging. In front of him a flock of oystercatchers skimmed over the swell, veering, scattering, condensing, while seagulls hovered and wailed in the updrafts above and below a single, solitary cormorant stood half-submerged on a bed of bladderwrack. I watched him for a long while and he didn't move. Until eventually he stood up and began to move back towards the cliff and the path. I would have been less surprised to see one of the stones get up and walk away.

I followed behind him on the path, quietly brushing aside the bracken that arched across it. I didn't want him to see me and it was easy to stay unobserved because he never looked up from his feet. He watched each footstep as though he were counting them, reckoning them up, and was uncertain whether he had enough of them to get back. He looked so frail and tired that I worried he wouldn't. This far outside of his cottage he seemed like a creature marooned in a strange and inimical element, tracking awkwardly through it with ill-suited limbs; a crab in the desert, a lion in the sea.

It took him nearly an hour to make his way the half a mile or less from the quarry to Tŷ Carreg. And yet five minutes later, when I followed him through the door, he appeared as full of energy as I'd ever seen him; but it was a frantic, slightly febrile energy, and there was something almost desperate about it.

He started talking the second I came in. He startled me by beginning with a question:

'Do you know how long I worked in that quarry?'

And I knew he'd seen me then, that he'd known I was there all along. I didn't mention it.

'No. I didn't know you'd worked there.'

'I worked there for fifteen years.'

He paused then, and I almost thought we were going to have a conversation.

'As a quarryman?' I asked.

No, they'd closed it by then. As a caretaker. They paid me to look after the buildings and machinery when they left; and they were meant to come back and collect what they'd left but they must have forgotten because it took them fifteen years to come back and get it. And so for fifteen years I walked in slow circles around that two hundred yards of stones, all during the day and sometimes through the night, that two hundred yards that wasn't quite the sea and wasn't quite the shore; a caretaker of nothing really, just a few rocks and a bunch of machinery that nobody would use and a building or two that nobody would live in.

And as I made my rounds things happened before and behind me. My nain and taid died and I wasn't allowed to go to their funeral. There were wars and elections and revolutions and I didn't take part in any of them. I used to spend my afternoons reading the old ledgers in the quarry houses, reading the names of ships and their destinations, making plans to leave and follow them. Because I knew that to find him, to find anything, I'd have to go to either of two places: I'd have to go out there across the ocean or back into the island to Llanysgerbwd. And I knew them both well enough. I'd read enough books and maps to find my way across the one, and my taid had told me so much about the other, and given me pictures and told me stories, that I might as well have lived there anyway. But somehow I could never properly decide which way to go and so I didn't go anywhere.

I tried twice. The first time I was twenty. A tinker had come by the quarry, an Irishman with a cart full of trinkets, and we'd talked for hours and he'd told me about all the places he'd been and how this travelling about was his whole life and that he'd not have it any other way. And when he was about to leave I'd determined to go with him for a bit, and he'd said fine, he wouldn't mind the company, and I'd raced off home to collect some clothes and provisions for the journey. But by the time I'd got down the stairs and to the front door my mother was there. She was crying and saying that if I left it'd be just the same as it'd been with my father, that I wouldn't come back, and that she'd barely lived through that happening and couldn't live if it happened twice. And I was furious and told her she hadn't lived for the past twenty years anyway so what difference would it make. I went to push her out of the way but she clung onto me, and when I'd pulled her arms off my shoulders she'd grabbed onto my legs and I tried to kick her off. But she wouldn't let go and with every kick my accumulated bitterness came seeping out and I was screaming at her, for not letting me go, for not letting me go to Llanysgerbwd, even when my nain and taid had died, even though it was where I'd belonged, because it was part of my father and she wouldn't share him with me; for not letting me go away to the sea, even though it was in my blood, for not letting me go away to America like Medicine had done, for not letting me go away to war like so many others from the island had done. And when I'd finished she was lying bloodied and barely conscious on the ground and I left her and ran down to meet the tinker but he'd gone already and though I searched the lanes for hours I never found him. When I got home she was sitting in the kitchen with her two plates and two knives and two spoons and I knew she thought she'd won, and I suppose she had.

As for the second time, well that was later and different and the same. I had one chance to live another life and I didn't.

After my mother died I decided I wouldn't make the same mistake as her: that if I was to stay here then I'd stay here properly; would live here properly, not in the past, not thinking of somewhere else, but right here. And perhaps I overcompensated a little. To stop myself dreaming and wondering and wanting I shut myself away, imagining that the less I saw the less I'd be dissatisfied, that the yearning would fade and flicker and vanish when I closed the door. But it never did. I found out that all I'd done was to close it in here with me. I was still living with him and looking for him and he was still everywhere I'd never been. And I was still living with her and she was still everything that had held me back. I was still living with all of them. I'd become the stationary custodian of all the journeys that had brought me here. The caretaker of all my pasts. And being the last one I couldn't just lock the gates and leave them behind. So I've stayed locked in here with them, almost my whole life, thinking that if only I could pass them on I'd be free and able to go.

Because it doesn't go away. It never does and I know now that it never will. The decision I had wasn't one that I could decide not to make, it was a decision I could at best defer, and keep on deferring. But eventually I'll have to make it. And as soon as I'm free and unencumbered I will decide. And then I'll start out.

9

For two days we searched for Johnny, even though there were hardly any places for us to look.

Bub and Nut went through their own fields; Bub on foot, Nut in his tractor. Goronwy and I chose the quarry and the surrounding coast; him the cliff tops above and me the stony beaches and jutting edges below. Sioned, who up to that point I'd heard of but never met, stayed in the cottage in case he came back. I rummaged between rocks and peered into tidal pools, sifted through clumps of seaweed and combed piles of flotsam and jetsam, wanting to find him but not wanting to either, secretly hoping we wouldn't.

It was the first day of August and it was hot and windless. The sea had settled into a stagnant calm, and the water near the shore had turned a rusty orange. An oily film of scum covered its surface, and a heavy, fetid scent filled the air above and around it; putrefying plankton, brine gone bad. People who I'd never seen before were lying on the beaches, splayed uncomfortably on the stones, burning in the sun, while their children paddled in the rancid foam. I thought how quickly he'd rot if he was in the water too.

Towards the afternoon of the second day a helicopter arrived and began circling up and down the coast. It was bright yellow and flew so low you could clearly see the men looking out of the open door on its side. The noise of its blades was deafening, a hard, percussive thrumming that you could almost feel when it hovered above you. The children on the beach waved up at the men inside when it came over them, and sometimes they waved back. I watched it with Nut and Goronwy from the top of the quarry. Nut got excited every time it came past. I was worried its noise might knock Goronwy over.

'Do you think it'll find him?' I asked.

'If he's there,' Goronwy replied, 'though a lot depends on the tides. They might have taken him further down the coast. But we don't know if he's in there at all, do we?'

But I think he did know. I think we all did. Where else could Johnny have gone?

'I reckon he's definitely carked it,' Nut shouted as the helicopter swept down over the sea in front us, churning up the surface of the water and drowning out our voices.

10

The next time I saw Johnny it was early in the morning and he was safely in his box. Sioned was tidying the lapels on his suit and I was looking down at his dead face – which is the only face I can remember – and while I was looking down at it, it was beginning to dawn on me what all these months had been about. I was beginning to understand what the game was. And if dead men can smile, then Johnny was smiling. When they found him he was only ten feet out from the quarry's edge, submerged beneath the water with two pockets full of stones. He'd finally escaped the calm.

I like to think he walked those last ten feet, down there on the seabed; that he hit the bottom and set straight off to wherever he wanted to go. And I hope, when the water began to fill his lungs and the seaweed tripped him, that he imagined he was getting there.

Inside his front room the fire had gone out and the heat had finally seeped away. Outside the window I could see Nut chafing impatiently against the starched collar of his shirt. The room didn't seem all that emptier without Johnny in it, just quieter. I could see the clock still ticking in the corner and I looked at its face and wondered where Johnny was now. And I wondered if it had taken him home, like we were about to take his corpse, and I wondered where it was taking me, because I didn't know.

Epilogue

Épilogue

1

After a few minutes Nut looked up from the tablecloth and said, 'Right, I'm off.' A quick glance over at Bub confirmed to him that this was permissible and so he got up from the table and went over to the door. Bub got up behind him and thanked Sioned for the tea, nodded to the rest of us at the table, and followed Nut towards the door.

'See yu,' Nut shouted as he went out.

I would have liked to have gone with them, but in the back of my mind I already knew that I'd spoiled all that.

The rest of us stayed around the table for about a quarter of an hour, not really saying anything, until finally Goronwy stood up to go. He went over to Sioned and thanked her, and I saw him reach down and gently squeeze her hand. I left with him. As I closed the kitchen door I saw her get up to clear the table.

Once outside, Goronwy and I made our way from the bottom of the village towards my cottage. Though he lived in the opposite direction he seemed happy enough to make the detour. For a while neither of us spoke and I looked about at the road which was entirely familiar to me, only to find that it had somehow, subtly, changed, and now appeared like those I had driven down earlier. It felt like I was seeing it through the window of a car, as an ever-receding strip of asphalt spidering through tunnels of green. And when I turned to Goronwy he also seemed somehow distant and remote, like I was looking at him through a telescope backwards. When I did speak I almost shouted.

'You know, it wasn't like I thought it'd be,' I said.

'You mean the funeral,' he replied, and I could hardly hear his voice. 'Well, I don't think it was what any of us thought it'd be.'

'No, not the funeral, the place – Llanysgerbwd. It wasn't what I was expecting.'

'And what were you expecting?'

'I'm not sure really. But from everything Johnny told me I guess I just assumed it'd still be there, that it'd be like he described it.'

'He never went there, you know.'

'Yes, and I'm kind of glad he didn't now. Imagine spending that long thinking of somewhere and then finding out it's hardly even there.'

'Well, we all do that a bit, don't we,' Goronwy said, and if anything it felt like he was drifting further away from me, was shrinking even as we spoke. 'And so perhaps Johnny was lucky in that respect. Perhaps. I remember when I came back here, after years of missing it, and thinking that when I did it'd make up for other things I'd missed out on in my life, that because I thought I'd missed it most of all it'd redeem those other lacks. And maybe it has. But maybe it hasn't. And I'm honestly not certain if I'll ever be sure which. So perhaps he was lucky, because he never had to look what lay beyond his longing.'

'But don't you think it might have been better if he had gone there, just the once, just to see it?'

'See it and then what? See it and know it was gone? Around here we tend to prefer spectacular disappearances, villages drowned in their valleys, castles gone under the sea, anything that allows them an afterlife, a lingering existence, anything that allows us to think that we never actually lost them, that they're only out of sight. Because the prosaic truth is much harder, the slow, gradual reality: the mine closing, the quarry closing, the farmers leaving, the ships not coming. And yes, you can call that disappearance change and transformation, but you also have to call it something else – because isn't a body in a coffin changing and transforming as well? Places die too you know. And that was something Johnny never had to find out.'

And then Goronwy had veered away from me, down the lane that led towards Seiriol's well. I watched him turn the corner, but he'd already seemed so far away that I hardly noticed when he'd actually gone. Instead I noticed how quiet it was. And it suddenly felt like I'd spent the last year living with nothing but voices.

2

I didn't know quite what to say when Sioned brought over the boxes. At first I thought she was taking them somewhere else. There were two of them, and as soon as I'd spotted her struggling down the lane with them I'd run out to help.

'Can I give you a hand with those?' I asked.

'Oh, thank you,' she said, heaving one of them onto the ground, 'that's kind of you. I don't know what he keeps in them but *Esgob*, they're heavy. It's worn me right out just getting them this far.'

I picked up the one on the ground and then reached over to take the one she was still holding.

'Oh no,' she said, 'don't you worry about it luv, I can carry this one just fine.'

After a slight pause I asked, 'Right, so where are we off to?' And then she gave me a confused look, as though she wasn't that sure what I was on about, as though she thought I might be a little confused myself. She gave me a few seconds to get my wits back

'They're meant for you. I was bringing them over to yours.'

I guess this was my cue to say of course, what was I thinking of, but I missed it because I wasn't sure yet why she'd brought them to me, or what was in them, although I was already beginning to suspect.

When we'd carried them inside I offered Sioned a seat and cup of tea. She sat down at my table and waited as the kettle boiled. She looked hot and a bit flustered and eager to get her breath back so she could speak. When I brought her her tea she asked:

'Aren't you having one yourself, luv?'

'No, I'm fine thanks. I've just had one,' I said, feeling embarrassed because I only had one cup. In fact I'd begun to feel embarrassed the moment she stepped through my door. It was so empty inside, and I'd seen her take this in with a single look. And because it was so empty I knew there was nothing, no 'nice place you've got' or 'isn't this cosy' to distract our attention from the boxes, which were pretty much the only things in the room. And by now I was certain they were Johnny's.

I'd not met Sioned until the day of the funeral, a week before. She was about ten years younger than him but was so sprightly and energetic that you might have thought she was much younger again. You could tell she wasn't that comfortable sitting still, or silently, and I could sense her almost twitching in her chair, wanting to be up and out of it, making, or tidying, or at least doing, something. My room must have seemed like

an affront to her: there wasn't anything you could do in it –
there wasn't even any dust settled in it. And as I watched
her shifting impatiently on the chair I suddenly became aware
of a scent in the room that was oddly familiar, although at
first, without the coal smoke that had previously cloaked it, I
didn't properly recognise it. And then I knew who the other
visitor had been and I wondered why Johnny had never
mentioned her; but then again he wasn't really in the habit of
talking about people who were still alive.

Sioned continued shifting around on her chair and I knew
one of us was going to have to say something but I didn't know
what and there were only the boxes.

'I don't know what's in them you know,' she blurted out
at last. 'He left instructions for the rest of them to be thrown
away, the ones them explosives people didn't take away, but he
wanted you to have these ones, he did, and I hope it's alright
for me to bring them and they don't get in your way or anything.'

'Oh, I think I might just about find room for them,' I
wanted to say but didn't.

'It was good of you to come last week Jonathon, it really
was; Johnny didn't have that many who were close to him you
know and I'm sure he'd have appreciated you being there and
everything.'

'It was a pleasure,' I said, and then instantly realised
pleasure wasn't quite the right word, not for a funeral, and
inwardly gave myself a kick. I wasn't sure of the etiquette for
these things. I'd never been to one, not even the one that'd
mattered most to me.

'He really would have, I can tell you that now. You've been
a great comfort to him these past months you have, and I know

317

he was glad of your company. It was good for him to have someone to talk to, you see, because he didn't have that many people to talk to and he didn't go out hardly at all. He was a bit strange like that was Johnny, private you know, but maybe too private, like he was hiding things and ended up hiding himself.'

Sioned's speech had begun to speed up, as though it was a substitute for movement, as though her tongue was doing what her body would've liked to have been doing. I could tell she was trying to keep her tone sombre, appropriate, but there was an unmistakable, agitated, edge to it, like she was arguing with him rather than talking to me.

'Was he always like that?' I asked.

'As long as I've known him, and that's a long time now. Ever since that day in the quarry I suppose. Locked up in that house on his own, it was no way to live was it, and I told him enough times but would he listen, no, he wouldn't listen to anybody, even the few who bothered to try to talk to him. A prisoner, that was what Johnny was, and I don't like to speak ill of the dead, and I'm not, but to be honest that's what he was and he was his own keeper.'

'He told me he tried to get away once,' I interrupted.

'Oh,' she said, with the hint of a blush spreading up her face, 'so he told you about that then.' And for a moment I thought that might be it. But after a few seconds she continued.

'Well, it was so long ago now there's no harm in it I suppose, no point in keeping it a secret. And with my Dylan gone too, no reason not to speak of it. I was only young then you see, and I didn't know what he was like, did I?

'It was that wink that did it, wasn't it. If I'd never seen it then maybe nothing would've happened and that would've been for the best I guess. But I did see it and I wanted to see it and you can't turn back time and close your eyes, can you. After I'd gone back from the quarry it was all I could think about for days I can tell you, and soon enough I was back up there on the cliff top wasn't I, pretending I was just walking or passing by, but really I was looking for him and waiting for him and it wasn't hard because the quarry was the only place he went. And he knew that, of course he did, he knew, but he made me walk past there for weeks anyway, watching from inside the buildings while I paraded myself up there above him, with the seagulls laughing at me, hoping he'd make some bloody sign or signal or just walk on up and meet me. Until in the end it was me who had to go down to him.

'I remember how nervous I was, taking those first steps down the path. There were brambles and bracken everywhere, catching onto my dress, and *Argwlydd* I'd spent all day getting it ready hadn't I, just to end up looking like I'd run through a hedge, but maybe that was better because by the time I got to the quarry I was so angry I wasn't nervous at all, not of him, not of anything, and when I saw him come out of the building I walked right on up to him and said, 'Look at me Johnny, look at the bloody state of me – don't they pay you to look after that path or something?' And he smiles he does and starts laughing and says, 'I'm sure they do Sioned, I'm sure they do, but I don't get that many visitors, do I.' And I was so surprised because he knew my name, I was so surprised and happy that I started laughing as well.

'After that I spent my whole summer at the quarry. I'd go down there every day. Johnny even cleared the path for me. And it was perfect for us, you know; we had the whole place

319

to ourselves and nobody ever disturbed us because Johnny and his dynamite had everyone thinking it was full of ghosts and bwgans and gave it a wide berth, when of course all the real ones were up in Johnny's head – but I didn't know that yet, did I. My mam'd say I was there more than my dad'd been there when he was working in the place, and she'd get angry with me, but not so angry that she stopped me going, or my dad either, because I was from a big family you see and if I'm being honest then I'd have to say that even though I knew they loved me and everything, maybe they wouldn't have been too upset to see me out of their house and into Johnny's. But that summer neither of us were planning to end up there.

'From the very first time I met him Johnny used to tell me these stories about all the places his dad'd been. We used to sit on the rocks together, by the water, with them old machines rusting above us, and he'd talk about deserts full of red stones and sand; and islands where men ate each other; and endless prairies where the people thought the world was a giant tortoise. I can hardly remember them all now, but I'd never been past Bangor then so it was exciting to me even if sometimes I didn't quite believe him, and I loved hearing him talking about them anyway because he'd get this big look in his eye you know, like he was seeing them right then and there in front of him, like he might just stand on up and step into them, and sometimes you can fall a bit in love with someone just because of what they want to see, and they can fall a bit in love with you just because of what they want you to see. So it didn't matter to me if these places were only words, as long as he was speaking them then I tried to think of them, to imagine them with him, until before long we were making plans to leave the island together, which sounds silly and romantic now, doesn't it, but it didn't then I can tell you. While we made them we meant them I think, and we must have meant them a bit because sometimes I'd worry that in the places he was describing, disasters happened and he'd tell me about them, about floods and volcanoes and hurricanes that his father always managed to escape, but I worried we might not. And he told me how lucky his family was so we wouldn't have to worry, but I knew even then that his family wasn't lucky, not even close to lucky, that his mother was a bit cucu and his dad'd died abroad somewhere, but from the way he spoke you'd think nothing bad'd ever happened to them, that his dad was still on the next ship home or that all he had to do to meet him was climb on board the next ship that left. So I knew there was something not quite right, I wasn't stupid, no, but I didn't know quite what it was and down there in the quarry with just the two of us it didn't seem to matter, nothing did. We could play with dynamite and get away with it.

'So I knew there was something not quite right, but it wasn't 'til later on that summer that I began to think there might be something wrong, properly wrong. I'd arrived early in the morning and Johnny wasn't there, so I spent an hour or so sunning myself until I got bored and then started to look through the old quarry buildings. There were three of them altogether, one where they'd had the office, one where the quarrymen had been allowed to sit and have their lunch when it was raining, and one where they'd kept the tools and dynamite. I'd been inside the first two, with Johnny, but also before when I was a child and had been allowed to visit my father at work. I remember him taking me into the office and

321

the people in there patting my head and me feeling all uncomfortable, and then going in for lunch in the other place and being much happier because the quarrymen would bounce me around on their laps and sing songs for me and I'd come out all smudged in white rock dust. But I'd never even been allowed near the third building, and when my curiosity got the better of me and I drifted towards it there'd always be someone around to guide me away and tell me it had dangerous things in it and was no place for little girls to be. So now, when I was a big girl and alone, and when I'd begun to believe that the whole quarry belonged to Johnny and me, it was this building that I gravitated towards, naturally. It was full of boxes, that much I knew, because I'd seen Johnny go in there to fetch the dynamite, but there was other stuff in them as well, I could tell, because sometimes when I'd arrive I'd find Johnny in there with pieces of paper and other things that looked like chunks of old fruit and bits of rag but that I never got close enough to see properly because as soon as he'd spot me he'd come scuttling out and shut the door behind him. Afterwards I'd ask him what was in there but he'd get all shifty and evasive and change the subject and get me interested in other things. That's what he was like sometimes, was Johnny, sly and careful and watchful, like an animal protecting its den, or a bird its nest, by making you look in another direction. And so when he was about I'd not think of it, but that day when he wasn't I wanted to look and see what was so important to him in there. But as I got to the door I found a padlock on it, a thick silver one streaked with rust, and I was trying to pry it loose when I felt him come up behind me and grab hold of me. He pulled me away he did, and not gently either, pulled me away and said, 'That's private Sioned,' and I said, 'Let go of me,' and he said, 'I'm sorry, but that's private,' and I said, 'So what's so special that I can't see it?' and he just kept saying that it was private and he was trying to get me off the subject but I could tell from the way he looked and the way his body was all tensed up that he'd probably hit me or something if I kept on at him about it and tried to get in there. And I knew there was something wrong then. And every day after that, when I walked past the building or even looked at it, I knew he was watching me and I knew there was something wrong.

'I didn't try to go in there again. I didn't want to. But I always think of that day as the end of that Summer, even though it was just August and the Autumn was a long way away. Because after that it felt like Autumn, like all the colour and brightness had started to drain out of things, like the sap had stopped in the trees, like the leaves were just hanging there, not growing but waiting, waiting for the wind, waiting to fall. In the days after I started to realise that the quarry wasn't quite what it had seemed a month, a week, before, that suddenly it was just a small, empty piece of shore, a little corner of the island filled with stones, and not the place I'd thought of first thing every morning and been excited by each time I spotted it from the cliff top. I really can't explain it, I can't, but whatever it was that was in that building it had managed to diminish everything around it, and whatever it was that had grown up between me and Johnny there, well that had begun shrinking and diminishing with it, and it felt like Autumn, it did you know. Because after that day I realised that I was waiting too.

323

'I could tell I was waiting, but for what I couldn't say. Maybe it was for Johnny and me to leave, though by then I don't think it was; I think I already knew he wouldn't, I think I already knew he was more in love with those boxes and whatever was in them than he was with me. And then I found that I couldn't see what it was he was trying to see anymore. I was bored of his stories, and I realised that they didn't make my life bigger, they made it smaller. I just wanted things to happen in my life and I didn't care if they happened here or in Timbuctu, I wanted things to happen and I didn't care if they were just normal things like what happened to everyone else. And so eventually I stopped visiting Johnny and things did start happening.

'It wasn't until years after, when I'd been married and had my second boy, that I began helping him out with his house. To be honest I never told my Dylan or anybody about what'd happened between us, because it was in the past then and I didn't think there was any reason for bringing it up and there wasn't, was there. It'd been over since that day. I went there first because I guess I wanted to know what had happened to him. I knew his mam'd died but apart from that I'd not heard anything. But as soon as I knocked on his door and he opened it I knew nothing had happened to him, that nothing had changed in his life except that even more of it was in his head than before, all hidden and stored and locked away. I couldn't even tell if he was glad I'd come, but it was a good thing I had because his place was in a hell of a state, like he hadn't tidied an inch of it since his mam'd gone. And I kept going back because I suppose I couldn't just leave him behind you know, not like that, because he'd been important in my life once and

I couldn't forget that, could I. I couldn't leave him totally alone and forget him when he was still alive, even if it wasn't much of a life.

'But now he's gone I don't know. Maybe I can forget him now. And I'm not being cruel or disrespectful or anything, I'm not, it's just that I've got so much else to think of you see. I've still got my sons and their children and my home. And the dead, well they don't need looking after, do they.'

She stood back up then and walked over to the sink and washed my only cup. And then she went to the door and before she closed it she turned back to me and said:

'I hope they don't get in your way luv. I haven't opened them you know. To be honest I didn't even want to.'

And I didn't either, because I already knew what was inside them. There was an axe and some letters and a journal and some bones and a bit of dried fruit called a 'Bornean Head' and a pile of made-up maps of nowhere and it was everything he had and he'd given it to me. So I took the boxes upstairs and put them with my own.

3

On packing days my mother and I would begin with the small things: she'd fold up towels and sheets and table clothes, and I'd gather together the cutlery and plates and cups and any other bits and bobs that happened to be lying about. Later, my father would come home from the pub or wherever he'd been and deal with the big things, like the television and the chairs and tables, hauling them outside to the van with puffed cheeks and a red face and a mouth full of expletives. After he'd finished loading it he'd stand at the back with his hands on his hips, looking through the open doors, and say, 'Christ luv, where'd we get all this crap!' Then he'd turn to me, smiling, and say, 'Bet you'll be glad to get out of here lad,' and with a gesture of his hands that indicated the street we were on, he'd continue, 'it's a shithole really, isn't it,' as though he'd only just that moment realised it.

I think these were some of the few times that I can remember my father being truly happy. It was an adventure for him, it really was. You could tell by the way he got all excited and carefree, like we were off on some exotic holiday. He'd jump around the van, checking the tyres and oil, making jokes and humming bits of songs, while my mother and I waited for him on the pavement. And maybe from the outside that's how it looked, because sometimes groups of children would gather around on the street to watch us (not to say goodbye to me – usually I'd hardly know them), sending furtive, jealous glances in our direction, wishing, I suppose, that they could be setting out on a thrilling jaunt just like us. And this would make my father even happier, and he'd prance around the van with augmented vigour like some great adventurer being waved away from the docks. But I knew better than them. I knew that an adventure is when you don't really know what's in store for you, when you don't really know what's ahead. And I knew exactly what was ahead of us: it was exactly what was behind us. Tomorrow we'd end up on another street, and another group of children would gather around and watch us unloading the van, curious about who we were and why we'd come, and in a few months, or a year, before they'd had time to find out, they'd be watching us again as we left.

But my father seemed blissfully ignorant of this. He had a stubborn inability to perceive the slightest hint of repetition in our wanderings, and treated each of our embarkations like they were the first. As soon as we got inside the van, with my mother and me sitting in the back, he'd start jabbering about what a relief it'd be to get to the next place – wherever that happened to be – and how much better it'd be than the last one, and how this was something we should have done years before. He must have had an unusual capacity for forgetting, an instinct for only looking forward. And I sometimes wonder where he is and if he's forgotten my mother and me, or if he's even now driving the van with his eyes fixed firmly on the road in front, jabbering away like we're both still there behind him, unable to look back, not noticing that we aren't there.

Because we invariably left at short notice – before the bailiffs, or worse, arrived – I'd always manage to leave something behind. No matter how careful I was, and no matter how careful my mother was, there'd always be some object that'd come to me once we were on the road. With the miles to go signs to our next destination diminishing as we swept onwards, I'd suddenly recall one of my toys in the garden, or a favourite book that I'd kept on the windowsill behind the curtain, and I'd shout out for us to stop so we could fetch it. But when I did my father would pretend not to hear me, until eventually we'd gone so far that he was able to say, 'Pack that in will you Jon. For fuck's sake, I'm not driving all the way back for that.' And there was nothing I could do and I'd start crying and my mother would hold my hand and tell me she'd get me a new one. But I didn't want a new one. I wanted that one. And all through my childhood I had nightmares about these things, where they'd become pieces of my body – fingers, thumbs, toes – and each time we set out I'd discover that part of me was missing, until in the end I'd be sat in the van looking like a zombie in a film, disfigured and digitless. And yet however many times I had these nightmares, however many times I woke up in a sweat with the fading image of my fingerless hands pressed against the window, it'd never stop me forgetting something the next time we set off. My mother would remind me to take a last look, she'd even look herself, she even gave me a special box to keep my valuables in, but without fail, after a few miles, I'd be shouting out again. What was worse was that as I got older I began to leave more and more important things behind; whatever it was that had come to mean most to me, then that was what I'd forget. My parents couldn't believe how absent-minded I was – in fact I'm sure they both suspected me of having some kind of mental defect – and soon enough they didn't even bother to listen when I called out. And after a while I didn't even bother to call out. The truth is that while these oversights remained inexplicable then, both to me and to them, I think subconsciously I was beginning to suspect that I was leaving these things behind on purpose, that I was contriving to lose them. And looking back now I'm sure I was. Because for as long as I can remember, before I could remember, I've had this masochistic urge to want things, to need things, to love things even, and then to leave them behind. My travelling has never been about accumulation, about all those clichés of augmentation – to see more, to experience more, to learn more, to accept more, to understand more – it's only ever been a slow, self-inflicted, self-lacerating process of dissipation, a way of discovering and jettisoning as much as possible. And one night I'll go to sleep and find myself in the van again, and this time I'll be no more than a torso, a few bones, a patch of dust on the seat.

Tammy and Nut both visited today, when I was inside packing my boxes. Tammy came first and I watched her as she

330

walked up to the door and began knocking. She knocked three times and then stood waiting by the door for ten, maybe twelve, minutes, waiting for me to open it. I watched her through the corner of my window and she just stared at the door, and when I didn't come she turned around and walked back down the track and onto the lane, and then I couldn't see her anymore.

Nut was louder. He banged his fist on the door and when I didn't answer he banged on the window. Then he stormed around to the windows at the back and banged on them as well. Before he gave up and left he shouted out to me, knowing I must be inside:

'Yer a twat yu are Jon, an' I know what yu did an' I told yu. An' yer gonna have tu come out sometime.'

And I will come out, first thing tomorrow when I go.

It's funny, but given two legacies it's my father's that I'm about to choose, yet again. For a while I didn't think I would. I thought I could take what my mother hid for me and keep it. I thought that was the least I owed her, and it was, but I can't stop here because I still haven't learned where here is. And I'm sorry for that.

I've put Johnny's boxes in the corner, where I won't see them when I leave. I kept them for as long as he needed me to and now I can pretend to forget them. There's a shadow falling in through the window as the evening comes, and behind it I can sense it all receding out of view – the lane, the straits, Bub and Nut's farm, Tŷ Carreg, Chwarel Wen, Ynys Seiriol, Llanysgerbwd, the whole island – and it's not dark yet, but it's getting there.

Acknowledgements

First and foremost I'd like to thank my family for their continued support of my writing. I also owe some other debts of thanks: to Martha, my god-daughter (sorry for the birthdays I missed); to Sian, for her friendship, kindness, and a trip we took to our island's California; to Joe, for his Dylan collection; to Tommo Sailor, for some nautical advice which, if it proves to be wrong, is entirely his fault; and to Gwen, my editor. I would also like to thank the Welsh Books Council and the Society of Authors for their financial assistance.